After Sophie

PENELOPE ABBOTT

TABLE OF CONTENTS

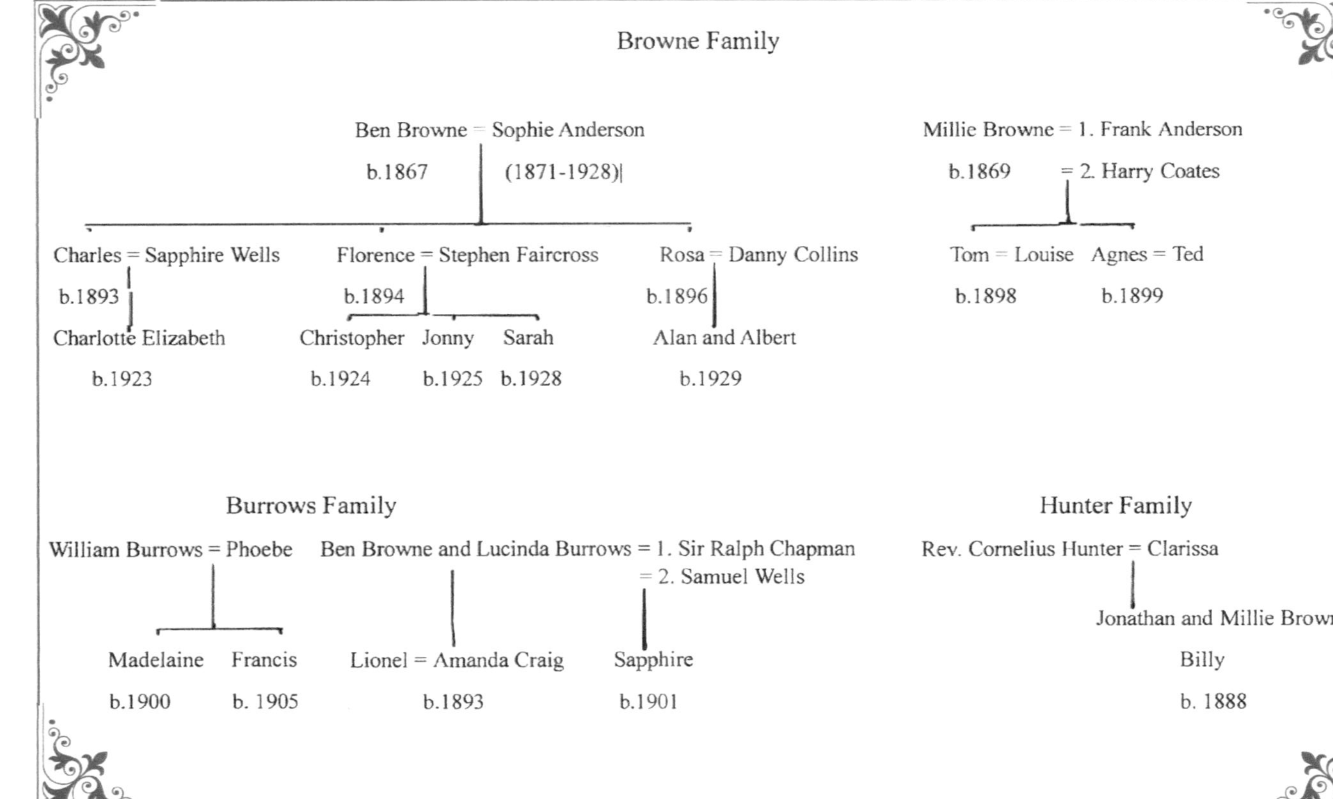

Browne Family

Ben Browne = Sophie Anderson
b.1867   (1871-1928)|

Charles = Sapphire Wells
b.1893
Charlotte Elizabeth
b.1923

Florence = Stephen Faircross
b.1894
Christopher   Jonny   Sarah
b.1924   b.1925   b.1928

Rosa = Danny Collins
b.1896
Alan and Albert
b.1929

Millie Browne = 1. Frank Anderson
b.1869   = 2. Harry Coates

Tom = Louise   Agnes = Ted
b.1898   b.1899

Burrows Family

William Burrows = Phoebe

Madelaine   Francis
b.1900   b. 1905

Ben Browne and Lucinda Burrows = 1. Sir Ralph Chapman
= 2. Samuel Wells

Lionel = Amanda Craig
b.1893

Sapphire
b.1901

Hunter Family

Rev. Cornelius Hunter = Clarissa

Jonathan and Millie Browne

Billy
b. 1888

CHAPTER ONE

BEREAVEMENT

S APPHIRE STEPPED CAREFULLY THROUGH THE wet grass. There had been a frost that night, and it had only just melted away as the sun rose, casting warm rays across the churchyard. She led Charlotte Elizabeth by the hand as they wove their way between the gravestones until they reached her mother-in-law's grave. The brown earth was heaped up into a mound, and some dead flowers lay on top. Sapphire removed them, allowing her daughter to place a small bunch of snowdrops on her grandmother's grave. The child then stood beside her mother, looking solemn and holding her hand tightly. They had gathered the spring flowers earlier from the sides of the lane that led to Forge Cottage.

Sapphire glanced at the smooth white gravestone, its carved letters crisp and clear.

Sophie Browne

Beloved Wife and Mother

1871 – 1928

Sitting in his chair in the kitchen at Forge Cottage, all Ben could hear was the steady ticking of the clock in the parlour. He looked round at the familiar objects in the room—the cast-iron range and kettle, the rows of coloured plates on the dresser shelves, the plain wooden table and four chairs, the patterned curtains hanging at the window. He would sit there in the afternoons, lost in grief and memories, thinking about his wife Sophie.

Suddenly the outside door opened, and in ran a young, bright-eyed little girl. She came straight towards him and flung her arms round his neck.

"Gandy! Gandy!" she cried.

She was followed by her mother. "Charlotte Elizabeth, you shouldn't run off like that without me!"

Her daughter paid no attention, climbing onto her grandfather's knee. He enfolded her in his arms, and Sapphire kissed her father-in-law on the forehead. "Hello, Ben," she said in a soft voice. He looked up and gave a faint smile as he held his granddaughter, who was feeling his beard with her fingers and laughing.

"Prickly Gandy!" she said. She looked at him with her wide blue eyes. "Granny's in heaven, isn't she?"

He held her close. "Yes, Granny's in heaven now."

Sapphire glanced around the room. It was obvious to her that Ben was not coping, despite his previous assurances. The table was strewn with the used crockery and the remains of his last meal.

"Charlotte Elizabeth, why don't you take those cups and plates into the scullery for Gandy?"

Her daughter clambered down from her grandfather's lap and eagerly busied herself with her task, carefully lifting each item off the table and taking it through to the back.

"How are you?" asked Sapphire.

He shrugged. "Not so bad. How are Charles and Lucinda?"

"Charles's antenatal clinic at the surgery keeps him busy. It seems half the village are expecting—except me," she added quickly. "My mother's gone shopping to London."

"Is she staying with Lionel and Amanda?"

"No, she'll be using her flat, but she will be seeing them."

"I'm glad they were able to come to the funeral. They live so far away, and I don't see much of them. It was good to see both my sons." He looked out of the window and stared into the distance for a few moments. Turning back to face her with desperation in his eyes, he said, "It was only three weeks ago."

"You should have a change of scene. Get away for a bit," responded Sapphire, briskly. "Everything here must remind you of Sophie. Charles and I are going away at Easter with Charlotte Elizabeth, would you like to join us? We're going to Torquay. The sea air will do you good."

Ben took his time replying. "Thank you, that's very kind of you to ask, but I don't think so."

"Charlotte Elizabeth will be disappointed."

He sat up and leant forward. "Oh, Sapphire, what am I going to do? I feel I can't go on."

She took his hand and held it. Just then, her daughter returned, having finished clearing the plates and cups.

"Leave the rest, darling," Sapphire instructed. She produced a story-book from her bag. "Perhaps Gandy will read this to you."

Charlotte Elizabeth's face brightened as she climbed up onto Ben's lap again. She put her thumb in her mouth and settled down to enjoy the book. Ben sat up in his chair in anticipation and opening the book began to read the words to her, talking about the pictures before he turned each page.

Sapphire finished clearing the table and took the rest of the things into the scullery. There was a sink in there, and she saw all the crocks waiting to be washed up. She'd noticed the range had not been lit in the kitchen, so there would be no kettle of hot water. Glancing down at her well-manicured hands, she decided to leave the plates and cups there. She put the remains of the food away and checked the pantry for anything that might have gone off. There wasn't much there, just some bread and cheese. She went back into the kitchen.

"You need someone from the village to give you some help," she said.

Ben stopped reading and looked up. "I don't want anyone coming and poking around." His voice was gruff. "I can manage!"

He turned his attention back to his granddaughter, giving her a little reassuring hug. Sapphire didn't reply but went upstairs into his and Sophie's bedroom. She gave a little shudder as she surveyed their bed. It was where her mother-in-law had languished for weeks until she'd finally passed away. Sapphire saw that the sheets needed changing, so she removed them and then looked inside a cupboard in the corner of the room and found some fresh linen. She made up the bed and then gathered the sheets together with a pile of dirty clothes that had been strewn on the floor. Walking downstairs, her arms full, she placed it all in the laundry basket.

"I'll get my daily to do these," she offered.

He thanked her. He had finished reading the story.

"Come along, Charlotte Elizabeth," said Sapphire. "It's time to go. I'm sorry it's such a quick visit, Ben, but Charles will be needing the motor for his rounds."

Ben hugged his granddaughter goodbye. "Thank you for coming," he said, his blue eyes showing some warmth as he looked at Sapphire gratefully.

"We'll come again soon," she promised, giving him a kiss. "Please think about the holiday."

He nodded and got up to see them out. Standing at the gate, he watched as Sapphire put the basket of washing in the back of the motor and settled Charlotte Elizabeth into her seat, then got in and started the engine. He waved as the motor sped away up the lane.

Turning slowly back into the cottage, he entered the kitchen.

"Damn that clock!" he muttered, closing the parlour door. Did he want to be reminded of time passing? He picked up the kettle and went into the scullery, where he saw the dishes waiting to be done. Deciding that they could wait, he filled the kettle, returned to the kitchen, and placed it on the range. Opening the front of the grate, he raked out the ashes from the previous day and, after adding fresh kindling, placed some coals on top. He then sat down and waited for the kettle to boil so he could make his solitary cup of tea.

As she drove home from Clayden village, Sapphire wondered what could be done for her father-in-law. They had not always got on. He had been hostile towards her when he learnt his son, Charles, wanted to marry her. The wedding had been hurried, as Sapphire had been pregnant with Charlotte Elizabeth. As soon as she was born, however, Ben had changed, and he doted on his first grandchild.

When she arrived back in Modbury village, she parked outside Acacia House surgery and hurried in, holding Charlotte Elizabeth's hand, looking for Charles. She found him in the small pharmacy situated behind the consulting room.

"Oh, there you are," he said as he filled his bag with various medicines from the shelves. "I was getting worried about having the motor."

Sapphire turned to her daughter. Bending down and putting her arm round her, she said, "Go and find Grandmama, darling."

The girl sped off to look for Lucinda.

"You should see the state of Forge Cottage," Sapphire exclaimed. "Your pa is not coping, and I'm worried about him. We've got to do something. He was just sitting there when we arrived, as if he'd lost all hope."

Charles stopped what he was doing and frowned.

"I suggested he get help from the village, but he flatly refused."

"If he won't be helped, what can we do?" he asked, looking bewildered.

"I think we should get the family together and decide something."
Charles nodded.

"I'll write to your sisters," Sapphire continued. "We'll have them over here, children and all, and discuss this."

"What about Lionel and Amanda? It's a bit much expecting them to come from Richmond, it's so far away."

"Yes, it's not possible for a day, but I'm sure Lionel would want to help his father in some way. I'll write to them as well."

"And Billy and Dorothy?" asked Charles, remembering his cousin and his wife.

"Yes, they need to know. I'll ask then all over for next weekend."

"Thank you, darling," said Charles, kissing his wife on the cheek. "You're wonderful."

Sapphire went out to fetch the basket of washing before her husband began his rounds. She went downstairs to the kitchen to find Mrs Harris, wondering how she was going to persuade her to do the extra laundry.

At dinner that evening, Charles told Sapphire he was pleased she had visited his father.

"Charlotte Elizabeth kept pestering me to take her there. She loves her Gandy."

"Do you think she understands that she doesn't have a granny anymore?"

"I think so. We put some snowdrops on her grave before we went to see Ben."

Sapphire sent invitations to the family, asking them to come to a meeting about Ben, and hoped they would be free to come. She arranged for the children to be cared for by her daily, Mrs Harris, together with the woman's teenage daughter, Susan. Sapphire was grateful Mrs Harris was good-natured, and her daughter would be helpful with the children. She knew they would be glad about the extra wages offered.

Ben's nephew Billy and his wife Dorothy were the first to arrive on the Saturday afternoon, along with their children, Frank and Clarrie. They lived in the nearby town of Kingsbridge, where Billy had a veterinary practice. Dorothy left to settle her two young children into Susan's care in the conservatory, while Billy joined Charles in the sitting room for a drink.

"How's business?" asked Charles as he handed his cousin a glass of freshly prepared fruit juice.

"Going very well," Billy replied. "I didn't realise there were so many dogs and cats in Kingsbridge. I'm glad of Dorothy's help in the surgery."

Charles nodded in agreement. "She does a good job with two young children to look after as well."

Just then Sapphire's sister-in-law Florrie and Florrie's husband, Stephen, arrived, preceded by their children, Christopher and little Jonny. Florrie looked flustered as she entered the room, pushing an unruly lock of hair away from her forehead.

"Boys!" she called as they ran into the room chasing each other. "I'm sorry!" she exclaimed, addressing her brother Charles. "They're *so* excited."

She greeted him and Sapphire, kissing both lightly on the cheek. Stephen rounded up his two lively sons and marched them into the conservatory. He came back looking relieved. "Peace and quiet for a short while!" he said thankfully as he took his drink from Charles and sat down.

Charles then excused himself to go and collect his other sister Rosa and her husband, Danny, from Kingsbridge Station. They had come up from Plymouth on the train.

When Charles returned with Rosa and Danny, Mrs Harris brought in plates of refreshments and hurried back to her child-caring duties. With everyone having arrived, they helped themselves to sandwiches and settled down, chatting animatedly. After a while, Charles stood up to speak, tapping the side of his teacup with a spoon and waiting for silence. The voices hushed, and heads turned towards him.

"We've asked you over here this afternoon to talk about Pa," he began. "Sapphire went to Forge Cottage recently and was very concerned about him. He simply isn't coping. Apart from not caring for himself properly, he's also very dejected and doesn't know how he can go on without Ma by his side." Charles paused, and there was silence in the room. "Of course, it's early days, and he's bound to feel like this having lost his wife, but it's not like my pa to give up, and we're worried."

"Can I suggest he has some help in the house?" asked Billy, his bright, open face looking hopeful.

Sapphire shook her head. "He's adamantly refused, he's quite capable of looking after himself—he's been helping Sophie in the house for years. He's lost the will to do so."

There were concerned looks from the rest of them.

"Perhaps my mother and stepfather can help out," Billy offered. "I'm sure they can provide some support, living nearby."

Charles looked doubtful. "My aunt Millie isn't getting any younger. We can't expect her to do all her brother's housework and shopping. Besides, she looks after her grandchildren while Agnes runs the village store."

Stephen stood up, glancing nervously at his wife beside him. "Can I say something, please?" He turned to address the group.

"Florrie and I have given this a lot of thought, and I would like to take this opportunity to put our idea to you all. We know that Ben will never want to leave Forge Cottage—he's lived there all his life. When I retire, we shall have to leave the schoolhouse, as it goes with my job as headmaster of the school. It's been perfectly adequate for us up until now, but not for much longer. We only have two bedrooms, and we shall need more space soon."

He looked at his wife, who was heavily pregnant with their third child.

Florrie grinned. "Stephen is determined to populate his school with our children."

Her husband smiled and looked slightly embarrassed. "We would like to ask Ben if he would consider our moving in with him to provide him with companionship and help, but we need to know if you all think this is a good idea and are happy about it."

He looked around the room to gauge the others' reactions.

"If Ben agrees, I think it would be just the thing," said Billy. This was met with nods of agreement from his relatives.

"It would be lovely for your children to grow up in the countryside," added Dorothy.

Stephen looked at his wife, who reached out and grasped his hand, smiling at him.

"What will happen to the schoolhouse?" asked Billy.

"It will provide the teachers with a staffroom and a place for meetings, and perhaps a small library." Stephen's eyes brightened as he explained his plans. "The two bedrooms could be extra classrooms, as the school is expanding."

"With or without your help," added Billy, winking at him. A ripple of laughter went through the room.

"I agree," said Rosa. "It would be a great relief to know Pa's being cared for properly, as long as it wouldn't be too much for you, Florrie," she added, turning to her sister.

Florrie gave a slight shake of her head. "I would be grateful for his company and help with the boys, especially as I am about to produce another."

"Maybe we should suggest to Ben you stay there on a trial basis first," suggested Danny. He turned to face the rest of the family.

Everyone nodded enthusiastically, and it was agreed that Charles would drive Stephen and Florrie over to Forge Cottage the following day to put their idea to Ben. Satisfied with the outcome, the families resumed their conversations until Mrs Harris arrived and whispered to Sapphire that "The children were getting tired and restless."

Ben was in the orchard behind the cottage when they arrived the following day. It was a chilly morning, but Ben liked to get outside. He could hear the church bells ringing as he raked up the windfalls from the apple trees that had been left the previous autumn. The brown and yellow fruits lay scattered in the grass, exuding a sweet, rotting smell. Sophie had not been well enough to gather them up and store them in the shed, as she had done in the years before.

Ben took a break from his work and leant on the handle of the rake as he listened to a blackbird singing in one of the trees, its clear pure notes cheering him a little. He looked up when Charles called to him as he came through the gate, followed by Florrie and Stephen. Ben wondered why the three of them had come. He put down his rake and hurried over.

"This is a nice surprise!" he said, greeting them all and raising his eyebrows. He led them into the cottage, through the kitchen and into the parlour. Charles glanced at Stephen nervously as they all sat down.

He cleared his throat before he began. "Pa, we've something to ask you. We're concerned about your living here on your own and wondered what we could do to help." He waited, but when Ben made no comment, he continued. "Florrie and Stephen have had an idea that they would like you to consider."

Ben bent forward to listen.

"We wondered if you would like Florrie, myself, and the boys to come and live with you at Forge Cottage," began Stephen.

Ben thought for a few moments, stroking his beard.

"Of course, if you agree, we could have a trial period to see how it works out," his son-in-law added.

Ben leant back in his chair to consider. *What would my Sophie want me to do?* he wondered.

She had left him far too soon. He had thought they would have a little longer together, but her heart condition had become steadily worse over the last year. It had been a difficult time. He still couldn't believe she wasn't there anymore. It had worn him out, emotionally and physically, caring for her. He tried to visualise a young family living in Forge Cottage once again, children laughing and running about, and his darling Florrie, her sleeves rolled up making bread, just as her mother had done. The family would be around him, loving him.

He sat up. There were tears in his eyes as he responded. "I think I would like that, very much. Thank you for thinking of me."

"You don't need more time to think it over?" asked Stephen cautiously.

"No, I think it sounds a good plan. But how will you get to school each day?"

"I was thinking of getting a motorcycle. Meanwhile, I shall have to cycle in."

"Well, when you do get one, I can fix it for you if it breaks down," Ben said. "I think I know a bit about motorcycles after working on them for several years." He turned to his daughter. "Did I tell you there's an omnibus going to Kingsbridge that now comes through the village?"

"That sounds just the thing for when the boys start school."

"I hope the two little horrors won't be too much for you," said Stephen, looking anxious.

"They'll keep me young," he said, looking at his daughter and smiling. "By the way, where are they?"

"At Billy's. We thought it best not to bring them today."

Stephen proposed that the move take place in the Easter holidays in two weeks' time, before their baby was due to be born. Ben agreed and insisted his daughter was to make the cottage her own when they moved in. He suggested they bring items of furniture as well as their belongings. He would welcome the changes.

"At the moment every room reminds me of your mother," he said.

"It's a great relief to us that you want to try out this arrangement," said Charles. "We've been worried about you."

Ben sighed and looked away, overcome with emotion.

"I wasn't prepared to lose your mother so soon. I haven't known what to do since, but with Florrie and Stephen living with me, I feel I can go on."

Charles gave his father a hug. "You know we're always here for you, Pa."

After discussing when and how the move would take place, the visitors all left, and Ben went back into the garden and sat on the seat in the orchard to think. He looked up at the blossoms on the trees. "Well, Sophie, what do you think about that?" he said out loud. "Our Florrie will be looking after me, so you need not worry".

He realised he would have to prepare Forge Cottage for its new inhabitants. He got up and walked back inside and began to look round, seeing everything in a different way. It had been many years since he and Sophie had brought up their family in these rooms. He went upstairs and saw that the two spare bedrooms needed a good spring cleaning. He had let things go when Sophie fell ill,

The following day he set to moving everything from the back bedroom into the adjoining one and then cleaning the floor and whitewashing the walls. It had been many years since he had mixed up bucketfuls of white paint. When Sophie had moved into Forge Cottage after they were married, the kitchen had been a mess; they had spent the first day of their married life clearing it out, and he had painted the walls, making them gleaming white and clean. His memories saddened him, but he began to feel cheered at the prospect of Florrie and her family living with him. He worked hard, washing the window and clearing out the fireplace. This was to be his room, since he would need somewhere to get some peace and quiet. He decided Florrie and Stephen would have the main bedroom and the boys the other one next to his.

Ben continued with his work over the next two weeks, finding renewed energy and purpose, and at the end of each day, he sat in his chair, content that he had done a good job getting everything ready for his daughter and her family.

The gabled stone schoolhouse stood behind the British National School in Kingsbridge and was situated on a hillside. There were several steep steps leading up to it, and Florrie had to struggle up these, often with a pram or heavy baskets of shopping, to reach the door. This opened into a small hall with a sitting room on one side and a kitchen on the other. A staircase between led up to the two bedrooms.

None of the rooms were very big. The house had been furnished when Stephen and his first wife moved in, and when Florrie married Stephen and had gone to live there, she'd had to make do with the same old, dark furniture. She told Stephen that she was glad to leave it behind and that she was looking forward to moving back into her old home. Her husband looked anxious.

"I hope we can all live together, and it won't prove to be too much for your father."

The following week, Florrie began to sort things out, ready for the move. She was on her knees clearing the items from the bottom shelf of a cupboard in the kitchen. Her two little boys were constantly getting in the way, interested in what she had found. The floor was strewn with pots and pans, an old pair of scales, and some cracked cooking bowls and stoneware storage jars. Florrie wondered how long they had been there. The back of the cupboard was dusty, and she kept a lookout for spiders.

She stopped what she was doing for a moment and sat up, feeling a little puffed out. Putting her hand on her swollen body, she felt the baby move. *Please, God, let it be a little girl this time!* She got up slowly and shooed the boys out of the room. It was time for their rests, so she took them upstairs. Jonny usually went off to sleep straightaway, but Christopher didn't always settle, and Florrie often had to read to him.

After she had finished his story, she tiptoed downstairs to put the kettle on. The teachers would soon be arriving for their tea. They came up to the schoolhouse for their morning and afternoon breaks, as there was no provision at the school. Stephen had asked her if she wanted to continue this arrangement when she'd moved in. She had told him it helped her feel part of the school now that she had left, and she was glad to let it continue. She liked to hear all the news and little anecdotes about the children.

There were four teachers altogether, including Stephen. Florrie had had the youngest class when she was at the school. The youngest member of staff, a probationer, had taken it over when Florrie left, and two older unmarried ladies took the middle two classes, with Stephen teaching the top class.

Florrie put a plate of her cakes out with the tea things. It was a Friday, and she always produced some home baking at the end of the week. Stephen stayed behind in his office to catch up on paperwork, so the teachers were able to chat freely. Sometimes one of them would inadvertently make a remark about him, and they would glance nervously at Florrie, who'd pretend she hadn't heard. She never repeated anything to Stephen, as it was important that they all got on in such a small school. She had learnt her wisdom from her mother.

Once the teachers arrived, she poured out their tea and then carefully took a cup down the steps to her husband's office. She placed it carefully on his desk together with a slice of cake, and he looked up from his work and smiled at her gratefully.

The following day, Florrie decided to tackle the boys' bedroom and start packing clothes and shoes. She looked out of the window before she began. She could see the schoolyard down below, where Stephen was taking a drill class. He was jumping up and down making windmill shapes, and the boys facing him in their singlets and shorts were doing likewise. It had been a frosty morning, and their puffs of breath could be seen in the cold air.

Florrie knew that the girls were inside, having their dance lesson to the music of Miss Page as her fingers fluttered over the piano keys. She imagined them moving round the small hall in their bare feet, bending their bodies and swaying from side to side. A new form of dance, which encouraged freedom of expression, had become fashionable. Florrie had never understood why the girls were considered too delicate to have their exercise in the fresh air outside.

She remembered the time a few years before when she had arrived for her interview and had looked up at the imposing school building. She had been shown into the schoolhouse, where she first saw Stephen.

Never in her wildest dreams had she imagined she would marry him and live there. It had all begun at the end of her first year, when he had surprised her by asking her out. She'd found him slightly restrained to begin with, but after sharing her concerns with her mother, she realised that he had been unsure of her feelings towards him.

How glad she was that she had met someone like him. He had proved to be a good husband and father to her children, and she knew him to be a good teacher and headmaster. Now they were about to embark on a new stage of their lives together when they moved to Forge Cottage.

Florrie saw that the drill lesson had ended, and the boys were filing back inside. She sighed contentedly and turned into the room to begin her tasks.

CHAPTER TWO

THE BIRTH

THE MOVE TO FORGE COTTAGE took place on the first day of the Easter holidays. The truck with Florrie's and Stephen's belongings arrived promptly, and Ben helped the men to unload. Billy brought Florrie and the two boys in his motor, and they arrived shortly afterwards. The boys ran around their new home excitedly, dashing upstairs and jumping up and down on their beds until Ben took them into the garden to keep them out of the way. Stephen insisted his wife sit down in the kitchen and not lift anything.

"Just tell us where to put things," he said.

Florrie made sandwiches while she waited, and a large pot of tea for the men. When they had finished bringing everything in, they all sat round the table for lunch. The removal men then left, and Florrie surveyed the muddle around her. They had not brought much furniture, but there were many crates and boxes to unpack. She looked bewildered, exclaiming, "I don't know where to start!"

"Plenty of time for all that," said her father. "Just tell me where the linen is, and I'll make up the boys' beds."

Florrie located the basket of sheets, and Ben disappeared upstairs with them. Stephen came in after seeing off the men and put his arm round his wife.

"Well, here we are," he said. "Your old home is now your new home."

Florrie looked round contentedly. "I'm so happy to have come back," she said quietly. "I wish my ma were here, though."

Stephen held her closer. "I think she is."

Florrie sighed and got up to find the pie she had made ready for their supper. The range was lit, and she eyed it unenthusiastically, thinking, *If only the village had a gas supply, like I had at the schoolhouse. Then I could ask Stephen if we could have a nice modern stove.* She remembered the reality of living in a cottage tucked away in the countryside. At least there was running water from a tap in the scullery.

Later that evening Ben, Florrie, and Stephen sat round the table for their meal, as the boys had been given their tea earlier and were now asleep in their new bedroom upstairs. Ben welcomed his daughter and her family to Forge Cottage and then tucked into the first good dinner he'd had since his wife died.

A week had gone by when a motor drew up outside Forge Cottage. Sapphire emerged and came in through the gate and straight into the cottage. She found Florrie in the parlour with her feet up, reading.

"Hello, Florrie. We've just got back from our little holiday. How's it all going?"

"We're just about settled in, thank you. How lovely of you to come."

Sapphire glanced round. "I came to see if I could help, but you look fairly organised."

"Pa and Stephen have worked hard. They're just a few boxes left to unpack."

"How long is it now?" Sapphire looked at her sister-in-law's stomach.

Florrie put down her book and sat up. "About two weeks."

Sapphire pulled a face. "Rather you than me, darling. How are the arrangements working out?"

"Pa seems very happy, although my boys will tire him out if he's not careful."

"Let us know if there are any problems."

Florrie nodded. "It's early days, but we all seem to be getting along. Pa has his little bedsitting room upstairs if he wants to get away from us all."

The women chatted happily until Ben came in with the boys. They had been out for a walk. His face brightened when he saw Sapphire. "No Charlotte Elizabeth?" he asked.

"Charles has her," replied Sapphire. "I think he's been invited to her doll's tea party. I can just imagine Charlotte Elizabeth in the future, surrounded by her friends, having afternoon tea and being very much in charge."

The two boys sat down at the table, and with some effort Florrie got up to get them their tea.

"I think I need to go home and rescue my husband," said Sapphire. "Charlotte Elizabeth's tea parties can go on rather a long time."

She moved towards the door. "Take care of her, Ben," she added as she left.

The remainder of the holiday was spent rearranging and sorting out the rooms in the cottage. Ben stayed well out of the way and allowed Florrie and Stephen to get on without him. He found himself overseeing their two lively boys and kept them entertained by kicking a football round in the orchard or taking them down to the nearby stream for walks. He could see they loved the freedom of the countryside after the constraints of the town. He remembered the walks he and Sophie had taken when they were courting. Now here he was with his two grandchildren watching them excitedly exploring the same pathways. Soon Forge Cottage would be welcoming another.

It was less than a week after the end of the holiday when Florrie went into labour. Stephen had gone to school as usual that morning, and Florrie was clearing away the breakfast things. She suddenly stopped and clutched her stomach.

"Oh, Pa!" she exclaimed.

Ben came quickly and helped her upstairs, wondering what to do about the boys. After explaining to them that he had to go out to get help, as Mummy's baby was coming, he told them to play quietly until he got back.

"You're not to bother Mummy," he instructed as he closed their bedroom door.

He hurried over to his sister's shop to ask his niece Agnes to send a telegram to Charles and ask Millie to come straightaway. There used to be a village midwife, but she had long gone, having been well on in years already when Sophie had her children. Ben hurried back, glad that his son was a doctor. Charles had insisted he should be called when the time came.

When Ben arrived home, he released his grandsons from their bedroom and took them downstairs. Soon after, Millie arrived breathlessly and went to sit with her niece.

A little over half an hour later, Ben heard Charles's motor draw up. He came in, greeted his father briefly, and went straight upstairs. Millie came down looking worried. She told Ben to go and ask Harry to take the shop van and fetch Stephen.

He arrived sometime later, looking very anxious. "Is Florrie all right, Ben? What's happening?"

Ben was unable to answer his questions. "Try not to worry, Stephen. Charles is an excellent doctor—we couldn't have better."

Stephen paced the room. After a while, Charles came downstairs.

"The baby's in a difficult position, but we shall just let nature take its course. It shouldn't be too long."

"Can I see her?" asked Stephen, anxiously.

"It's best we don't disturb her," Charles replied. "She has a bit of work to do yet. I'm hoping not to have to perform a caesarean section, but I can't rule it out at this stage. You'd better occupy those two boys." He turned to his father. "Lots of hot water, please, Pa."

Ben jumped up to refill the kettle, and Stephen went outside to where the boys were playing. Ben could hear his daughter moaning and sometimes calling out as he placed the kettle on the range. An hour later, Millie came downstairs.

"It's not been easy, Ben, but she has her little girl."

She collected another kettle from the range, and an excited Ben hurried outside to tell Stephen, who then sat on the seat and put his head in his hands, saying, "Oh, thank God!"

Both men went back inside, followed by the boys. Stephen sat at the kitchen table and put an arm round each of his sons. "Mummy has had a baby girl," he told them. "You have a little sister."

Christopher seemed to understand, but Jonny looked bewildered.

"You can see her in a little while," began their father, but at that moment, Millie appeared with a bundle in her arms and deposited it on Ben's lap. The boys peered at the little screwed-up red face.

"Baby," said Jonny, staring at it.

"Charles says you can go up, Stephen," Millie told him.

Taking a quick look at his daughter, he dashed upstairs. Millie spoke quietly, "The birth was very painful because of the baby's position. Florrie's exhausted, poor thing."

Ben looked troubled as she took more hot water upstairs. As he held his new granddaughter gently in his arms, his thoughts turned to Sophie. *How she would have loved seeing this latest addition. But why had Millie brought the baby downstairs? Was his daughter all right?*

Stephen came back downstairs, and Ben handed the child over to him.

"She's lost a lot of blood," he whispered. "The birth was difficult, and she needs lots of rest. I'm so glad she's all right!"

Charles came downstairs and said he needed to examine the baby. He listened to her heart and checked her arms and legs. He looked a little concerned but didn't say anything. Ben asked if he could see his daughter.

"Just go to the bedroom door and look in, Pa. I think she's sleeping."

Ben went up to find Millie sitting by the bed with Florrie looking very peaceful as she slept. He tiptoed back downstairs to where his son was waiting, and Charles told him he would return the next day, but they were not to hesitate to contact him if they were concerned. He said to get the baby feeding as soon as Florrie woke. "She's an experienced mother, she'll know what to do."

When he'd gone, Ben made some tea in Sophie's big brown teapot and took a cup up to Millie. When he came down, he and Stephen discussed what needed to be done.

"I doubt if I can get any time off school, there's simply no one to replace me. I shall come straight home each day and bring my work to do here. Will you be able to manage the boys? And who will look after Florrie?" Stephen seemed overwhelmed with worry.

"I expect Millie will be over each day," Ben assured him. "I'm sure we'll manage. We'll take each day as it comes." He looked at the little child wrapped up in her shawl in Stephen's arms. "This one's going to be special."

Charles came back the next day, and Stephen took him to see Florrie, who was sitting up in bed, looking cheerful. She put out her hand to greet her brother.

"Thank you so much for helping me through yesterday."

"You did all the work."

"But you gave me confidence by being there."

"I don't know why I didn't spot the baby's position at my last examination," he said, seriously. "She must have shifted afterwards."

"All's well now. She's lovely, isn't she?" answered Florrie, looking tenderly into the cot by her bedside.

Charles sat on the bed and took his sister's hand in his. "Florrie, when I examined her yesterday, I detected a heart murmur."

Stephen put his arm round his wife and looked concerned.

Florrie withdrew her hand. "Why is that? What have I done wrong?"

"Nothing at all. There are many causes. It means we shall have to keep a careful watch over her. She may grow out of it, or it may cause problems as she grows up. I will arrange regular appointments with a heart specialist. You do not have to wrap her in cotton wool all her life, just be vigilant of any changes. Please don't spend the rest of your life worrying about her. Enjoy her, and I know you and Stephen will take good care of her."

Florrie smiled weakly and took her brother's hand again. "Thank you," she said.

"I'll come again tomorrow, and every day this week. Can I bring Sapphire? She's longing to see you."

Florrie brightened up. "Oh, yes, that would be lovely."

"Is she feeding well?" Charles said, looking at his new niece.

"Yes, a bit slower than the boys."

"I forgot to ask. What are you calling her?"

"Sarah."

Charles picked up his bag and kissed his sister goodbye. "Rest while you can!" he called out as he went down the stairs.

Later that day a basket of gifts arrived from the shop. Florrie was delighted when Ben handed it over and she saw what it contained. Her sons were getting used to the new addition to the household, and Florrie gave them the sweets that Agnes had put in, telling them they were good boys.

Her brother and his wife came later that week, and Sapphire gave Florrie a big hug as she put a large bunch of flowers on the bed. "How are you, darling?" she asked. "Charles told me it was all pretty ghastly."

Charles, who was examining Sarah, looked up. "No, I didn't. I said she had a bad time of it."

Sapphire laughed and said, "It amounts to the same thing. Now listen, darling, you and I must have a chat. You don't want to go through *this* again. Three is quite enough for a civilised woman."

Charles raised his eyes, which made Florrie laugh.

"Sarah's doing very well," he said, carefully putting the covers back over her. Florrie smiled contentedly as she watched Sapphire looking at the baby in her cot. She gently touched her cheek with her finger. "I'm so glad you have your daughter. I hope she turns out better than ours—she's such a handful!"

Charles looked exasperated again and shook his head.

"We have good news," announced Sapphire. "Billy and Dorothy will have your boys for a while. Dorothy insists she can manage, although I can't imagine how. She's a great girl, I must say. Sorry I can't help, darling. You know what a hopeless mother I am."

"No, you're not," said her husband.

Florrie looked relieved. "As long as she thinks she can. I've been worried about Pa coping with them all day."

"We're going to take them there today. You'd better tell me what to pack."

CHAPTER THREE

EMERGENCY

Florrie was nursing Sarah, and she was thriving. Now the boys had gone to their uncle Billy's, the cottage was peaceful, interrupted only by the baby's cries for her next feed. Florrie doted on her. The child had become even more precious since she and Stephen had learnt of her heart complaint. Millie continued to call round, sometimes twice a day, to see that all was well, and Ben prepared the meals and kept the cottage in good order. As Florrie's anxiety for Sarah began to lessen, she was able to enjoy the little girl she had always wanted.

On the third day after the birth, she came downstairs, and Ben fussed round her, insisting she have his chair to feed Sarah. Stephen came home as soon as he could each day. At the end of the second week after the birth, he said he was worn out cycling into school and had decided to get a motorcar instead of a motorcycle.

"If I'm bringing schoolwork home, I need to keep it dry," he pointed out.

Florrie agreed, but she knew how expensive they were.

"We could go and see Stan, Danny's boss," Ben suggested. "When I worked for him a few years ago, he had several in his back yard of his garage waiting to be done up and sold on. He may be able to find a second-hand one for you."

Stan ran a motor repair business in Plymouth. Danny had worked for him for some years, and he was a good friend. Ben said he would write to Rosa, and if she agreed to a visit, they would go the following weekend.

Stephen discussed the expense with Ben. "I don't know how much I shall need. I've put aside some money for a motorbike, but I know it won't be enough for a motor."

Ben reassured him. "We can probably find one that needs some repairs, which will make it cheaper."

That evening, Ben went round the cottage looking for items to sell. He found a gold chain that had belonged to Sophie in the chest of drawers in his bedroom. He had given it to her the Christmas after his love child, Lionel, was born. He also took out his gold watch, a gift from Millie and Harry when they returned from their trip to New York to see their son, Tom. At the back of the drawer was a small box containing Sophie's wedding ring, which he took out and held up, studying it for a few moments. Putting it gently to his lips, he returned it to its box and replaced it carefully. He said nothing to his son-in-law about the extra cash he hoped to raise by selling these two items. He realised how important it was for Stephen to get to school each day and hoped they could obtain a suitable motor when they went to Stan's garage.

Rosa replied, saying they would love to have them, so Ben and Stephen caught the Plymouth train the following Saturday morning and then a bus to Rosa and Danny's road. Rosa was thrilled to see them, asking about the birth of her niece and looking concerned when she learnt about Sarah's condition. She said she would visit Florrie as soon as she had some leave.

The three men walked round to the garage, and Danny went to find Stan. While he waited, Ben spotted his friend Joe, who was cleaning one of the cars.

"Hello, Joe," he called out. "Good to see you again."

Some years before, Joe had helped Danny when he was in trouble, having been accused by the police of a crime he had not committed. Joe had provided evidence to prove his innocence, and because of this, Ben had found him employment at Stan's garage.

Joe looked up when he heard his name and grinned. "'Ello, Mr Browne," he replied. "I'm still 'ere!"

Ben looked pleased. "That's good to hear. How are you getting on?"

"Danny's a good mate," Joe replied. "I'm nearly as good as 'im now, mending the motors."

Ben grinned to himself. Why shouldn't the fellow have some self-belief? Just then, Stan appeared round the corner with Danny.

"Hello there, Ben! I understand you're wanting a motor," he called out.

Ben introduced him to Stephen. "This is Mr Faircross, my son-in-law. He needs a second-hand motor."

They shook hands.

Stephen looked at him anxiously. "I must be honest, Stan, I haven't much money. I need something small but reliable."

Stan blew through his moustache. "You and half the population of Plymouth!" he replied, scratching his head. "Come round the back and see what's there."

They followed Stan as he trudged round to the other side of the garage, where several used cars were parked along the wall at the back of the garage. Most of them had been there for years and looked a sorry sight with their rusty bodywork, cracked windscreens, and deflated tyres.

"Welcome to the old banger's graveyard." Stan laughed.

They began examining the motorcars, but none of them appeared particularly roadworthy. Danny was looking intently at one at the end, an old black Ford, when Ben strolled over to him.

"It's a Model T," Danny explained. "They're very good cars overall. This one needs some parts replaced, but I can help with that."

Ben stood back, surveying the row of battered vehicles they had already looked at, and realised they had all seen better days. He knew motors were becoming more reliable, but many early models had tended to break down and were not always worth repairing. Garage repair shops were kept busy, but demand was outdoing supply, and many motor owners simply bought new and better models. He respected Danny's opinion, so he went to speak to Stephen.

"Danny thinks he's found something suitable, the one at the end."

They went over to look at it. Danny assured them it was the best one there.

Stephen looked hopeful. "Should we make an offer then?"

Ben called over to Stan. "How much do you want for this one?"

Stan stood fiddling with his moustache. "Thirty pounds."

"Twenty-five" replied Ben.

"OK, twenty-five."

Stephen looked alarmed. "I've only got twenty pounds."

"We'll put the twenty pounds down and let him have the rest later," suggested Ben. Before Stephen could protest, he turned to Stan and said, "Done!" The two men shook hands on it.

Stan said he would let Danny work on it in slack periods. Joe had sauntered round and was watching with his hands in the pockets of his overalls.

"I could 'elp, too," he said.

Stan looked at him sternly. "You'll do as yer told, young man!"

Joe shrugged and grinned. Danny winked at his mate as they returned to the front of the garage.

On the way home, Danny spoke to Stephen and told him he thought he could get the vehicle up and running in a couple of weeks. "I know that motor, I remember when it was brought in and what's wrong with it, Stan doesn't. It's worth a bit more, really. We don't have the time to get them going with all the other repair jobs, so they go to scrap. Stan says they're not worth saving, but some of them are, like that one."

"I don't have twenty-five pounds," said Stephen, still fretting.

"You will have by the end of the day," said Ben. "You two get back—I know you want to see your parents, Stephen. I'll see you later."

Stephen looked puzzled as Ben left them, walking towards the High Street. He was looking out for a jeweller's shop. When he spotted one, he went in and placed the gold chain on the counter. After some minutes hard bargaining with the jeweller, he took the five pounds offered and walked out. He still had his watch in his pocket.

"Thank you, Sophie," he said quietly to himself. Returning to the garage, he settled the bill with Stan. He then returned to Rosa's and informed his son-in-law that everything had been taken care of.

The following day, Danny set to work on the engine in his lunch hour and after work. Joe helped when Stan wasn't there, and they eventually got it going. Danny slammed down the bonnet and wiped his hands on an oily rag. "We've done it, Joe! I'll get Rosa to let Ben know to come and collect it."

Ben arrived back at Danny's house as soon as he heard. He found the repaired motor standing ready outside. Ben couldn't believe what he saw. Danny had cleaned and polished the vehicle so that it looked almost new. He thanked Danny for all his efforts getting it going so quickly.

"Good luck," said Danny as Ben got into the driver's seat. He went round to the front to crank up the Ford. The engine spluttered and rumbled into life. Danny returned the starting handle, and Ben steered the car carefully down the road and round the corner.

The journey took three hours, and the engine frequently ground to a halt. There were many times when Ben had to get out and poke about under the bonnet or top up the water in the radiator.

"If this gets Stephen to school and back, it will be a miracle," he muttered as he closed the lid of the bonnet for the fifth time.

When he finally arrived home, his hands were black with oil. As he drew up beside Forge Cottage, Christopher and Jonny ran to the gate to greet their grandad.

"Motorcar," yelled Jonny. "Brmmm!"

Florrie followed them, carrying Sarah. "I'm so glad you're back, Pa. I was getting worried. How did it go?"

"Don't ask!" exclaimed Ben. "Let's say it just about got me here."

He told her to keep the boys inside the gate. Turning the car round, he reversed it slowly into his old workshop. Danny had given him a box of spare parts, which he took out of the back and put on the workbench. Behind the building, Ben's old motor stood rusting away. He had bought it when their old horse died many years earlier. It had been old when he bought it, but it had lasted a few years. He wondered if it could provide a few spare parts for repairs on Stephen's motor.

When Ben told Stephen about the extra five pounds for the car, he had insisted on paying it back when he could. Ben adamantly refused, explaining the money was from a piece of Sophie's jewellery, and he knew she would have wanted them to have it. Ben suggested he drive Stephen to school for the first week or two in case the car broke down, which he said was "highly likely." He showed him one or two things he could do if that happened.

"If you can't get it going, you'll just have to walk the rest of the way," he added, holding both hands out.

Ben worked on the car all week, ensuring it would go well. On Saturday he took his son-in-law into Kingsbridge to obtain his driving licence, then took him out for his first driving lesson on Sunday afternoon. Stephen came back elated.

"Thank goodness I don't have to cycle to school anymore," he said to Florrie when they returned.

"I had to do it for two years," she reminded him. "Even when it rained, and Pa forgot to come and get me!"

Ben laughed. "I did take you in for the rest of the week, if you remember."

The Ford proved to be more reliable than Ben had anticipated, and after a few days, Stephen was managing on his own. He set off for school at seven-thirty each morning, and afterwards Florrie would give Sarah her first feed of the day. Ben got the boys up and gave them their breakfast, although his first job was always to light the range. Later he would go to the shop for a few provisions or take the boys for short walks. He often had jobs to do round the cottage and outside.

Ben was content with his life, especially having his grandchildren around him. He was sitting one afternoon in his chair holding his little granddaughter in his arms. He commented that she was looking very bonny as he passed her to her mother for her next feed.

He went to his room to rest, leaving Florrie to feed Sarah in peace. When she had finished, she winded her, gently placed her carefully in her cot, and went about her chores. A short while later she returned to check on her child and as she did, she started back in shock, clasping her hands to her chest and calling out.

"Pa! Pa, come quickly! Something's wrong!"

Ben rushed downstairs and looked at his granddaughter in her cot. Her lips looked blue, and she was struggling to breathe. Florrie was standing over her, clutching her face in disbelief. Ben took Sarah out and sat down with her on his lap. He placed her on her back and began the procedure that Charles had taught him, rhythmically pressing the baby's chest gently with his fingers.

"Get Agnes to send a telegram to Charles and one to Stephen as well," he ordered.

Florrie fled out of the door. Ben continued the treatment, trying to keep himself calm while he waited for his daughter to return. How thankful he was that that they had the post office in the village and telegraph wires were now connecting them to Kingsbridge.

Florrie came rushing back. "How is she?" she asked breathlessly, looking at her baby daughter in Ben's arms.

"She seems a little better," Ben answered as calmly as he could. "I think I'll continue this treatment until Charles comes."

They both waited; the time seemed to go by so very slowly. At last they heard the door of a motor slam shut, and Charles rushed in. He went straight over and looked at Sarah.

"Well done, Pa," he said. "She's looking nice and pink now." He asked Ben to stop resuscitating and listened to Sarah's heart with his stethoscope. "She's recovered. I want her to go to the hospital, though. Pack a bag quickly, Florrie, and I'll take you there."

Florrie soon returned with her bag and a few things for the baby, and they both prepared to leave.

"What about Stephen?" she asked as they hurried out. "He should be here soon."

"We can't wait—he'll have to follow." Charles dashed out to his car and opened the door for his sister. Florrie was just getting in when Stephen's car drew up. "Is she all right?" he asked anxiously, jumping out of the driver's seat. He ran over to look at his child and got in quickly beside Florrie. They drove off.

Ben watched them go as they disappeared round the corner. As he went slowly back inside, he could feel he was shaking slightly.

"Where's Mummy gone?" asked Christopher, coming downstairs after his nap, followed by Jonny.

"Baby Sarah isn't very well," replied Ben. "They've taken her to the hospital to make her better. Now, what do you two want for your tea?"

Christopher looked pleased. He thought for a few minutes. "Fried bread!"

"Fwide bwed!" repeated Jonny, jumping up and down and clapping his hands.

"Fried bread it is, then!" said Ben, getting out the large pan and putting it on the range. He took the jar of fat drippings out of the pantry and put a spoonful into the pan. As it sizzled, Ben began slicing some bread. Turning, he saw his two grandsons sitting eagerly at the kitchen table. He gave them a knowing wink.

"And then what happened?" asked Lucinda, anxiously.

Charles had returned home from the hospital later that evening and was describing the dramatic events of the afternoon to his mother-in-law and Sapphire. He told them a paediatrician had seen Sarah and had called in a heart consultant. They had decided to keep the baby in a few days to observe her.

"Poor Florrie," said Sapphire. "What an awful thing to happen when Sarah seems to have been doing so well."

"It's a good thing Ben was there," added Lucinda. "Florrie and Stephen moved in with him at the right time. I hope he's managing with those boys."

The next day, Stephen appeared back at Forge Cottage. He said he was hoping to collect Florrie and Sarah from the hospital the following weekend. He thanked Ben for all he had done.

"You probably saved her life."

"I only did what Charles had told me to do," replied Ben.

Stephen asked how the boys had been.

"Very good," his father-in-law assured him. "They'll be glad to see you home."

"Thank you, Ben, for all you do."

"Your coming to live here is working out well."

Stephen nodded. "I think you have us for life now!"

Stephen returned to his duties at his school, grateful that Ben could look after the boys while he was at work. By the end of the week, he could see that his father-in-law was getting worn out. He arranged for Millie to have the boys on Saturday to give Ben a well-earned rest, and then set off early for Plymouth to collect his wife and child.

He returned later that day. As Florrie carried Sarah carefully into Forge Cottage, she was met by Christopher, who was holding his great Aunty Millie's hand.

"Is Sarah better now?" he asked anxiously.

"Yes, she is," replied his mother. "But we have to take great care of her."

She sat down and let him see his sister, explaining what had happened. Christopher listened intently. "I'm glad she's better," he said.

Florrie thanked her aunt for stepping in and looking after the boys. She assured her that Sarah was a lot better.

"The poor little thing," replied Millie. "Such a thing to happen when she's so young."

The following day was a Sunday, and Charles and Sapphire arrived, bringing Charlotte Elizabeth with them. Charles looked Sarah over and said he thought she had recovered remarkably well. Florence gave a broad smile.

While Sapphire and her daughter fussed over the baby, Charles saw that Stephen still looked very concerned. He drew his brother-in-law to one side.

"She *will* be all right," he assured him. "The specialists at the hospital said there was every chance she will grow out of the condition."

"Yes, I know, it isn't that. I haven't the means to pay for the cost of her treatment." He glanced nervously at his wife. "I shall have to take out a bank loan or something. If it comes to it, I'll have to sell the car. Do they allow you to pay it off in instalments?"

"You have no worries on that account," said Charles. "The hospital costs were paid for by someone who wishes to remain anonymous. And before you ask, it wasn't me, much as I would have liked to help you out."

"I…I don't know what to say," Stephen began. "That was extraordinarily kind, and I wish I knew who it was so I could thank them and show my gratitude."

Charlotte Eizabeth had gone outside to play with the boys, and she shortly returned, appearing in the kitchen doorway. "Jonny's stuck, Gandy."

"Not again," said Ben. "All right, I'm coming."

He hurried out to the orchard and gently lifted his little grandson down from the apple tree he had been attempting to climb.

"You must be careful, boys," he instructed. "The branches can break easily, as the trees are getting old."

There were a few scattered ones on the ground that he would need to clear away. He hadn't had much spare time since Florrie and her family moved in.

When he got back inside, she was making her guests a pot of tea. "I've had an idea," said Ben as she passed him a cup. "I think I'll cut down some of the old dead and dying trees in the orchard and plant new ones. Every new fruit tree will be dedicated to one of the family, and the first one will be in memory of your mother."

Florrie looked at her father with tears in her eyes. "That sounds wonderful!" she said.

While the grownups had their tea, Charlotte Elizabeth hung around Sarah's cradle in the corner of the kitchen, peering at her.

"Would you like to hold your little cousin?" asked Florrie, lifting her daughter gently out.

Charlotte Elizabeth's eyes shone as she nodded enthusiastically. She sat down, and Florrie placed the baby gently on her lap.

"Put your arm under her head," she instructed.

Sarah stirred and made a slight noise as Charlotte Elizabeth took her, which made the girl laugh. She held her carefully for some time, until her aunt said she needed to feed her. Florrie disappeared upstairs, and Charlotte Elizabeth sidled over to her mother.

"Can we have a new baby, Mummy?"

"No, we can't," replied Sapphire tersely. Charles raised his eyebrows, and he and Ben exchanged looks.

When Florrie retuned with the baby, Sapphire announced it was time for them to go. "I think Mummy would like a visit from you sometime, Ben," she added.

"Tell Lucinda I can't leave Florrie at present, but I'll come and see her when I can."

"You could come on a Saturday when Stephen's home—then you could use his motor," suggested Sapphire.

"That's a good idea," said Florrie. "You go, Pa."

After they had left, Stephen told them that someone had paid for Sarah's treatment. Florrie wondered who it was.

"It could be Sapphire, I suppose," she said. "Or maybe Lucinda?"

"Or even Lionel?" suggested Stephen. "It would be good to find out."

Ben was driving Stephen's Ford through the lanes on his way to Acacia House to visit Lucinda. The motor was running smoothly, and Ben made a mental note to ask Florrie to write and reassure Danny that he had made a good choice. When he arrived, he parked at the bottom of the High Street, unsure whether he would make it up the steep hill. He walked the rest of the way, passing Charles's smart Tourer, which was parked outside the house, and giving it an admiring glance as he went by. Mrs Harris opened the door and showed him straight up to Lucinda's apartment.

"Ben, darling! Lovely to see you," she said as he entered, her eyes shining.

Ben kissed her lightly on the cheek and sat down, looking round. "You have a lovely room here, Lucinda."

"Thank you. I try to give Charles and Sapphire time to themselves, so I often sit in here. I have a good view of the garden this side of the house."

Mrs Harris brought in a tray of coffee.

"Well, Ben, what a lot of drama at Forge Cottage." Lucinda looked intrigued as she poured him a cup. "Charles told us all about it. How is little Sarah?"

"She's doing very well. We're so thankful to Charles for his quick response getting her into hospital."

Ben put his cup down and looked directly at her. "Lucinda, what you did was very kind and generous, and I'm enormously grateful to you."

"You know, then."

"I'm afraid it was obvious, knowing you. Charles didn't tell me."

"Do the others know?"

"No."

"Please keep it to yourself. I would appreciate that."

"Of course. I'm glad I know, and I admire you for it. It was a kind gesture. Can I suggest to Florrie and Stephen they ask you to be Sarah's godmother?"

"Tell them I would be delighted."

They drank their coffee quietly, each in their own thoughts. Suddenly there was a knock on the door, and Sapphire entered with Charlotte Elizabeth, who immediately ran towards her grandfather and hugged him.

"Will you read me a story, Gandy?"

Ben enveloped her in his arms and kissed her. "Yes, of course I will."

CHAPTER FOUR

THE PIANO

THERE WAS A SENSE OF relief at Forge Cottage. Florrie felt reassured that their daughter would be all right now she had been seen by a specialist. The doctor had explained that as Sarah grew stronger there would be less likelihood of another episode.

It made her happy that her father went about his tasks whistling and humming to himself. Little Jonny followed him like a shadow, continually asking questions. Baby Sarah was feeding well and seemed content. Florrie would sometimes sing to her, and Sarah seemed to respond, smiling and fixing her little blue eyes on her mother.

"I think Sarah's going to be musical," remarked Florrie to Stephen one evening when he had finished his schoolwork. "She loves it when I sing to her."

Florrie was knitting Sarah a matinee coat as they sat together in the parlour in front of a roaring fire.

Ben looked thoughtful. "There's no one on my side of the family who was. Sophie told me she learnt to play the piano when she was young." He turned to Stephen. "We are depending on your side to introduce some culture."

"My mother had piano lessons for a while." He frowned slightly, thinking hard.

"I should like Sarah to have lessons," said Florrie earnestly. "We need to get a piano. Perhaps Dorothy would teach her."

Ben gave a chuckle. "It'll be a while before she'll be ready for lessons!"

"I wish I could play." Florrie sounded wistful. "Then we could have family singsongs."

The two men glanced at each other and grimaced.

Florrie would often stroll up the lane for a short walk with Sarah in her perambulator. One afternoon she returned with some news.

"When I walked past Clayden House, it looked empty," she informed Ben as she struggled through the narrow door, carefully manoeuvring the baby carriage into the kitchen.

Ben got up to help her. "Yes, I heard that old Mrs Wilmott-Smith had moved out and gone to live with her son, Philip. You remember, the boy Ma taught when she was the governess there?"

Florrie knew her mother had worked there before she had married her father. Sophie had told her she had been tormented by her employer's eldest son, which had led to her being dismissed.

"Yes, I do remember. It was Uncle Harry who got her reinstated, wasn't it?"

"Uncle Harry would have done anything for her."

"He liked her too?"

"Yes, Harry used to tell me all about her when we went drinking together. The first time I saw Sophie coming down the lane, I smiled at her and said hello, but she just put her nose in the air and walked past me!"

Florrie laughed. "You won her in the end, though. I wonder what will become of the place—whether it will be sold or let."

Clayden House was a large brick-built mansion situated at the top of a hill, away from the rest of the village and surrounded by laurel bushes and large trees. Over the years these had grown and now almost hid the house from view. A flock of jackdaws lived in the eaves and outbuildings. Florrie would hear them chatter and caw whenever she walked past. The house always made her shudder slightly. Her father had told her that the family never involved themselves in the village, not even attending the church, although Mr Wilmott -Smith knew the rector well.

Sophie had said the family and servants would say prayers daily in the library.

A week later Florrie saw a flier in the shop saying that Clayden House was to be sold and announcing an auction of the contents that was to take place the following Saturday.

"I think we should go and see if there's anything worth having," she said to her father when she got back from her shopping. "I would love to have a look inside!"

Ben agreed, and on the day of auction escorted his daughter up the lane to the house.

"Have you ever been inside?" Florrie asked her father as they strolled along together.

Ben gave a short laugh. "Huh! Wilmott-Smith wouldn't have wanted *me* in his house. He told Sophie I was a disreputable character and forbade her to see me."

"And is that why Ma left?"

"Yes. I told her to get paid, then walk out. Apparently, he was furious."

They arrived and went through the main door. Florrie smiled knowingly at Ben as they entered. "I don't suppose Ma would have been allowed to come in this way," she commented.

An attendant asked their names, then gave them an inventory of the articles for sale and invited them to walk round to view them. Ben and Florrie walked through the spacious reception rooms on the ground floor. These contained pieces of furniture as well as pictures, carpets, rugs, mirrors, and various smaller items, such as clocks and ornaments, all arranged and labelled, ready to be examined by prospective buyers. Florrie looked astonished as she surveyed the contents, stopping to look at anything that caught her eye.

"These are fine pieces of furniture," she observed, examining a rosewood cabinet. "I wonder if that clock is here. You know, the one Ma was accused of stealing?"

"There are so many clocks," answered Ben, looking round. "I wouldn't know."

"You told me Mr Wilmot-Smith *was* a banker," replied Florrie. "He was obviously very well off."

They moved on to the bottom of the wide staircase. Florrie slid her hand along the shiny mahogany banister as they ascended to the first landing. They passed through more rooms and Florrie gasped at the four-poster bed in the master bedroom.

She leant over to whisper to Ben. "I don't think we can afford anything here. Let's go up to the other rooms."

They mounted another set of stairs to a smaller landing and entered the schoolroom where the furniture was of a lower grade. Florrie felt very strange seeing where her mother had once taught many years ago. She gave a sideways look at her father. He caught her eye and put his arm through hers, and they stood in silence. Suddenly, Florrie gasped and nudged him.

"Look," she whispered.

In the corner was a dusty old upright piano.

"I think I remember your ma telling me that there was one here," Ben said, "but it was stored away behind a lot of junk. Wilmot-Smith did not want her to teach music; he said his sons were not that way inclined."

"I wonder what we could get it for." Florrie was excited. "Can you bid for it, Pa?"

Her father looked uncertain. "I'll try. I've only done this once before, when we bought some furniture for the parlour years ago."

Florrie left her father to continue looking round and made her way down to the kitchen in the basement to view several items she wanted. She marked them in her catalogue and then joined her father in the library, where the auction was to take place.

The room was very crowded, full of all sorts of people, from finely dressed men and women to working class men in caps and womenfolk in shawls. Florrie recognised a few people from the village and nodded to them. The buzz in the room suddenly quietened as the auctioneer mounted the rostrum at the front to commence the bidding. He was a large red-faced man wearing a smart suit and waistcoat. Across his ample front he had a gold watch chain. He perused the catalogue in front of him and then raised his gavel.

Ben had been given a card with a large number printed on it. They had to wait some time for the items in the schoolroom to come up, and these included desks, a blackboard easel, rocking horse, and globe.

Finally, the piano was announced. Florrie stiffened and glanced nervously at her father, who was looking straight ahead, concentrating on the proceedings. They were at the back, and Florrie had to stand on tiptoe to see the auctioneer over the heads of the crowd when the bidding began. She glanced round the room as hands were raised and the price gradually rose. Ben waited a short while, then joined in. Eventually it was between him and one other person. Ben put his hand up one final time, and the gavel went down.

"Sold!" shouted the auctioneer, pointing at Ben's card.

"Oh, Pa," exclaimed Florrie, jumping up and down and gripping his arm. "You did it!"

Ben looked very pleased with himself. "I paid a little more than I should have," he said. "But I know how much you wanted it."

Florrie exclaimed, "Thank you!" and kissed him.

"Now we need to get it transported to the cottage. I'll see if Harry can round up a few lads."

Florrie stayed on to bid for her kitchen items, which were announced right at the end of the afternoon and managed to obtain some of them. When she went to look for her father, she found him sound asleep in the main sitting room in one of the large comfy armchairs.

The auction people had insisted that the buyer remove the piano from the upstairs in Clayden House. Ben had fetched Harry, and they had thought long and hard about how to get the instrument out without damaging it or the stairway. Ben returned to his workshop to get some planks and ropes, and Harry left and returned with Agnes's husband Ted and two other strong-looking men from the Twin Foxes tavern. They managed to manipulate it down the stairs, but it wasn't easy.

"If I'd known what a heavy old brute this was, I wouldn't have bid for it," grumbled Ben as he stood watching the others pull and heave. They steered it outside and wheeled it the rest of the way down the lane, through the gate, and into the cottage, where it was positioned in the parlour.

Florrie was very excited when it finally arrived and thanked the men for their efforts in getting it there. Ben and Harry took their companions to the Two Foxes to buy them drinks, leaving Florrie to admire her new acquisition. Holding a dusting cloth in her hand, she lifted the lid and pressed a few keys to see how it sounded. When she heard the notes, she realised it would need some tuning. *I'll get Dorothy to come over and have a look at it,* she decided.

CHAPTER FIVE

SAPPHIRE'S TRIP

SAPPHIRE WAS IN THE SITTING room holding her daughter as she tried to wriggle free.

"No, I won't!" shouted Charlotte Elizabeth, managing to release her arm and running away from her mother.

Sapphire could see she was tired and wanted to get her to bed. She decided she would have to get her mother's help—she could always manage the girl when she was in one of her moods.

Charles came into the sitting room just then at the end of evening surgery.

"I need a drink, darling," said Sapphire. "That child is getting worse."

Charles calmly poured two, gave one to his wife, and kissed her cheek. "I think the time has come for her to have a governess or nurse-maid or something," he said. "She needs the discipline."

"I think she's a little young for that."

Charles sat down and put his feet up. "What do you suggest then?"

"I don't know," said Sapphire, fiddling with her glass.

"She needs someone to play with," said her husband. "The child's probably bored living in a house full of adults." He got up and poured himself another drink. "Perhaps Billy and Dorothy would have her for a while. It would give you a break, and I'm sure she would love playing with Frank and Clarrie."

Sapphire sat up. "What a good idea!"

"I'll telephone him and see what he says. I hope they don't think it's an imposition."

Charles went through to the hallway. They had only recently had the telephone installed, and he still felt slightly nervous as he picked up the receiver to dial Billy's number. When he came back, he said, "All fixed. They would love to have her. I'm free tomorrow, so we'll drive over there."

"Oh, thank you, darling!" Sapphire flung her arms round his neck. "I do so need a break."

After lunch the following day, they drove to the veterinary practice Billy had set up with his wife Dorothy in Kingsbridge after they married. It was a red brick detached house that had been extended to include a surgery, a treatment room, and a recovery room for the animals.

Charles greeted his cousin and his wife, and Dorothy took Charlotte Elizabeth to see the animals recuperating at the back of the surgery. Frank and Clarrie were running about on the bare floor, making quite a noise. Billy quietened them down, then turned his attention to Sapphire, who had sunk into one of the chairs.

"You look tired," he said.

She smiled sweetly at him. "Yes, I am. To be honest, I'm finding my daughter a bit of a handful. We think she needs some friends and something to occupy her." She glanced at Charles, who was looking out of the window at the wooded garden at the back of the house.

"I'm sure Charlotte Elizabeth can make herself useful, and Dorothy would probably like her company and help with the other two. She can stay as long as you like." Billy looked fondly at his young son and daughter. They were playing with their toys, which were scattered all over the floor.

"That would be perfect, as I'm planning to go away for a few days."

Charles swung round and raised his eyebrows but said nothing.

Dorothy returned a little later with Charlotte Elizabeth and said it was time for tea.

"Am I sleeping here, Mummy?" asked her daughter, clasping her hands together in delight.

"Just for a few days, darling. You must be very good and help Aunty Dorothy."

Dorothy smiled kindly and went to bring in the tea things, and when she returned, she asked Charlotte Elizabeth to help. Sapphire watched as she passed round a plate of cakes. *Why is she good here and so difficult at home?* she wondered.

Charlotte Elizabeth put the plate back on the table and began telling her mother about the animals she had seen. "Uncle Billy's making them all better. Some of them have got bandages on. Aunty Dorothy let me help feed a kitten. Can I have a kitten? *Please.*"

"I'll think about it," was the response she got.

When tea was finished, Charles and Sapphire prepared to leave.

"Now, be a good girl," Sapphire instructed as she kissed her daughter goodbye. "Then we'll see about that kitten."

As they drove home, Charles asked his wife about her plans to go away.

"Didn't I tell you, darling? My cousin Madelaine has asked me if I would go with her to Le Touquet, in France. We're going to fly there."

Charles looked astonished, gripping the steering wheel tightly as he drove along. "You're what?"

"Don't sound so shocked. It will be perfectly safe, and great fun!"

Charles fixed his eyes on the road ahead. "I must say you never cease to amaze me. Whatever will you be doing next? Hunting tigers in India, I suppose."

Two days later, Sapphire packed her bag, and Charles drove her to Kingsbridge Station to catch her train. He kissed his wife as she boarded her first-class carriage and stood back and waved.

"Goodbye, Sapphire! Safe journey."

He watched the train as it drew away, wondering how safe her trip would be. Air travel was relatively new and was often dangerous. What if the engine cut out during the sea crossing? Why did his beautiful wife want to put herself in danger, especially when they had a child? Why had he agreed to let her go? His thoughts raced on as he drove home, and he tried hard to overcome his fears. He could not contemplate life without her.

Back at Acacia House, he let himself in and went to find Mrs Harris. "I'll dine in the breakfast room," he instructed, and for the next few days, he spent his spare time reading his medical books and trying not to worry about what his wife was up to.

Sapphire met up with Madelaine in Exeter, and they continued by train to London. There, they hired a taxicab to take them to Croydon, south of London, where there was a small airfield. Both had taken warm coats, as the air travel company had told them the flight would be noisy and chilly. They had also been advised to bring flat footwear, so they were in their tennis shoes. They had each taken a small case of essentials and changes of clothing.

"Isn't this exciting?" Madelaine exclaimed as the taxi rumbled on. "Charles didn't mind you coming, then?"

"Oh, no! He knows I must get out of the village sometimes, otherwise I'd go spare."

"Can he manage Charlotte Elizabeth on his own?"

"She's staying with his cousin, Billy, and his family. He has a veterinary practice, and she loves helping to look after the animals."

They arrived at the airport and drew up outside a large white structure in the Neoclassical style. The taxi driver told them that the terminal building and control tower had only just opened at the beginning of the year. Inside, a man in uniform sitting at a desk checked their passports and then briefly looked inside each of their cases. They made their way to the departure lounge, where they could view the airfield through the large window. The room was furnished with comfortable chairs and side tables, and there was a bar in the corner. Sapphire and Madelaine sat down and ordered tea from the waitress.

As Sapphire peeled off her gloves, she looked round at their fellow passengers. A well-dressed middle-aged couple sitting nearby smiled at them. The woman had a fur tippet round her neck, and her husband was wearing an overcoat.

Two young men standing at the bar introduced themselves as brothers. They were both wearing blazers and fashionable wide flannel trousers and had sleek, combed hair.

"Is this your first flight, ladies?" asked one of them.

"Yes, and we hope it's not the last," replied Madelaine. They all laughed nervously.

"And yourselves?" enquired Sapphire.

The other brother replied, "We've flown before, as we're having flying lessons. We fancied going a little further on this trip."

Four more passengers arrived, making the total number ten. The small airport lounge was now full. The cousins finished their tea, and after a short wait, the uniformed man reappeared and asked everyone to get ready to board. Sapphire glanced at Madelaine nervously. A steward took their cases, and they were led across the field to the waiting machine, a Handley Page W9 biplane. Sapphire had never seen an aircraft before, and as they approached, she was impressed by its size, noticing the huge propellers, one at the front and one on the fuselage. The double wings, separated by six pairs of struts, spread out on either side, and the plane was supported by four tyred wheels. She found it hard to believe that this machine was going to leave the ground shortly and take her into the sky above.

Sapphire and Madelaine climbed up the few steps to the doorway and followed their fellow passengers into the cabin to find their seats. From their comfortable cane chairs, one on each side of the aisle, they could see out of the curtained windows. The steward settled them in, providing small rugs to wrap round their legs and explaining that the flight would be chilly.

The pilot appeared and welcomed them on board. He told them a little about the flight and explained the safety precautions. He left through a canvas doorway at the front, and shortly afterwards, the engines revved up, and the aeroplane taxied round slowly, moving towards the main runway. Sapphire reached across and gripped Madeleine's hand.

The brothers, who were sitting behind, laughed. "Wait until we land!" teased one of them.

As the plane gathered speed, the noise increased. The wheels rumbled along the runway, and then suddenly they were moving along smoothly and had left the ground. Sapphire looked out of the window and saw how quickly they had gained height. Below them, aircraft were scattered about on the airfield, looking like toys. They rose rapidly, then levelled off, the engine emitting a continuous loud hum as they continued to fly below the cloud line. They had been told that the cabin was not pressurised. The other passengers talked quietly, pointing out features they could see on the ground.

Sapphire sat without speaking for a while. She had never experienced anything so thrilling and wanted to enjoy every moment. The steward brought round drinks and little dishes of cheese and biscuits on trays, but Sapphire could hardly eat anything—she felt compelled to look out of the window the whole time. The aeroplane passed over white cliffs and then out across the English Channel, and she could see the steamships below forging their way through the waves, leaving white trails behind them.

They continued to fly over the sea, and all too soon the coast of France appeared. The plane began to descend and curve round and down towards the airfield at Le Touquet. They bumped a few times on landing and eventually came to a halt.

Sapphire looked at Madelaine with relief, her eyes shining with excitement. "We made it!" she gasped.

After passing through passport control, they followed their fellow passengers as they left the plane and made their way out of the airport to the line of parked vehicles at the front. Here they hailed a taxicab to take them to their hotel. Sapphire took in their surroundings as they drove along the seafront. The beach was flanked by many hotels and tall apartment buildings. In front, the wide expanse of almost white sand stretched far and wide, edged by dunes covered with tufts of marram grass. The May sunshine made the sea sparkle, and Sapphire could feel a wave of excitement surging through her.

"I hope we shall be able to swim," she said, turning to Madelaine, who looked doubtful.

"I think you'll find the sea is still quite cold."

They arrived at the hotel and were shown to their room. Sapphire went straight to the window and was pleased to find that they had a sea view.

"What did you think of the flight?" Madelaine asked as she unpacked her case and put her clothes on the bed.

"Brilliant! I've never experienced anything so thrilling."

"I suppose one day they'll manage to heat the cabin. It was a bit cold."

"I was too busy looking out of the window to notice," replied Sapphire. "To see the world from the sky was very strange."

By now it was late afternoon, so they ordered a light supper to be brought to their room and then retired early. It had been an exhausting, if exciting day.

The next morning, they explored the waterfront, enjoying a bracing walk along the promenade. They held onto their hats, their silk scarves flapping wildly in the sea breeze. Afterwards they visited the shops, buying clothes and choosing souvenirs to take home.

Back at their hotel, they spread their purchases out on the beds and tried on their new garments.

"How exciting to have something with a French label," enthused Sapphire, holding up a blouse she had selected. She carefully wrapped everything away in tissue paper, and they went down to the restaurant for dinner.

"Can you read any of this?" Sapphire asked Madelaine as she picked up the menu and studied it.

"Yes, I think so. My French isn't too bad."

"Maddy, you're such a swot! I have none. The lessons at school were so boring."

Her cousin translated the menu, and the waiter came and took their order.

"Tomorrow, I want to buy a little gift for Charlotte Elizabeth," said Sapphire, sipping her glass of red wine. "And something for Mummy and Charles. He's such a swell, letting me off the leash occasionally."

Sapphire was more relaxed on the flight back home two days later. She knew what to expect and looked forward to it, and they soon landed safely back at the airfield. She felt relieved, as she had read in a magazine that an aircraft like theirs had ditched into the sea, all lives being lost. Flying was still a risky business.

Sapphire and Madelaine parted company at Exeter railway station but had promised each other they would take another trip soon. "Though perhaps not flying," added Madelaine. "It's *so* expensive."

On her arrival home, Sapphire was full of her new adventure. She greeted her husband enthusiastically, flinging her arms round his neck when he arrived to collect her off the train. "Charles, you must try it! Flying is so exciting."

"And dangerous," he replied, taking her small case from her. "I'd rather keep my two feet on the ground, thank you."

"You are an old fuddy-duddy. Everyone will be flying one day, you'll see."

He looked unconvinced.

Charles had to do evening surgery, so Sapphire spent the time with her mother, describing her experiences in detail. Her husband joined them for pre-dinner drinks, and Sapphire handed over her gifts.

Charles undid the ribbon tied round his small box. He opened it and looked pleased. "These are smart," he said, taking out a pair of gold cufflinks.

"A little thank you for letting me go," said Sapphire, smiling happily.

Charles put his arm round her, drew her towards him, and kissed her. "Thank you, darling. I'm glad you're home safe and sound."

Lucinda thanked her for her gift, unscrewing the top of a bottle of perfume and sniffing it.

"When are we going to collect Charlotte Elizabeth?" asked Charles, putting the cufflinks back in their box.

"If she's happy, she might as well stay where she is," replied Sapphire. She wasn't in a hurry to have her daughter back.

"I would like to have her home soon. She'll be missing us."

Sapphire shrugged.

"Did I tell you I'm thinking of getting a secretary?" Charles went on. "There's so much paperwork to do. It should free me up so I can spend more time with Charlotte Elizabeth. I'll speak to Brian about taking on more responsibilities. I was wondering if his wife would be interested."

Sapphire smiled. "That's a splendid idea, darling."

"But it wouldn't solve the problem of finding her some friends her own age," Lucinda pointed out. "I've been thinking—we do need a nursery for young children in the village. It's something the church could be involved in, and I'm sure it would be welcomed by the mothers."

Lucinda had been attending church every Sunday since she moved into Acacia House some years before and had made several acquaintances. She and Caroline Bailey, the previous doctor's wife, were firm friends.

"I'm not sure I want our daughter mixing with village children." Sapphire wrinkled her nose.

"Why ever not? Children are all the same at that age," Charles argued. "I do think we ought to bring Charlotte Elizabeth home tomorrow."

Sapphire sighed and reluctantly agreed.

They collected their daughter the following day. Dorothy told them that her visit had gone very well; she had loved caring for the animals at the surgery and had been no trouble at all. Charles suggested that Frank could come over to Acacia House to play once a week with her, as he was almost her age. Dorothy thought the arrangement was a good idea.

It began well, but two weeks later, Sapphire informed her mother that there were problems with Frank's visits. "They don't seem to be getting along, Mummy. It amazes me that in a roomful of toys, they both want the same one at the same time."

"They're both strong little personalities. Do you think we ought to tell Dorothy?"

Charles agreed it would be best to end the visits when told about the situation. Sapphire was disappointed the arrangement hadn't worked out. She remembered the kitten Charlotte Elizabeth had wanted and asked Charles if she could have one. He had no objection and said he would ask on his rounds in the village. He soon found a litter, and they took Charlotte Elizabeth to choose one. She decided on a small black-and-white cat and named him Nipper, as he had tried to playfully bite her hand.

The nursery was soon set up in the village. It was supported by some of the better-off women, including Lucinda. The church had provided a room, and some of the village mothers had offered as volunteer helpers. The rector's wife was very enthusiastic about the project and had bought some toys and equipment. Other donations of toys started to come in, and the nursery opened.

Sapphire was adamant she did not want Charlotte Elizabeth to attend when Lucinda suggested she could go there. She told her mother and Charles she had seen the state of some of the children and they looked dirty.

"There's one rather sweet little girl," said Lucinda. "Her name's Molly. Her mother runs the haberdashery shop in the High Street. She works all day, so she has Molly in the shop with her in the afternoons. I was talking to her the other day. Perhaps she could come and play with Charlotte Elizabeth."

Sapphire pulled a face. "Her mother works in a shop?"

"You really must come off your high horse," said Charles testily. "You used to work in a shop, if I remember."

"That was different. It was a high-class department store, and I would have made it into management if it hadn't been for your making me pregnant."

"Sapphire, please!"

Charles glanced at Lucinda, who was trying not to laugh.

"Come and see her," she suggested, smiling sweetly. "I think she would make a charming playmate for Charlotte Elizabeth."

The following morning, Sapphire accompanied her mother on a visit to the nursery while Charles looked after their daughter. Sapphire observed Molly and agreed that she played very nicely and seemed a well brought up little girl. Lucinda introduced her to Molly's mother and arrangements were made for Molly to come to their house for two afternoons a week.

CHAPTER SIX

AMANDA'S EXHIBITION

S APPHIRE HAD JUST JOINED HER family for breakfast one morning when Lucinda held up an invitation card she had just opened. "Amanda's asked us to an exhibition of her work," she announced. "It's a weekend at the beginning of June."

Sapphire poured herself a cup of tea. "That sounds exciting, not long then."

"It counts me out," said Charles, looking up from his newspaper. "I'm on duty, and I know Brian wants that time off for a family event."

"*This* is a family event," said Sapphire.

"I'm afraid I can't go either," said Lucinda, putting the invitation down. "The nursery is having a fundraising sale, and I said I would help. We need the money—I can't let them down."

Sapphire frowned. "That leaves just me, then."

"Who'll look after our daughter?" asked Charles, pointedly. "You can't take her."

"Oh, I'll sweet-talk Mrs Harris or ask Dorothy." She stirred her tea, deep in thought. "I could ask Ben if he would like to come."

"He can't leave Florrie, darling," said her mother. "Not alone with a young baby and those boys."

"It's over the weekend," said Sapphire. "Stephen will be there."

"You'd have to travel up on the Friday afternoon and return on the Monday morning," said Lucinda.

"I expect Millie will help her," Sapphire answered airily.

"You always expect everyone to fit in with your arrangements," said her husband in an exasperated tone. "It might be inconvenient for them."

"Oh, Charles, don't be cross!"

He swallowed his tea down and got up to go. "I'm off to surgery. I'll let you two sort this out."

Lucinda maintained her silence.

"I'm not being selfish, Mummy. I just thought it would be nice for Ben to have a break."

"That's kind of you, darling, but I'm not sure you'll persuade him. Will he like going to an art exhibition?"

"It will be something different, and he will want to see Lionel. I'll visit him later today and ask him, if Mr Grumpy will let me have the car."

Sapphire was always glad of an excuse to go to London, and later that day she set out to Forge Cottage to see Ben. He was getting the boys' tea ready, and Christopher was sitting at the table.

"Hello, Aunty Saffy," he said, giving her a bright smile.

"Hello, little monster!" She tousled his hair.

Florrie came in carrying Sarah, followed by Jonny. "Hello, Sapphire, is everything all right?"

"Yes, thank you. I've come with an invitation for Ben."

When she explained what it was, Ben was doubtful. "I don't think I can leave Florrie at the moment," he said.

"You go," said Florrie immediately. "A break will do you good."

After a little more persuading, Ben agreed.

Sapphire gave him a hug. "Charles will collect you on the Friday morning."

The weekend of the exhibition, Ben and Sapphire set off to catch the early train to London. It was a fine spring morning, and as Charles drove along the lanes past the fresh green hedgerows, Ben felt a sense of relief. It was good to get away from the hectic life at Forge Cottage for a bit. There always seemed to be a baby crying or the boys scrapping with each other, and Florrie would get tired and edgy. Sometimes she and Stephen would have an argument over something, and he would have to retreat to his room until it passed. Fortunately, that didn't happen too often, Overall, they all got on well together, but it wasn't the quiet life he had been used to before Sophie died, however.

Having arrived at Kingsbridge Station, Sapphire went straight to a first-class carriage and opened the door. Ben looked surprised.

"I know you think I'm a posh snob, but I can afford to be!" she said, laughing.

They settled into their seats opposite one another, and Ben began reading his newspaper. Sapphire opened her magazine. After a while, she looked up, and he smiled at her.

It took all morning to reach Paddington Station. Lionel was waiting for them as they walked to the gate at the end of the platform. He embraced them both and took their bags.

"Amanda's so looking forward to your visit. She was thrilled you could both come. She's worked hard at her sculptures and hopes to sell a few."

Ben looked at his and Lucinda's son and felt proud of him. He had made a good marriage to a lovely talented girl and was working successfully as a solicitor at his own practice. He was grateful his son's illegitimacy had not hindered him in any way.

When they arrived at Lionel's stylish house in Richmond, Amanda came out to welcome them. She and Sapphire had lots to talk about, so Lionel took Ben into the sitting room and put a glass of whisky into his hand.

"Let me show you round while the girls catch up with each other," he said with a wry smile.

Lionel and Amanda lived in a large two-story Victorian house. The rooms were furnished in the new art deco style, and each room contained well-designed pieces obtained from top London stores, such as Heals and Maples.

When the tour was over, Ben turned to his son. "You have a beautiful house here," he stated. "How Sophie would have loved seeing it."

Ben regretted his late wife had never made the journey to Richmond. She had become too ill to travel far.

"Of course, Amanda has done all this," said Lionel, waving his hand. "We are very fortunate to be able to afford such luxury."

Lionel took his father to see his wife's sculpture studio at the back of the house, where she had clay models in progress and several completed figurines waiting to be cast.

"Amanda's pieces are beginning to sell," Lionel explained. "She has had many of them cast in bronze, and those should fetch good prices."

Ben looked carefully at the statuettes and looked impressed.

"They're all very good," he acknowledged. "She has great talent."

Lionel smiled in agreement and led the way back to the sitting room. As they entered the room, Ben saw that David had arrived.

"My father's joining us for dinner," said Amanda. "I think you already know each other."

Ben and David had briefly met six years before at Lionel and Amanda's wedding banquet. He and Sophie had found the man rather eccentric.

David approached, holding out his hand. "May I offer my sincere condolences on the passing of your wife, Ben," he began. "I am fully aware of what you are going through, having experienced it myself, albeit many years ago. One is never the same, but we must be thankful for our dear children."

"Thank you," said Ben, shaking his hand, feeling surprised at David's little speech.

Amanda steered the conversation towards more cheerful subjects. "I hope you'll enjoy the exhibition," she said. "I've been working hard to get ready for it."

"I'm sure it will be a great success," Sapphire reassured her. Amanda asked after Florrie and said she would write to her. "I'm so glad she has her little girl," she added, looking wistful.

"Speaking of little girls, how is that lively daughter of yours, Sapphire?" asked Lionel.

"Rather a handful," she replied. "As she is an only child, we think she needs some other children to play with, so we've arranged for a little girl to come."

"Amanda grew up without brothers or sisters," announced David. "It didn't seem to do her any harm."

Lionel frowned and went to refill his glass.

During dinner, Ben looked intently at David as he began to hold forth on art and artists. Sapphire remarked that her mother had always thought that he was a true artist.

"That's very kind, but I've never thought of myself primarily as simply an *artist*," responded David, leaning back in his chair. "We craftsmen are really artisans. What would you say about blacksmithing, Ben?"

He looked straight at Ben and waited for his answer. Lionel pursed his lips and glanced at his father.

After a few moments, Ben said, "Blacksmithing may not be an art, but it is a functional craft. For example, creating a perfect shoe for a horse is gratifying in that the horse can continue to do his work in comfort, and the farmer can rely on that."

David looked surprised. Lionel smiled and continued to enjoy his dinner.

"The Arts and Crafts movement validated all artisans," added Amanda brightly. "William Morris said every created thing should be seen as beautiful as well as functional. I hope my work can give pleasure to people and perhaps inspire them, but I admire all craftsmen who have trained long hours to perfect their work, and our society could not do without them."

Lionel shot a look of admiration towards his wife.

The conversation moved on to other subjects, and at the end of the meal, the ladies left, and Lionel got out the cigars. Ben declined, telling them he had to be careful with his chest.

As they drank their glasses of port, David took a puff of his cigar and suddenly announced, "Lucinda and I are going on a trip to Edinburgh. I wrote to her, and she has agreed to come once she has finished with all this nursery business. My friend is an artist and has a studio there, and he's going to paint her."

Ben gave him a hard look. "I believe there's already a rather fine portrait of her hanging in her sitting room."

"That was done years ago," said David dismissively. "She said she would like a more recent one."

Ben turned to Lionel and asked how his work was going, and Lionel began telling him about his practice.

David puffed another plume of smoke and stubbed out his cigar. "I think I will join the ladies." he said, getting up to go.

There was an air of excitement when the small family party arrived at the art gallery in Chelsea the next evening. Other artists had also been invited to exhibit, and Amanda's work was on the first floor. Ben followed Lionel and the others up the stairs and into a room where there were several white plinths and pedestals, each with a single bronze figurine mounted on the top. Around the walls were framed sketches of figurework and some portraits.

The room was already full of guests and was buzzing with animated conversation. Ben walked round, examining each piece and trying to catch a glimpse of the title labels between the jostling bodies. As he wandered, he made sure to keep well clear of David, who was in one corner, surrounded by a group of enthusiastic acquaintances.

Ben continued to study the bronze statuettes, which he found interesting. On several occasions in the past, he had fashioned ironwork and had made a few objects of his own design. *I think I must be something of an artist, or artisan, as David said,* he thought to himself. He had made Lucinda and her husband Samuel a free-standing wrought-iron candle holder for their wedding, which he knew she still had in her apartment.

Amanda came up to him, pushing through the throng of people. "Hello, Ben! I hope you're enjoying yourself," she called above the noise.

"Yes, I am," he replied enthusiastically. "This is all a new experience for me, and I love your work."

She smiled warmly and thanked him.

"I don't think I'll be buying any, though," he said, with a twinkle in his eye. She laughed and was then drawn away.

Ben grinned to himself and proceeded downstairs, where he helped himself to a drink from a tray of champagne flutes on a side table. There were plates of light refreshments, and he sampled a few, finding the food rather strange. He went back upstairs and settled into a quiet corner from which he could observe the proceedings for the rest of the evening. He was finding it all very entertaining.

Two days later, Sapphire was back home. It was Monday evening, and Charles had just joined her and Lucinda for their usual pre-dinner drink in the conservatory. Her mother had asked her about the exhibition. "I think Ben really enjoyed it," she said. "It's a very different world for him, but he told me he liked seeing Amanda's work."

"What pieces did she show?"

"Mainly small bronze figurines, but there were some drawings for sale."

"I do hope she managed to sell some."

"Not as many as she had hoped. There was a lot of competition there."

Lucinda sat down in one of the cane chairs amongst the potted palms, and Charles joined her.

Sapphire remained standing, looking directly at her mother. "He says David's taking you to Edinburgh to have your portrait painted."

"That's right. I really don't know why I let myself be talked into it."

"Are you going to go?"

"I don't want to go on my own, darling. Will you come with me?"

"Yes, if you want. What shall we do about Charlotte Elizabeth? Charles is far too busy to have her, and I can't keep asking Mrs Harris."

"How about asking Amanda to take her for a few days? We could drop her off on the way."

Sapphire agreed it was a good idea. She was pleased at the prospect of another trip away.

Presently her daughter came running in, preceded by Nipper, who fled under the plants. She was ecstatic on being told she would be staying with Aunt Amanda and talked about it continually over the following two weeks.

The day before they were due to leave, Sapphire was in her bedroom with her mother. She shut the lid of her weekend case and closed the closet door. "I hope I've packed the right clothes," she said. "I don't know what I shall do with myself while you're swanning off with David."

"I had hoped we would stay together," replied Lucinda calmly.

"I wouldn't want to play gooseberry."

Lucinda gave her an arch look. "I don't know what you mean. I'm only going to see about this portrait. I expect there are some good shops and department stores in Edinburgh. David won't want to trail round with the two of us if we're shopping."

Sapphire looked more hopeful. She always loved buying new clothes.

Charles drove them to Exeter station to save their having to change trains. Charlotte Elizabeth insisted on carrying her own small case until they boarded, when all the luggage was stored in the racks above their seats. The girl hung out of the window, waving to her father.

"Bye, darling! Be good for your aunty. See you soon," he called to her as the train pulled out.

Sapphire hauled her daughter back into the carriage, and they settled down for the journey.

When they arrived at Paddington Station the three of them took a cab to Lionel and Amanda's house.

Amanda welcomed her niece warmly. "We're going to have a wonderful time together," she exclaimed.

She had planned a few excursions to London Zoo and Richmond Park, and she described these outings to Charlotte Elizabeth while they had their tea. The child was tired and overexcited after her journey, and Amanda settled her into her bedroom and let her sleep. The following days were going to be busy.

Lucinda and Sapphire left to catch the night sleeper to Edinburgh. David was to meet them at King's Cross, and when they arrived, he was waiting in the station restaurant, as arranged. He closed his newspaper quickly and rose to meet Lucinda and her daughter.

"Ladies, how lovely to see you! I trust your journey went well?" He embraced them both and then enquired after his daughter.

"She was very excited about Charlotte Elizabeth's visit," replied Lucinda.

"It's high time she had her own child. No sign yet, alas." He sighed.

"I think her work keeps her very busy."

"Ah, we artists!" said David, waving his hand in the air.

Sapphire looked around for a waiter. "Shall we order some tea?" she asked.

Towards the end of Charlotte Elizabeth's short visit, Amanda took her into her studio and showed her how she moulded the clay. The girl told her aunt she liked drawing pictures and colouring them in.

"Would you like me to draw you?" asked Amanda.

"Oh, yes, please, Aunty!"

"I might decide to make a model of you too."

Her niece's eyes shone with delight.

Amanda showed her where to stand and asked her to remove her dress. "Because I want to draw your arms and legs," she explained.

She got Charlotte Elizabeth ready and showed her the pose she wanted. She asked her to stand with her legs together with her hands folded in front and her head slightly to one side. Grabbing her sketchbook she quickly made some rapid drawings in charcoal as she began to form an image in her mind of a small figurine of a child. She had to draw quickly, as Charlotte became fidgety. She allowed her to have a short rest, then resume the pose so she could carry out some more detailed drawings in pencil.

When she had finished, the child jumped off the low platform and came to see Amanda's drawings. She clapped her hands together.

"Ooh! You are clever!"

Amanda smiled and closed her sketchbook.

Charlotte Elizabeth danced round the room. "I'm going to be an artist when I grow up," she declared to her bemused aunt.

Charlotte Elizabeth and her aunt had grown close during the few days of her stay, and eventually Amanda had to tell her that her mother would be collecting her the following day.

Sapphire was on her own when she came for her daughter. She told her sister-in-law that her mother had gone to an art gallery with David for the day, and they were to meet up later.

Charlotte Elizabeth told her mother all about her various visits. "Aunty Amanda took me to the zoo, and I saw a huge elephant! You could have a ride on him, but Aunty Amanda said it was too high up." She chattered on, and finally Sapphire announced it was time to leave.

"Before you go, I want to show you these," said Amanda, opening her sketchbook, which lay on the table.

Sapphire's expression changed as she examined the drawings. The sketches were done in a very free style, showing a good likeness of Charlotte Elizabeth posing in her chemise, her arms and legs left bare.

"What do you think you were doing, drawing half-naked pictures of my daughter?" exclaimed Sapphire, looking up angrily.

Amanda was stunned. "I didn't mean any harm. I would like to make a sculpture of her, that's all. Charlotte Elizabeth was happy for me to sketch her."

"You think it's acceptable for my child's body to adorn some stranger's sideboard for all the world to see? Really, Amanda, what were you thinking?"

"No one would know who it was. It would just be a figure of a young girl."

"I would know!" Sapphire raised her voice, making Amanda wince.

"Sapphire, I've been kind enough to look after your child while you've been off enjoying yourself, and this is the thanks I get. You're always expecting other people to look after her. You don't deserve such a lovely little girl!"

"How dare you say that! This is not the last you will be hearing of this. Wait until Lionel finds out."

Sapphire stormed out, holding Charlotte Elizabeth's arm, pulling her through the door. Amanda was left in tears. She felt bewildered at such a violent reaction over a few drawings.

By the time they reached Paddington, Sapphire had calmed herself down. Charlotte Elizabeth sat beside her mother in the taxi, not saying anything. Sapphire did not mention the upset to her mother when they met up later. Charlotte Elizabeth was very quiet on the journey home.

"Did you have a nice time at Aunty Amanda's?" asked Lucinda, putting an arm round her.

"Yes, thank you, Grandma," the child replied.

When they arrived back at Acacia House, Sapphire told Charles what had happened when she had collected her daughter.

"I'm sure she didn't mean any harm, Sapphire, but I agree, she should have asked you first."

"I'm going to write to Lionel. He should know about this," she said adamantly.

"Don't you think it might be better to wait for it to blow over?" asked Charles.

"No, I want an apology. Amanda is in the wrong."

He sighed. "If you write this letter, I must insist on seeing it first," he said, firmly.

Sapphire showed him her letter the next morning, and he agreed she had voiced her concerns well.

The letter reached Lionel a day later. He and his wife were having breakfast together.

"Amanda, what's this all about?" he said, handing the letter to her, having opened and read it.

Amanda took it from him and glanced at its contents.

"I was going to tell you, but it's upset me." She described Sapphire's reaction to her drawings.

"You shouldn't have done it without asking first."

"Charlotte Elizabeth didn't seem to mind when I asked her."

"That's not the point. She wants an apology, Amanda. I hope you will write to her."

"I don't think I've done anything wrong." Amanda tossed her head defiantly. "It's all a bit of fuss."

Lionel shrugged. "It's up to you, but I think it would be better to apologise."

Charlotte Elizabeth had been subdued since her return home but became more like herself when Molly's visits resumed. They played well together, and if Charlotte Elizabeth tried to be bossy, Molly was able to stand up to her.

Sapphire continued to wait for a letter from Amanda, but none came. Charles could see she was fretting about it. He was due to attend a conference on childhood illnesses and immunisation at University College Hospital in London, and later that week, he left early to catch his train.

After the lectures had finished for the day, he set off to Richmond to see Amanda and Lionel, arriving early in the evening. The house looked quiet and dark when he rattled the knocker. After a short wait, the door opened a little way, and Amanda peered round.

"Oh, it's you, Charles!" She opened the door wider. "Sorry, I wondered who it was. I'm on my own in the house; Lionel is away. Please come in."

Appearing ill at ease, she led him into the spacious sitting room with its stylish furnishings. Charles surveyed his surroundings, thinking how well his brother had done for himself to have such a lovely home.

"Lionel's visiting a client in Birmingham," Amanda informed him. "I'm sorry you've missed him."

They sat down opposite one another.

"I really came to see you," said Charles.

She nodded and got up quickly. "Can I get you a drink?" She walked over to the sideboard. "What would you like?"

Charles asked for a whisky and soda, which she poured out and handed to him. She didn't get herself one but sat down again, clasping her hands together.

"Amanda, this upset with Sapphire—it needs to be sorted out."

She stared at the floor.

"I don't know why she was so angry with me. I meant no harm. They were just simple drawings."

"Can I see them?"

Amanda went to fetch her sketchbook. When she returned, Charles was standing with his back to her, staring at the fire. He turned round.

"Here you are," she said, laying the sketchbook open on the coffee table. He bent down to examine them.

"I must say you've captured a good likeness. You're very talented." He looked at her with an expression of admiration, and Amanda relaxed a little.

"Thank you," she said in a quiet voice.

"Personally, I see nothing to object to in these pictures, but Sapphire gets very precious about our daughter at times. I feel as her husband I should support her, but it isn't easy. She's never been one to keep her opinions to herself, as you know."

He sat down, and Amanda closed the book.

"Would you consider writing a short letter admitting you should have asked her before getting Charlotte Elizabeth to pose for you?" he asked tentatively.

"I really don't think I did anything wrong, Charles. If I had made a figure from the drawings, I would have shown you both first. I would probably have given it to you. It wasn't my intention to make money from it."

"I don't think Sapphire was objecting about that."

"I was very hurt she shouted at me."

"And she was upset when you said she didn't care for her daughter."

After a few moments of silence, Amanda said, "I so enjoyed having Charlotte Elizabeth to stay. I would love a daughter like that. Sapphire doesn't know how fortunate she is."

Charles finished his drink and placed his glass carefully on the table between them. After a short pause he said, "May I ask how long you and Lionel have been trying for a child?"

"Long enough—about two years now."

"Have you sought any medical advice?"

"No, Lionel refuses to discuss it with me. He says it will happen when it does."

"You both need to see someone, Amanda. I can recommend a consultant in Harley Street if you wish. You must insist that Lionel talks to you. If he doesn't, let me know."

She began welling up. "Thank you, I'll do that," she said, wiping her eyes. "I'll write Sapphire an apology and destroy the sketches."

"Well done, old girl!" Charles got up and gave her a hug. Suddenly, he drew back and turned away.

"What is it, Charles?"

"You're right in one respect, Amanda. Sapphire *is* always trying to palm Charlotte Elizabeth onto someone else. I don't feel we're a family. I know my work makes it difficult sometimes, but we don't do anything together. Sapphire is always off on some trip or visit, leaving her daughter with Lucinda or someone else. I don't understand why she doesn't spend more time with her. She says they don't get on."

"Have you spoken to Lucinda about it? Try to get her on your side and then talk together. You've just given me much the same advice, Doctor!"

"Yes, you're quite right. We both need to talk about our concerns." He paused for a few moments. "Thank you for agreeing to write to Sapphire. I'll ask her to reply and make things up. Now, I really must be going."

Amanda saw him to the door. "Thank you so much for coming, Charles." She stood there, watching him go.

He ran down the steps. At the bottom he turned and said, "Did Lionel ever say you have lovely eyes?"

"Be off with you!" she said, laughing, and closed the door.

CHAPTER SEVEN

A NEW VENTURE

HARLES WAS IN HIS SURGERY looking out of the front window at the row of prams parked outside. He was about to begin his weekly mother and baby clinic. It was a part of general practice that was important to him, despite Sapphire complaining about the noise.

Diphtheria had reoccurred in the village, and he needed to spot any new cases before they became acute. He wished he could offer immunisation to these young babies, but the vaccine, although used effectively in America, had not yet reached the shores of Britain.

The mothers chattered together happily in the waiting room with the babies in their arms or sitting on laps. Charles realised that each child was precious and hoped the disease would not break out, as he had little he could offer in treatment. He called in the first mother and enquired about the child's progress. Sometimes a mother would voice a worry or have a query. Charles enjoyed these sessions when he was able to reassure them and give advice.

Eventually the last mother and baby left, and he washed his hands carefully and then sauntered into the conservatory, where he joined Sapphire and Lucinda, who were sitting talking together. Charlotte Elizabeth was playing with her new kitten, who was running in and out between the potted plants.

"Nipper, come here," the girl commanded, but the cat ran further away. "Oh, Mummy, he's so naughty!"

"Yes," her mother replied. "Now you know what it's like for me when you don't do as you're told."

Charles frowned slightly. The child wasn't bad, she just played her mother up for attention. She was always compliant with him. Charlotte Elizabeth pouted and went to sit beside her father. He put his arm round her, and she snuggled up to him, putting her thumb in her mouth.

"Don't do that," her mother instructed. "You're not a baby."

Mrs Harris brought in the afternoon tea and asked Charlotte Elizabeth if she would like to do some baking. She often asked the girl to help in the kitchen. When they had gone, Charles got up to pour out the tea.

"When I was in London, I went to see Amanda," he said, passing a cup to his mother-in-law.

Sapphire looked up sharply. "Why on earth did you do that?" she demanded.

"Because I wanted to clear up this upset between you. I told her I thought it would have been best to ask you before she made those drawings, and she has promised to destroy them. She also agreed to apologise, and a letter should be arriving soon."

"How did you manage to persuade her?" asked Lucinda, taking her tea from him.

"Turned on the charm, did you?" said Sapphire.

Charles put down the silver teapot. "I hope you'll have the generosity to accept her apology and make friends again," he said sternly.

Sapphire looked uncomfortable and didn't reply.

"Well, will you?"

She shrugged. "I suppose so."

"Sapphire, I wish I could understand you better. What *is* the matter? You're becoming a bit, well, unpleasant."

Lucinda began to get up to leave.

"Please stay, Lucinda." said Charles. "We need to discuss this all together."

She sat down again.

"If you must know, I'm bored," stated his wife.

Her husband sat down next to her. "Go on."

"You know I'm not mother material. I don't know why. I saw those mothers today enjoying their babies at your clinic, and I wish I could be like them. I can't seem to get interested in your work, and I don't want to do all that paperwork for you. I feel useless. Molly's mother came round today to tell me that she's giving up the shop and they're moving away to be nearer her mother, so I shall have to find another playmate for Charlotte Elizabeth."

Charles thought for a few moments, then asked, "Does that mean the shop will be available?"

"Yes, as far as I know. She's going next month. I believe she rents the premises."

"Then why don't you take it on?"

"Darling, I don't want to sell knitting wool for the rest of my life."

"No, I don't mean that. How about opening a little art gallery or gift shop?"

Sapphire looked ecstatic, clasping her hands together. "Oh, Charles, what a brilliant idea! How did you think of it? Oh, I would just love to do that. And, Mummy, you could help me choose the pieces of art. I can't wait to get started!"

She had suddenly come alive. The shop was on the High Street. Charles pointed out more tourists were now coming to Devon and might stop as they drove through the village.

"I suppose once you establish the gallery, people will come to you," observed Lucinda.

"It will give my travels a purpose too," Sapphire said. "I could go on buying trips."

"You'll have to use your own money for this," Charles pointed out. "You know I could never fund it for you."

"Yes, of course, I understand. I could even sell Amanda's work for her!"

"You would have to spend long hours in the shop," he said. "What about Charlotte Elizabeth?"

Sapphire looked at her mother.

"I can take on the childcare if it helps," said Lucinda. "She'll be going to school soon. It's a shame she's lost her little friend. It seemed to be working out so well."

Amanda's letter arrived the following morning. She had written a conciliatory account of her intentions and acknowledged she should have asked Sapphire's permission before she drew her daughter. She concluded by saying she hoped they could resume their loving friendship. Sapphire replied straightaway, gratefully accepting her apology and telling her all about her new venture.

When Amanda's other letter to Charles came, it contained good news. She had managed to persuade Lionel to visit the specialist Charles had recommended, and they were undergoing tests and receiving advice. It was a sensitive subject, and Charles did not divulge the contents to his wife or mother-in-law. He answered wishing the couple every success and wrote that he hoped there would be 'an announcement' before long.

Charlotte Elizabeth said goodbye to Molly when the girl's mother came round to collect her for the last time. She hugged her new little friend goodbye and offered her a small gift, which Molly took, saying a quiet 'thank you'. Mrs Andrews thanked Sapphire for allowing her daughter to come and play.

"You've helped us," Sapphire told her. "We shall be sorry to see you both go."

"I know Molly will miss Charlotte Elizabeth. She has always enjoyed coming here," replied the woman, looking emotional.

Sapphire wasted no time securing the tenancy of the shop after Mrs Andrews had left and began arranging the alterations needed to make it into an art gallery. As promised, Lucinda looked after Charlotte Elizabeth and kept her occupied by playing games and reading to her. She found her quick to learn, and so began to teach her the alphabet using a set of wooden letters.

Ben came to see her one afternoon. He had caught the bus from Clayden village, changing at Kingsbridge. Lucinda was full of the news of Sapphire's proposed art gallery.

"It's a new venture, which we hope will keep her occupied," she explained excitedly. "She's been spending all hours there getting it ready. It needs redecorating and some refurbishment. I've been looking after Charlotte Elizabeth in the meantime."

Ben looked surprised. "What will she sell?"

"Paintings by local artists mainly. She tells me local landscapes and seascapes should do well. She's made a few contacts already. She wants me to go to Richmond with her to choose some of Amanda's work, but I told her I would not leave Charlotte Elizabeth."

"Couldn't she go too?" asked Ben.

"I think Sapphire wants to be free from child duties while she's away."

"Bring her over to Forge Cottage," he suggested. "I would love to have her, and Florrie could perhaps do a few lessons with her."

"But poor Florrie has three children now. How will she manage with one more?"

"I'm often off with the boys for long walks, and little Sarah's very good."

"I know, but Florrie's still breastfeeding. She will feel very tired with having to cope with another child, especially a lively one!"

"It would only be for a few days. I'll ask her and Stephen about it."

"Thank you, Ben. I would love to go with Sapphire."

Ben left to catch his bus home, and he broached the subject with Florrie as soon as he arrived

"I'm very fond of Sapphire," replied Florrie. "But she does expect others to look after her daughter rather a lot."

Ben looked disconsolate. "The child's lonely. Her little friend has just moved away. Sapphire won't allow her to go to the nursery, and Charles won't let her have a governess yet, and she is too young for school. It would only be for a few days, maybe a week."

Florrie could see her pa was very fond of his granddaughter, and she relented. "Yes, all right, we'll have her. You'll have to help, though!"

Charles brought Charlotte Elizabeth over the following weekend. Ben made a great fuss of his granddaughter, and she played happily with the boys. Lucinda had written a short note, which Charles had given to Florrie. She had asked Florrie to give her some advice about teaching Charlotte Elizabeth her letters.

When Charles came to collect his daughter a few days later, Florrie handed him her reply. She had suggested that Charlotte Elizabeth could come to Forge Cottage every Saturday morning for a lesson. Stephen could have the boys, and Sarah would be having her morning sleep, so she was quite sure she could manage. She said she missed teaching and would be delighted to help her niece learn to read.

When Charles and his daughter had left, Florrie searched for the teaching aids she knew her mother had once used when she had tutored all her children many years before. They appeared rather old-fashioned, so Florrie asked Stephen if he could let her have a few early readers from his school. She rigged up a small blackboard ready for lessons to resume once again on the kitchen table at Forge Cottage.

CHAPTER EIGHT

ALARM

HARLOTTE ELIZABETH WAS VERY EXCITED when she was told that Aunty Florrie was going to teach her to read. She began to pick up the words quickly and was soon reading her first primer book. They had made a good start together, and Charles was always very impressed with her progress when he came to collect his daughter each Saturday morning.

A few weeks later, Florrie was giving her niece her lesson when she noticed that her pupil was lacking concentration.

"Are you feeling all right, Charlotte Elizabeth?" she asked.

"I've got a sore throat, Aunty."

Florrie felt the girl's forehead, and it was hot. She gave her a drink of water and quickly cleared the books away. When Charles arrived and saw her, he looked alarmed. He immediately examined her and asked her to open her mouth. When he looked down her throat, his expression changed.

"I think she may have diphtheria," he said, quietly. "I had a case in the surgery earlier this week."

Florrie gasped and put her hand to her mouth.

"You must keep calm," said Charles. "When we've gone, I want you to clean everywhere Charlotte Elizabeth has been. Then change your clothes and wash your hands before you go anywhere near Sarah."

Florrie nodded adamantly. "What will happen if Sarah gets it too?" she asked. "Especially with her heart condition."

"If you do as I say, everything should be all right. This illness is caused by bacterium, so we must prevent cross contamination. You'll know what to do. Remember your days nursing in the war?"

Charles lifted his daughter into his arms and carried her out to the car. As soon as they had gone, Florrie set about her tasks. She had just finished when Ben and Stephen came in. They were both shocked at the news, and Ben sank into his chair looking distraught.

"I hope to God she'll get better," he said.

"What else did Charles say?" asked Stephen.

"Only that we should be safe, as none of us—except me—has been in close contact with her. He told me to clean down everywhere and change my clothes, and I've done that."

"Poor Charles and Sapphire," said Ben.

At that moment, the two boys rushed in from the garden.

"Is it lunchtime yet?" asked Christopher.

When Charles arrived back at Acacia House, he took his daughter upstairs, laid her on the bed, and went to find Lucinda, who came quickly on hearing her grandchild was ill. She told him Sapphire was at the gallery.

"Can you ask Mrs Harris to go and fetch her, please?"

She hurried off to the kitchen, and when she came back, she helped Charles put Charlotte Elizabeth to bed. The child looked very sleepy.

"What can we do?" asked Lucinda.

"Keep her sponged down when she runs a high temperature and give her lots of fluids. That's all at present. Maybe a crushed-up aspirin will help."

Lucinda bustled round preparing everything, and soon Sapphire arrived, breathless.

"How is she? Oh, Mummy! What are we going to do? What does it mean? Will she get better? Oh, my poor little girl!"

She knelt by the bed, putting her hand on her child's burning cheek.

"Please don't panic. With careful nursing, she will get better," said Charles.

"I'll stay with her, Sapphire," said Lucinda. "You and Charles decide what needs doing."

Charles led his wife out of the bedroom, and they went downstairs together. "We must all be in quarantine for now," he said. "I'll get Brian to do surgery for the rest of the week until Charlotte Elizabeth starts to get better."

"How did she catch it?"

"I had a case in the surgery earlier this week."

Sapphire looked alarmed. "You've brought it into my home!"

"I'm puzzled as to how it got in," he replied.

"I knew this would happen one day," exclaimed Sapphire angrily. "Your dreadful mothers have put my child in danger!"

"Calm down, and don't talk that way," Charles replied. "I always wash my hands after surgery, and I don't hold the babies. They sit on their mother's laps when I examine them. I throw the spatula away, and all my instruments are sterilised. I put them in a lidded container, and Mrs Harris takes them to the kitchen to boil them."

They looked at each other.

"Charlotte Elizabeth is always in the kitchen helping. Could she have touched something?" wondered Sapphire.

"Perhaps we'd better ask Mrs Harris about it."

Charles went down to the kitchen, and his wife followed. Mrs Harris was preparing the evening meal. She looked up when they entered.

"How is the little poppet?" she asked.

"Not too good, I'm afraid," Charles said. "I think she has diphtheria."

"Oh, Lord! How ever did she catch that?"

"That's what we're trying to find out. Can I ask you about the disposal of rubbish from my surgery? Where exactly does it go?"

Mrs Harris put down her wooden spoon. She looked frightened. "Well, Doctor, I bring the wastepaper basket in here, and I tip it into the rubbish bin, over there." She pointed to the waste bin in the corner.

"Do you handle the rubbish?"

"I suppose I might. I sometimes pull it out with my hand when I'm emptying it. Oh, Doctor, I haven't given it to her, have I? Please don't tell me I'm to blame!"

"We're not here to blame you. This is my fault for not setting up proper procedures for disposing the rubbish. I use wooden spatulas for examining throats, and then I throw them away. I've been careless, not you. In future, all waste from the surgery must go straight into the dustbin outside, not come through the kitchen."

Mrs Harris nodded her head vigorously. "Yes, Doctor. I'll see to it."

"You'll have to continue to sterilise the instruments in here, but always wash your hands after handling them."

Again, she nodded.

"Meanwhile, we are in quarantine, but you can go home—just wash your clothes." Charles could see his housekeeper was near to tears. "Please, don't get upset. As I said, you were not to know."

Tears welled up in Mrs Harris's eyes as they left.

Sapphire returned straight to her daughter's bedroom and made up a bed for herself in there. Her mother was sitting by Charlotte Elizabeth administrating the cold sponges. By morning, when Charles examined her, there was no change. The three of them stood round the bed, looking helpless.

"I'm going to London," announced Charles. "When I was at my conference, I learnt that one of the hospitals is conducting trials for treatment of diphtheria, so I'm going there to see if I can get some of the medication. I know I'm breaking quarantine."

He set off straightaway that morning. Lucinda and Sapphire took turns nursing Charlotte Elizabeth and were both becoming increasingly exhausted. Sapphire sat by her daughter's bed listening to her rapid, laboured breathing and coughing fits all through the following night. The child seemed to be fighting for breath, and her mother could see and hear her getting worse. She took Charlotte Elizabeth's limp hand and began to quietly sob.

She must have drifted off, because she was awoken by a noise downstairs. Lifting her head, she blearily looked at the clock on the chest of drawers. It was six-thirty in the morning. The bedroom door opened, and Charles entered. He immediately strode over to Charlotte Elizabeth and looked at her intently.

"Any change?"

Sapphire shook her head. "Oh, Charles, we're losing her! I know we are."

Her husband put a reassuring hand on her shoulder to steady her. "I have the medication, and by all accounts it will work."

Sapphire sat up. Was there a glimmer of hope?

Lucinda had also heard Charles coming in, and she now joined them, wrapped in her grey silk dressing gown. She was hugging herself tightly, her face pinched with anxiety.

"Charles has something to give her!" Sapphire exclaimed.

They sat up a sleepy Charlotte Elizabeth between them while Charles administered some liquid from a bottle in his hand.

"She needs to take this every two hours," he said. "We should see an improvement by tomorrow."

"Please God, make her better," Sapphire murmured as they laid their daughter gently down.

She and Lucinda again took turns sitting with Charlotte Elizabeth while Charles went to bed.

Later that afternoon they all took a break while Mrs Harris sat with the patient. She had left them a tea tray in the sitting room with a large fruit cake. Lucinda poured out the tea while Charles cut three large slices.

Charles told them he had caught the early morning train, and it had been a tiring long journey to Paddington. He had eventually arrived at the hospital and had to wait some time to see someone.

"After some persuasion I managed to get one of the research doctors to allow me to join the project involving the use of antitoxins. I need to submit a report as to how the treatment works."

Sapphire regarded him anxiously. "Oh, Charles. It will work, won't it?"

He reached out and grasped her hand. "Charlotte Elizabeth is a strong, healthy little girl, and I see no reason why not."

All through that night they took it in turns to administer the medicine. The following morning Sapphire was sitting with her daughter when suddenly she became aware that her breathing was slightly better. She called out to Charles, and he hurried in and felt the girl's forehead and took her pulse.

"She's definitely turned the corner," he said, smiling broadly. "It's still early days. She has a way to go yet."

Sapphire burst into tears, and her husband comforted her. "It's all right, darling. She will be better, trust me."

Two weeks later, Charlotte Elizabeth was sitting up in bed, propped up by pillows. She looked drawn and pale, but Charles assured everyone she was making good progress. She was delighted when her grandfather walked through the door.

"Gandy!" She held out her thin arms to him.

"Hello, my beautiful, best girl in the world!" greeted Ben. He enfolded her in a gentle hug.

"Mrs Harris made me ice cream," she announced.

"Did you save some for me?" asked Ben.

She shook her head and laughed.

"I could put it in my pocket and take it home," he said, his eyes twinkling at her.

"It would melt, silly!"

"I'm glad you told me that. It would have gone all down my leg."

This reduced Charlotte Elizabeth to a fit of giggles, and Ben continued to tease her and make her laugh. Lucinda came in with a dish in her hand.

"Here we are, young lady. Mrs Harris has made you some jelly today."

Charlotte Elizabeth ate ravenously. Ben stayed a while longer, and they read some storybooks together. Afterwards he went up to Lucinda's apartment to sit with her. He said the family were relieved at his grandchild's recovery, and he was writing to Rosa to tell her all about the medication Charles had obtained. He knew she would be very interested, being a nurse.

"Charlotte Elizabeth will have to spend two more weeks in bed to recover fully, and then she will have to convalesce," Lucinda told Ben. "Charles wants to take her to the seaside."

"Thank God she recovered. What would we have done without her?"

"I can't bear to think about it, Ben. I'm so glad you were all safe at Forge Cottage."

"Florrie was beside herself with worry. She kept cleaning everything."

"The nursery here in the village was closed down during the epidemic," Lucinda told him. "Altogether I think there were just three cases, and all recovered, thankfully. Charles says there is a vaccine for diphtheria, and it's being used successfully in America. It will be wonderful when all children here are immunised. The hospital asked him to submit a report, which will be added to the trials they're conducting. He's very interested in childhood diseases and wants to do some further study. It might mean that he takes a sabbatical."

"It sounds as if something ought to be done," said Ben, looking serious. He rose to go. "I'm so glad she's getting better. My life would not be worth living if anything had happened to her or my other grandchildren. I have a lot to be thankful for."

CHAPTER NINE

ROSA'S VISIT

Rosa replied to Ben's letter saying she was upset to hear about Charlotte Elizabeth's illness and interested in the treatment she had received. She had nursed several children with diphtheria at the hospital in Plymouth, and some had not been so lucky as her niece. She asked Ben if she could come and stay for a few days. It would just be her—Danny couldn't get time off work, and his mother would be there to look after the house and Digger, the dog.

Ben met Rosa at Kingsbridge Station, and as he took her small bag from her, gave her a kiss. When they got back to Forge Cottage, she was instantly overwhelmed by the two small boys flinging their arms round her as she appeared through the gate.

"Aunty Rosa's here!" shouted Christopher.

"Come in, Rosa," said Florrie, emerging from the cottage door. "It's lovely to see you. Sorry about the boys—they've been so excited."

Rosa hugged her two nephews and rummaged in her bag for the sweets she had for them. This quieted them down, and Ben told them to go and play in the garden.

"They're getting a bit wild," he said. "The best place for them is outside."

Florrie fetched Sarah from her cot and placed her in Rosa's arms. Her aunt regarded her fondly, smiling as she gently cradled her.

"How has she been?" she asked anxiously.

"Absolutely fine, no more frights," Florrie reassured her sister. She turned to her father. "Pa's had a wonderful idea."

Ben explained how he planned to plant a tree in the orchard for every member of his family. "Why don't you come and see what I've done already," he said, eager to show her.

Rosa carefully handed Sarah back to her mother and followed him outside to the orchard where some new trees had been planted.

"I haven't finished yet," said her father. "Let me show you the first one." He led her over to a sapling planted in a central position. "This is a Comice—it was Sophie's favourite pear. This is her tree," he said proudly.

They both stood in quiet contemplation, until Rosa spoke. "She would have loved you doing this for her, Pa."

Ben showed her a few more trees he had put in, pointing out Charles's and Florrie's. "I haven't done yours yet. What would you like?"

Rosa thought for a short while, finally saying, "A morello cherry, please, Pa."

He nodded in agreement. "A good choice. I'll see to it this autumn."

As they strolled round the garden, Rosa asked Ben how it had been, living with Florrie and Stephen and the boys.

"I'm so glad they came. The boys are a bit of a handful sometimes, but they keep me active. It's good having Florrie doing all the things my Sophie used to do, and I get on well with Stephen, although I was a bit nervous of him at first."

"You must make sure Florrie has some sort of life, Pa, not all drudgery."

"She has talked about going into the school to help when Sarah's a little older," Ben explained. "She misses her teaching."

"Will you be able to cope with all the children?"

"I brought up the three of you," he replied. "I think I remember what to do. We're talking about a few years hence, and one of the boys, if not both, will be at school then."

Ben fell silent for a while, and they continued walking slowly, arm in arm. "I'm concerned about things when I go," he began. "Florrie and her family are settled here for the foreseeable future. The property should be divided three ways, but I know Charles will forgo his as he is relatively comfortably off. That leaves you, Rosa. I want you and Danny to have something, but I have nothing else to leave. I have thought about this a lot lately, and all I can suggest is that Stephen offers you money for your share. They're living here rent free, after all. This is what I shall put in my will. I don't want any upset, and I will let the family know my wishes."

"What about Auntie Millie?" asked Rosa. "Shouldn't she inherit some of Forge Cottage?"

"My father left it to me. Millie knows that. She's been left comfortably off by her first husband, Frank, and the shop and post office are doing well. But I will speak to her about it."

"I don't like all this talk about wills, Pa, but I see it's necessary." She pulled him closer to her. "I hope we shall have you for a while yet. You still need to plant up the orchard."

They sauntered round the trees, stopping every now and again to examine one, and Ben would describe its history. He was quite knowledgeable, as his father had told him about the old varieties when he was a boy.

"Pa," began Rosa, "I would like to know a little more about your family."

Ben sat down on the bench he had made for Sophie in the corner of the orchard. He patted the seat next to him, and Rosa settled down to listen.

"I can only just remember my grandfather. He was a blacksmith before my father, and he set up this smithy. He and my grandmother had this cottage built. It replaced an old one that was nearly falling down. He also planted the orchard and grew vegetables in the garden, something I've never done, I'm afraid. Grandfather lived with us when he got too old to work. He would hobble round in leather gaiters strapped round his legs—I think he had rheumatism rather badly. I don't remember my grandmama. I think the men in this family have a habit of outliving their women folk."

Rosa reached out and squeezed her father's hand. "Perhaps all that hard work in the smithy kept them fit and healthy."

"It was tough at times," he went on. "My pa worked long days but never made much money. He had to engage a man to work the bellows and help with the difficult jobs. The forge was kept very busy in those days, as many more horses were used for farm work and pulling carts. We had the horses from Clayden House stables, hunters and carriage horses, all constantly needing new shoes. Despite working long hours, we were never very well off when my father took over. He was often paid 'in kind' and sometimes not at all. Prices were kept low, although the landowners did well. I was using this system of payment when I married your mother until she put a stop to it."

"When did you start working in the forge, Pa?"

"My apprenticeship began when I was thirteen years old. I was supposed to stay on at school until I was fourteen, but my pa took me out early. Nobody seemed to mind. My pa was a mite too fond of going down to the Two Foxes, and that got worse after my ma died. Poor Aunty Millie was left to keep house, even though she was still very young. After Pa died, she got pregnant with Billy by the rector's son, so I had three mouths to feed."

Rosa looked sombre. "Difficult times, then."

Ben nodded. "We just got on with everything as best we could."

"Where did you go to school?"

"Millie and I went to school in Kingsbridge. We had to walk there every day. We thought nothing of it—back then, folk would often travel long distances on foot. Sometimes a farm worker going into town would give us a lift on his cart. Everyone helped each other."

"What about your ma's family?"

"All I know is that she was a farmer's daughter, and she met my pa at the weekly market in Kingsbridge. Lots of farmers came to sell their animals, as they do today. It was always quite a day out then."

"That must be why Auntie Millie took to dairy work," Rosa observed.

"Things were very different when I was a boy growing up. Life was quieter, and we didn't know much about the outside world. Everybody knew everybody else and all your business. Most folks never went very far, and travel was slow. It's a very different world now with all this automation. When I took over the forge, farmers had begun to use steam-driven threshers and binders for the harvest. I had to turn my hand to repairing these contraptions, because they were always going wrong. I devised a portable fire box to do my repairs on the machines, as they were too big to bring to the forge. I soon realised that the nature of black-smithing was changing, so I decided to build and repair bicycles as there wasn't enough work coming in."

"And then you set up your garage business with my Danny," Rosa added with a smile.

"Yes, I remember when motor cars first appeared in the lanes, the horses would rear up at the sight of one. Your ma had to give up driving our pony and trap, as she was nervous of them. I realised this was the future of travel, and garages were being set up to repair them. We thought trains were a marvel, but now folks are flying. I would never have believed it."

He shook his head slowly and stared at the ground. After a few moments, he looked up and said, "Life is better now, Rosa. Everything is getting better, especially healthcare. I'm so thankful both my grand-daughters have survived." He gave his daughter a hug, and they got up and strolled back to the cottage.

During her stay, Rosa met up with her brother at Acacia House, and while she was there, she asked him and Sapphire about Charlotte Elizabeth's treatment.

"It worked surprisingly quickly," Charles explained. "Of course, we need to wait awhile before we can administer this drug to the public. I was able to use it as I had agreed to be part of the trial. I knew the risks, but I had seen that the antitoxins were working in most cases of diphtheria."

"I have never been so frightened," added Sapphire. "I thought we were going to lose her."

She knelt and put her arm round her daughter, who was playing with her dolls on the floor. Rosa joined her niece and began to admire them. Charlotte Elizabeth told her their names as she sat them round in a semi-circle. The three of them played together for a short while, and then Mrs Harris came to fetch the child for her tea.

"My dolls haven't finished theirs yet," said Charlotte Elizabeth firmly as she picked up the toy pot from her dolls' tea set.

"You mustn't keep Mrs Harris waiting," said Sapphire.

"Would you like me to give them their tea for you?" asked Rosa. "I do the teas at the hospital where I work."

Charlotte Elizabeth readily agreed and got up to take Mrs Harris's hand.

"Goodbye," said Rosa. "Next time I come, we'll play doctors and nurses."

The girl looked pleased and kissed her aunt goodbye. When she'd gone, Sapphire said, "You seem to have a gift at playing with little girls. You'll have to give me lessons."

Rosa laughed. "I did enjoy my times in the children's ward."

"Are you and Danny going to start a family any time soon?"

"I don't know. I want to continue nursing for as long as possible."

Sapphire suggested she might like to see her new gallery, and Rosa agreed enthusiastically.

The refurbishments had been completed, and the bare walls were waiting to be filled with pictures. Sapphire took her round the empty rooms and explained how she planned to source pieces of artwork by contacting some local artists.

"I do admire this venture of yours," commented Rosa, clearly impressed.

"I can't tell you what it means to me," replied her sister-in-law. "It's a bit stifling living in a small village. I'm looking forward to getting out from time to time."

They returned to the surgery, where Charles had just finished his surgery session. They convened in the sitting room where tea was waiting.

"Before I go," began Rosa, helping herself to a cup, "I think Charlotte Elizabeth is still looking rather pale." She gave some advice on what her diet should be. "And she needs plenty of fresh air," she added.

"Charles and I are taking her to the seaside," Sapphire reassured her. "She tires very easily at present, but she should be strong enough to go soon."

On the ride back to Forge Cottage with Charles, Rosa commented that Sapphire seemed very excited about the art gallery.

"Yes, I'm glad she's found something to do. Modbury's a quiet village, and I have always worried she would get tired if it," he replied.

"Has she thought of a name yet?"

"A few, but 'Browne Gallery' doesn't sound very glamorous. I think she's decided on 'Wells Fine Art.'"

"She'll retain her maiden name to run it?"

"Yes, she thinks it sounds more professional."

Charles and Rosa exchanged looks and then burst out laughing.

"You have to let Sapphire do whatever she wants," said Charles, waving his hand in the air.

CHAPTER TEN

A THEFT

SAPPHIRE WASTED NO TIME FILLING the gallery once Amanda had arrived with several of her bronze sculptures and a few framed paintings and drawings. She had also brought some small stained-glass panels from her father's studio.

When they had finished arranging them, the two women stood back to view the pieces on display. They both agreed that the white walls set the exhibits off to great advantage, and Amanda's sculptures stood out well on their white plinths.

"I still need lots more paintings," said Sapphire, looking at the spaces that had not yet been filled.

"Where will you get them?" asked Amanda. "It's going to be very expensive if you have to purchase good ones," she added.

"I won't buy them, darling. I'll just sell them for the artists and take a hefty commission."

Amanda laughed. "Well, I wish your penniless artists good luck!"

"I won't treat you like that," said Sapphire quickly. "I'm grateful that you've let me have some of your work."

As they left, she locked up the premises, and they walked back to Acacia House arm in arm.

"I'm so glad we're pals again," said Amanda. "Quarrelling with you made me so miserable."

Sapphire drew her closer and patted her hand. "Me too," she replied. "I think I overreacted. I'd just had a horrid trip to Scotland, and I shouldn't have spoken to you like that."

"Why was it horrid?"

"I had convinced myself that Mummy might be contemplating getting married again."

"To Daddy, you mean?"

"Yes. You must have noticed how friendly they're getting."

"Yes, I did at one time, but I think they just share a love of art."

"I think you're right. I was being very silly. I don't want to lose Mummy to anyone—I like her living with us. I know that's very selfish of me."

"I'm sure she would never do anything that would make you unhappy."

"She's decided not to go ahead with this portrait. It's too far to go for sittings."

The women walked a little further on.

"Some good came out of our quarrel, you know," began Amanda. "When Charles came as peacemaker, I told him that Lionel and I had been trying to start a family, but we had been unsuccessful. He gave me the address of a consultant, and we are now expecting our first child!"

Sapphire stopped and looked at her sister-in-law with amazement. "Darling! I'm so pleased for you! Lionel must be thrilled."

"Yes, he is. We both are. It's still early days, though. We have waited such a long time, and I began to think it would never happen."

"Good old Doctor Charles," said Sapphire as they continued down the hill.

On their return, everyone gathered in the conservatory before dinner. Amanada looked nervously at Lionel as Charles poured the drinks and gave her husband a small nudge.

"Ahem!" he said, rather loudly. After gaining everyone's attention, he took his wife's arm and raised his glass.

"We have an announcement. We are delighted to tell you that we are expecting!"

Lucinda was overjoyed and hugged them both with tears in her eyes.

"This is wonderful news!" she enthused. Turning to Charles, who had been standing quietly in the background, she said, "You'll keep an eye on her, won't you?"

"Oh, yes," he said. "I certainly will. Congratulations to you both!"

Charles had known in advance. Amanda's letter to him had arrived earlier that week. He and Amanda managed a share a quick glance and a smile while Lucinda went to find some champagne.

After her visitors had returned home, Sapphire spent all her spare time obtaining works of art from the local area and beyond. She found some small galleries that put her in touch with various artists, and several took her up on her offer to sell their work. She bought a few watercolours, and gradually the rest of the gallery walls were filled with oil paintings and prints to be sold on commission. She was particularly pleased with a large seascape in oils, which held pride of place opposite the entrance.

When all the pictures were hung and labelled to her satisfaction, Sapphire invited her family to an informal viewing. Holding Charlotte Elizabeth's hand, she led the way through the rooms, followed by Charles and Lucinda.

"You have a good eye, my love," her husband said when they had finished their tour. "This is a very good selection of fine art."

Lucinda agreed. "I'm tempted to buy some. But I will resist!"

"I can now arrange the opening reception," announced Sapphire, enthusiastically.

"Before that, I think we ought to go away for a week or so," Charles began. "As Rosa recommended, Charlotte Elizabeth needs some sea air to recuperate." He looked fondly at his little daughter, whose face had lit up.

"Yes, of course! Mummy, you'll come too?"

"I'd love to," replied Lucinda. "If Charles doesn't mind."

"Not at all. And what about asking Ben?"

"Perfect!" Sapphire clapped her hands together. "I can't wait!"

They booked the holiday, a week together in a hotel in Salcombe. Ben needed a little persuasion, but once he'd made sure Florrie would have help from Millie, he agreed to come.

A week later Charles packed up the motor and they all piled in, squashed together for the journey. It wasn't far to their hotel, and everyone emerged, glad to have arrived. Charles stood and breathed in the sea air. The sun was shining brightly, and they had a splendid view of the sea from the terrace of the hotel.

Having settled into their respective rooms, Ben went for a walk by himself. He had unhappy memories of Salcombe. He and Sophie had lived there for a short while with Millie and her first husband, Frank. It had been many years earlier, and something had happened that had nearly wrecked his marriage. It was there that he'd had his affair with Lucinda.

He walked until he came to the top of a hill, where he could see the Lodge in the distance that Frank and Millie had made into a guest house for holiday visitors. He looked at the solid, square white building, wondering who was living there now. He recalled the fine, high-ceilinged rooms where the guests had stayed, and the bedroom he'd shared with Sophie. It had a veranda from which the sea could be seen, and although it had been early in the year, the sun had been bright. He remembered how he had returned each day from his work at the stables at the Hall, knowing he had betrayed his wife. He felt an overwhelming desire to tell Sophie again how sorry he was, as he had done so many times during their marriage, still feeling the weight of guilt in his heart. How would she feel if she knew he was staying with Lucinda and her family here? It was something that troubled him, but he pushed it to the back of his mind. He turned and walked slowly back.

When Ben returned, he entered the lounge where Lucinda was sitting with her family. She glanced at him as he came in, and he knew she had probably guessed where he had been. Charles and Sapphire had booked the hotel, not knowing it was situated close to the Hall where Lucinda had lived with her first husband. She had rarely spoken about her past to her children.

Memories were soon forgotten as they enjoyed their time on the beach, and it was agreed that Charlotte Elizabeth was soon looking a lot better.

Most days Ben and Lucinda would sit in their deckchairs watching Charles and Sapphire splashing in the waves with their daughter. They would return, wrapped in towels, always complaining that the water had been cold.

One afternoon, Charles and Sapphire took Charlotte Elizabeth to get an ice cream. When they returned, Ben got up and told them he was going for a paddle. "Come on!" He held out his hand to Lucinda.

She laughed and shook her head, so he left her sitting with her silk shawl draped elegantly round her shoulders.

She watched as Ben, his trousers rolled up above his knees, shuffled along the shoreline in the waves and raised her hand. He waved back to her.

After their holiday, Sapphire completed the final arrangements for the opening of the art gallery, sending out invitations to family and friends.

On the day of the event, she waited excitedly for her guests to begin arriving. The first to come were Lionel, Amanda, and David. Her cousin Madelaine brought some friends, and Caroline and Donald Bailey came with both daughters and their husbands. Charles had collected Ben, and the small premises was soon full of chattering guests. Mrs Harris and her daughter circulated, offering drinks and refreshments.

The evening was a huge success, and Sapphire was kept busy talking about the artists and works of art on display. She sold several pieces, and there were now gaps on the walls. She mentioned to Charles afterwards that it would mean another trip sourcing more pictures.

"You'll have to find someone to help run the gallery if you keep going on buying trips," he commented.

"Yes, I know. I was thinking of asking Caroline."

"She sounds just the person. I hope she agrees." Charles put his arm round his wife. "I'm so glad you've found running the gallery exciting. I used to think you might go back to London because you were bored here with me."

Sapphire gave him a kiss. "I'm not bored with you," she answered.

A week later Sapphire's mood had changed.

"Oh, Charles!" she exclaimed at dinner. "Is anyone going to buy my pictures? So far, it's only been a few inquisitive villagers."

"Haven't you sold anything?

"No."

Charles frowned and drummed his fingers on the tabletop. "I'm sure you will. Don't worry."

Sapphire was unconvinced. She began to think her venture was doomed to failure. Each day she sat behind her small desk in the gallery facing the door. She had placed some watercolours in the window and hoped they would interest any passers-by.

A few holidaymakers began to wander in to see the exhibits, admiring what they saw, but not buying. Then one morning a couple came in and bought one of Amanda's pieces. Sapphire wrapped it up carefully and handed it over with a friendly remark. She realised that most of the money she'd received would have to go to Amanda.

The following day, a well-dressed man came in and wandered around for a while, examining each exhibit carefully. He came over and spoke to Sapphire.

"I'm interested in one of your oil paintings," he said. "That one over there."

He pointed to the large seascape opposite the door. Sapphire knew it was one of the best pieces in the gallery, and she had hung it to best advantage to be seen. She told him a little about the artist and the location of the view.

"You've just opened, I believe," the man said. "Have you had a lot of interest?"

"It's growing."

"Your prices must be an attraction. I have a gallery in London where pictures can fetch much more." He helped Sapphire take down the painting, and she began to write out the invoice.

"I'll take this while you do that. My motor's just outside."

Sapphire looked up. "I would prefer it if you would wait—"

Before she could finish her sentence, the man had picked up the painting and was walking out of the door. She put down her pen and watched through the window as he placed it carefully into his motor and closed the back up. He then walked briskly round to the driver's side, hopped in, and drove away.

Sapphire stood transfixed. "Oh, Lord!" she said, putting her hand over her open mouth.

She rushed out of the gallery and looked up the road, but there was nothing to see. She quickly dashed back, found her handbag, and fumbled in it for her key. Locking up the gallery, she ran as fast as she could down the road to Acacia House.

"Charles! Charles!" she called as she hurried through the door.

He came out of the surgery. "Sapphire! Whatever's wrong? Are you all right?"

"Oh, Charles," she cried out breathlessly. "I've been robbed!"

Sapphire, Charles, and Lucinda were sitting in the conservatory. Charles had managed to calm his wife down, as she had been shaking when she came in. He and Lucinda were listening avidly to what had happened. Sapphire looked pale as she related how the man had stolen the best painting in the gallery. Lucinda gasped as the story unfolded.

"You didn't see what the car was?" Charles asked hopefully.

Sapphire shook her head. "I'd know *him* if I saw him again," she stated.

"Did you buy that picture?" asked Charles.

"No. The artist had agreed for me to display it, and I was to take a commission when it was sold."

"How much were you asking?" When his wife told him, he raised his eyebrows. "I don't suppose you are insured?"

"No, I was looking into it, but it was hard to set a premium because the value of the artwork varies from month to month. I was waiting a few months to get an average price."

"I think we ought to tell the police," said Lucinda.

"Not very good publicity for your new gallery," observed Charles.

Sapphire bent her head down in despair. "I'm so sorry. I feel so foolish."

He put his arm round his wife. "You have nothing to apologise about, darling. You've been taken advantage of." He could see Sapphire was still in shock. He rose to go to his surgery. "I'll give you something to calm you."

"I still think we ought to report it," persisted Lucinda. "It might be happening to other galleries in the area."

Charles nodded. "Yes, you're right, I'll drive over to Kingsbridge police station with Sapphire after tea. This has raised several problems that we must think about. How safe is it for you to be in the gallery on your own? It was very easy for this man to do this."

Sapphire agreed wholeheartedly. "We'll talk about it when we get back," she said. "What I need now is a cup of tea!"

Mrs Harris brought in a tray while Charles left to get Sapphire's medication and was astounded when they told her the news. "I've never heard of anything like that happening here before," she said, wide-eyed.

Sapphire swallowed her pills, and when she had finished her tea, Charles asked her if she was up to going to the police station.

"Yes, definitely. This man's not going to get away with it if we can help it."

Sapphire sat quietly while Charles drove her through the lanes. Suddenly she raised her head.

"This has spoilt everything! I was *so* enjoying myself in this new venture. It's given me some real purpose, and now I feel like a naïve amateur."

Charles placed a reassuring hand on her knee. "Darling, you mustn't let this set you back. It could have happened to anyone. You were just very unlucky this rogue picked on your gallery."

At the police station they submitted their report, and the sergeant took the details, licking his pencil from time to time and writing very slowly. Finally, he completed his notes and looked up.

"Thank you for reporting this. We'll make some enquiries, but I must say it looks doubtful if you'll ever see your painting again. It's probably in London by now."

Sapphire and Charles walked slowly back to the motor.

"That was interesting, what he said," remarked Sapphire as Charles op0ened the car door for her.

Charles gave a puzzled look.

"The man who took it said he had a gallery in London."

"What are you inferring?"

"It might well turn up somewhere."

Back home, she and Charles made some decisions regarding the running of the gallery.

"Don't move the artwork until it is paid for," recommended Charles.

Sapphire nodded vehemently. "I realise that now."

"It might even be wise to wait for the cheque to clear, if they pay that way, and ask the customer to come back to collect their purchase. I'm afraid you'll have to reimburse your artist. Does he live far away?"

"No, just along the coast, I know where. I'll drive over tomorrow."

When she returned later the following morning, she told Charles that the artist had been very understanding and was grateful to her for paying him. "He's given me a receipt and a written description of his painting. I can prove it does belong to me now, if it's ever found."

"I've been thinking about that," said Charles. "Why don't we ask Amanda to keep a look out for it? You said she frequents the galleries around central London and Chelsea trying to sell her work."

Sapphire's eyes brightened. "What a good idea! I'll write giving her a full description and the name of the artist. Oh, Charles, do you think it *will* turn up?"

"Not yet awhile. It may appear in a few weeks, even months. I strongly suspect that your thief wants to make some money quite soon, though."

Sapphire wrote her letter to Amanda and waited.

CHAPTER ELEVEN
SLEUTHING

S APPHIRE RECEIVED A RESPONSE FROM Amanda straightaway telling her she would certainly keep an eye out for the stolen painting. "Art dealers are a slippery lot," she wrote. "I don't trust any of them!"

Meanwhile, interest in the gallery grew steadily, and Sapphire was hard-pressed to keep up with demand at times. Newspaper articles about the theft seemed to have helped sales rather than hindered them, as they gave the business publicity.

Caroline agreed to help some afternoons, and Sapphire closed the gallery on Sundays and Mondays. Another letter from Amanda arrived three weeks later.

Dear Sapphire,

I have good news! I think I might have located your stolen painting. It's in a gallery in Bond Street, and I have put a reserve on it to prevent it being sold. I have not said anything to the art dealer, but I think you had better come as soon as you can to verify it. He said he would keep it a week for me. Telephone me when you will be arriving.

Much love,

Amanda

Sapphire showed the letter to Charles, and he agreed to go with her. They travelled up to Richmond together the following day and met up with Lionel and Amanda in the station café to discuss what they would do.

"What a stroke of luck, coming across it!" exclaimed Sapphire as she joined them at their table.

"I'm pretty sure it's your painting," Amanda said excitedly. "I can't wait to take you there."

They settled themselves down while Lionel ordered at the counter

"How are you going to approach this?" asked Lionel, returning and putting the tray down.

They all helped themselves to their cups of steaming coffee.

"I have the letter from the artist," Sapphire stated, getting the piece of paper out of her handbag. She passed it to her brother, who read it carefully, then passed it to his wife.

"This will help," he said, "but we need to contact the police first to deal with this. The dealer may be reluctant to believe us, and he may even be working with this man who stole it."

"The world of art dealing sounds a bit murky to me. As Lionel says, we'll have to tread carefully if we're to get the painting back," agreed Charles.

They finished their drinks, eager to get on with the matter in hand. Having hailed a taxi outside the station, they arrived in Bond Street and looked up and down at the row of smart galleries and shops.

"It's the one over there," said Amanda, pointing.

Lionel enquired from someone as to the location of a police station, and they walked the short distance there. Inside, a police sergeant advised them to visit the gallery and, if the situation was not resolved, to return, and he would send an officer round.

They returned to Bond Street and entered the small gallery that Amanda had identified. Sapphire quickly agreed it was the painting. She let Lionel approach a smartly dressed man who was sitting behind a desk to explain the situation. The man asked them to come to his office at the back of the gallery.

They entered a room that was full of pictures stacked against the walls and a desk covered with paperwork.

"May I ask what evidence you have to claim this painting?" the man asked. He appeared slightly annoyed as he peered at them over his half-moon spectacles.

"Let me introduce you to the owner of the gallery where the painting was stolen," said Lionel, turning towards Sapphire. "This is Miss Wells." The smart man greeted her briefly. "She has a letter from the artist. Perhaps you would like to read it?"

Sapphire gave it to the man and waited.

After studying it, he handed it back to her. "I'm afraid this proves nothing. It could be a forgery for all I know."

"We can bring the artist here to verify his work and explain his arrangement with Miss Wells," answered Lionel. "The theft has been reported to the police, and we have been advised to contact them if you do not hand it over."

"I'm not about to hand anything over."

"Then we will go to the police," stated Lionel firmly.

"Can I ask who you are selling the painting on behalf of?" asked Sapphire.

"Certainly not."

"We'll leave now." Lionel looked straight at the man. "But you haven't seen the last of us."

He ushered everyone through the door, and they stood outside, wondering what to do.

"The police will find out who brought it to the gallery." Charles sounded hopeful.

"We'll go there now and return with an officer," said Lionel, who had taken charge of the situation.

The station sergeant agreed to send an officer with them but asked for an interview first. Sapphire said she would answer any questions. After the meeting, the officer examined what he had written down and went over the details once again. He asked Sapphire if it was all correct, then picked up his helmet.

"Right, let's see what we can do."

When they returned to the gallery, the smart man looked furious. "What's the meaning of this?" he snapped. "I have clients to see!"

"That will have to wait, I'm afraid, sir," the officer answered calmly. "I need to ask you a few questions."

He was shown into the office at the back, and the door closed. A short time later, he emerged.

"You'll have to let us make some enquiries, sir," he said, addressing Lionel. "I suggest you come back to the station and give me your contact details, and we will be in touch."

Sapphire looked desperately at him.

"We'll have to do as he says," Lionel told her.

After they had finished their business at the police station, they made their way to a nearby restaurant.

Sapphire sat staring at the menu card. "I don't think we're going to get it back."

"I shan't ever use *that* gallery to sell my work," said Amanda. "I'll make sure word goes round that they're not to be trusted."

"I really thought we would get it back straightaway. Why didn't he believe us?"

"Don't worry, we'll get it back," answered Lionel. "Even if we have to bring a civil action. That dealer's hiding something, I'm sure of it."

"Let's hope the police can get to the bottom of it," said Charles. Then he added, "I think I'll have the salmon."

Sapphire continued working at her gallery, and nothing more was heard from the police. She told Charles she had little hope of ever seeing the stolen painting again. "I'm going to put the whole ghastly business behind me," she said.

Lucinda continued to be involved with the village nursery and was not always available to look after her young granddaughter, so Sapphire would sometimes take Charlotte Elizabeth to work and let her play there. She gave her crayons or paints, and her daughter would spend a happy morning creating pictures. Sapphire had promised she would frame a special one and maybe hang it in the gallery, saying, "It will have to be very good."

The gallery had begun to attract more visitors, but there were times when it was quiet. It was a month since the picture had been taken.

Sapphire was thinking about locking up early one day when she heard a motor draw up outside. She looked up, and when she saw who it was, she was horrified. Her hands gripped the sides of her chair as she rose to meet the man entering her gallery. He was carrying a large painting.

"Miss Wells, we meet again," he greeted, placing the picture carefully against the wall.

"You've got a nerve!" began Sapphire.

He held his hands out, as if to look innocent. "I'm afraid there has been a huge misunderstanding," he continued, quite unperturbed. "I really was under the impression that you had asked me to take your painting to London. Unfortunately, it hasn't sold."

"I informed the police, as I believed you had stolen it. Why didn't you leave a name or a receipt?"

"Didn't I do that? How remiss! I do apologise. I thought I was doing you a favour."

Sapphire had to think quickly. "Excuse me a moment," she said. "I just have to check on my child."

She hurried to the room at the back of the gallery, where Charlotte Elizabeth was busy at her artwork. "Darling, don't be frightened, but run home as fast as you can and tell Daddy to come to the gallery, as Mummy wants him urgently."

Her daughter jumped up eagerly. "Go out of the back door," Sapphire instructed.

Charlotte Elizabeth ran out, and Sapphire waited a few minutes before returning to her visitor. He was standing with his back to her, his hands in his pockets, looking at a painting. He swung round. "I do hope there are no hard feelings?" He gave a charming smile. "Perhaps I can help you out in the future, if you would like me to?"

"I don't think I will be trusting you with any more of my pictures, Mr…?"

"Campbell, Angus Campbell, at your service!"

"If I remember rightly, you had told me that you wished to buy the painting, but you never paid for it."

"Forgive me, but I think your memory doesn't serve you right. Don't you recall my telling you about London prices?"

"Yes, we spoke of that, but I didn't ask you to sell the painting for me."

"I was under the impression you had done."

"And I was under the impression you wished to buy it from me."

At that moment, Charles came through the door.

"Oh, thank God!" said Sapphire under her breath.

"I'm Doctor Browne, Miss Wells's husband. Can I ask you what the devil you're doing here?"

Angus held his hands out helplessly again. "I came to return your wife's picture. I'm afraid it didn't sell."

"The one you stole, you mean. I don't know what your game is, but the police have been informed."

"Yes, they've been to see me, but when I explained that it had all been a misunderstanding, and I was working in accordance with your wife's instructions, they seemed satisfied." He gave a self-complacent smile.

"You're a liar. You know that's not true!" Charles was beginning to get angry.

"My word against yours—difficult to prove, I have to say."

"Get out!" demanded Charles. "I know what you and that dealer are up to. You're lucky I won't bring a civil action against you, now we know who you are. Now get back to your grubby little scams, and don't show your face round here again!"

Angus smiled again as he swiftly passed Charles on his way towards the door. Outside, he got into his motor and drove away.

"Let's hope that's the last we see of him," said Charles.

Sapphire flung her arms round her husband, "Oh, darling, you were magnificent!"

"It was all I could do to stop myself giving him a black eye."

His wife threw her head back, laughing. "You sound just like your father!"

CHAPTER TWELVE
STEPHEN'S TROUBLE

FLORRIE WAS SLICING BREAD FOR the boys' tea when she heard Stephen's car draw up. She glanced at the clock—it was a little past four. *He's back very early,* she thought to herself.

Her husband came through the door with a pile of exercise books under his arm, which he deposited on the table in the parlour. Without saying anything, he immediately went back to his motor and returned with another armful of books and his briefcase.

Florrie paused as he walked past her. "Is everything all right?" she asked.

"Yes, yes, why shouldn't it be?" he answered tetchily.

"Is the end of term getting to you?"

"I said, there's nothing the matter."

Just then, the boys burst through the door, followed by their grandfather.

"Daddy's home!" exclaimed Christopher, followed by Jonny's "Daddy! Daddy!" They both hugged their father's legs.

"That's enough, boys," said Florrie. "Let Daddy sit down. Go and wash your hands."

Ben ushered them out into the scullery, and Florrie poured her husband a cup of tea.

"I'll make a start on the marking before supper," said Stephen and went into the parlour, taking his tea with him.

Florrie frowned. Stephen hadn't even kissed her when he'd come in or asked her about her day. She sighed and continued to butter the bread.

After tea, Ben put the boys to bed and came downstairs. Stephen emerged from the parlour and sat down at the kitchen table without saying anything.

"Would you like me to help with the marking after supper if there's a lot to do?" asked Florrie, dishing out the potatoes onto their plates.

"Yes, that would be a great help," Stephen replied. "Can you do the essays, and I'll finish the arithmetic?"

Florrie said she would be glad to and continued serving the meal.

They ate in silence until finally Ben said, "Out with it, Stephen. What's happened? Is it something at the school?"

Stephen stopped eating. "Yes," he replied, putting down his knife and fork.

Florrie and her father glanced at each other.

"Something *has* happened." Stephen looked distraught. "I'd better explain. All this year, we've had a probationer, a young woman called Miss Allen. I think I might have mentioned her to you?"

"Yes," Florrie said. "I remember, you had concerns about her teaching."

"That's right. She hasn't turned out to be a very good teacher, and despite my efforts to help her, she hasn't improved. Her teaching is poor, and she has no discipline over the children. I have had no alternative but to fail her. I went to her classroom yesterday after school to warn her and to say I had done my best. She didn't say much, so I left it at that. Today, after school, she came and sat herself on my desk and compromised me."

Florrie gasped and put her hand to her mouth.

"Go on," said Ben. "What did she say to you?"

"She said that I had always looked at her in an admiring way, and she thought we 'had something.'" He looked at his wife. "Florrie, there's never been anything like that. She's making it all up to try to get me to give her a pass."

Florrie reached out and held his hand. "I know, darling," she said quietly.

"She said she hoped I would give her a second chance. I told her to remove herself from my desk and under no circumstances would I change my mind. I also informed her she was very much mistaken about me, and I was not attracted to her in any way. I said I was a married man with a family, and she said why should that matter?"

"Certainly not teacher material, then," said Florrie.

"I asked her to go back to her classroom and told her she was lucky I wasn't going to report her to the chairman of governors. She became quite unpleasant and told me I should watch out as she would report *me* for harassing her if I didn't give her a pass. You know how damaging that sort of accusation can be." Stephen put his head in his hands. "What am I to do?"

"You must inform your chairman of governors," said Ben. "Do you know where he lives?"

"Yes, in Kingsbridge. I've been there a few times."

"Go now, this evening—don't wait until tomorrow. Tell him everything you have just told us. Would you like me to come with you?"

Stephen looked up hopefully. "Yes. I'll go. I'll be all right, Ben. You stay with Florrie."

He hurriedly finished his meal and left. After he had driven away, Ben put his arm round his daughter. "His chairman will know what to do. He must believe Stephen to be an honourable man and a good headmaster."

Florrie nodded and went into the parlour to finish her husband's marking, waiting patiently until he returned. Later that evening, he came back looking more relaxed.

"Mr. Fraser has suggested that we threaten her with a civil action for attempted blackmail," he said, as soon as he came in. "She would have to make her accusations under oath and pay costs if she lost. He said the school would pay for a lawyer for me, and he would be prepared to contribute towards the case himself, if need be. He said he valued my headship and would stand by me."

Florrie breathed a sigh of relief. "Oh, Stephen, I'm so sorry this has happened. You don't deserve it!" She put her arms round him and gave him a kiss.

"What will happen tomorrow?" asked Ben. "You have to stop her making these accusations."

"Mr Fraser is writing a letter, which he will hand to her as soon as she arrives in the morning."

"Do you think it will work?" Ben looked doubtful.

"Mr Fraser seems to think so. Her reputation will be on the line if she appears in a court of law. He says the fact that she is going to fail her probationary year makes it obvious what she is up to."

The following morning, Stephen kissed Florrie goodbye and left for school. All day Florrie worried about what would happen. What if the young woman stuck to her story and refused to be intimidated?

When Stephen returned later that afternoon, she could see he looked relieved. "She's gone," were his first words as he came through the door. "It worked."

He embraced his wife and held her close to him. "Florrie, I would never do anything to hurt you and our children." He went over to baby Sarah's cot. "What a little treasure," he said, touching her cheek.

Florrie fetched Ben, and Stephen told them both what had happened that day. He said that Miss Allen had been handed the letter before school and had left straightaway.

"What about her class?" asked Florrie.

"I had to divide them up between the other classes for the day. The children loved it, but I wasn't very popular with the teachers. I won't be able to get a replacement this late in the term." He looked desperately at his wife. "Florrie, I don't suppose that you would step in. It's only two weeks."

"I would love to, but it depends on Pa." She waited for his reaction.

"You could bring Christopher and put him in the infant class," suggested Stephen. "Perhaps Millie would have Jonny."

"Sarah is taking the bottle now to supplement her feeds. I could just about manage if Ben agrees."

"Yes, I can manage," her father assured her.

"I'd bring you home as soon as school's finished," added Stephen. "Then I could return to do my work. I know it's a lot to ask of you."

"It will be strange to be in the classroom again," Florrie mused.

The boys were in bed when Stephen had arrived home from school, so Florrie decided to tell them about the arrangements the next morning.

At breakfast she explained to Christopher she was going to take him to Daddy's school that day. She told him how he was to behave in the classroom. "You must call me Mrs Faircross," she instructed.

"But you're Mummy," he replied, looking bewildered.

"I'm going to be your teacher. That's what all the other children will call me." She put her arm round him. "You'll love school. We do lots of interesting things, and you'll make some friends."

"What do I call Daddy?"

"Mr Faircross. Daddy is in charge of everybody at school. All the teachers call him Mr Faircross." She turned to Jonny who was spooning porridge into his mouth, listening intently. "You're staying at home with Grandpa," she instructed. "And you are to be *good*."

Jonny met her eye contact and nodded. She then got Christopher ready, kissed Sarah goodbye, and followed Stephen out to the motor. They set off quickly, and Ben watched them go, standing in the doorway. He turned round to find Jonny had left the table and was tugging at his trouser leg.

"Where's Mummy gone?" he asked.

"She's gone to school with Daddy. Christopher's gone too."

After clearing away the breakfast things, Ben put Sarah in her pram, then took Jonny by the hand, and they went outside.

"Where we going?" asked his grandson.

"To the shop to see Aunty Millie."

"Can I have sweeties?"

"No, not this time. You'll be staying with Aunty Millie. You must be very good."

"Then can I have sweeties?"

"If you're very good."

Jonny nodded.

When they arrived, Ben went to the cottage near to the shop where Harry and Millie lived. Millie answered the door, looking alarmed. "Is everything all right?" she asked.

Ben explained the situation, saying that a teacher had left suddenly, and Stephen needed Florrie to help. "Can you have Jonny for me? I have all the housework to do, and meals. I would be grateful."

"Yes, of course." Millie patted the boy on the head. "Come on in, love. I have Agnes's two here today, so the more the merrier!"

"I'll come back at lunchtime," said Ben.

He kissed his grandson goodbye and pushed Sarah back to Forge Cottage. She had been sleeping after her early morning feed but would be waking later, and he needed to have her bottle ready. He did his chores, then got himself some bread and cheese. After an early lunch, he wheeled Sarah back over to Millie's to collect his young grandson.

"Did you get your sweeties?" he asked.

Jonny looked up at him and grinned, which was all the answer Ben needed.

Back home, it was time to rest, although Sarah took time to settle after she had her bottle, and Ben realised he had forgotten to wind her. When Florrie came home at four o'clock, he gave a sigh of relief. It had been a tiring day for him. Stephen said a quick hello and then went straight back to school.

Christopher was full of chatter about his day. "Mummy let me play with the train set, and then we all went out to play, then I did some painting, and then it was lunchtime, and we had sausages!" He paused to draw breath.

"Do the children do any lessons?" Ben asked his daughter. "Or do they play all day? It wasn't like that in my day."

"It isn't 'your day' now, Pa. Times have changed."

Ben said no more but made Florrie a cup of tea while she fed a very hungry Sarah.

"How's she been?" she asked him.

"Absolutely fine."

"And Jonny?" She looked round. "By the way, where is he?"

Ben put the kettle down and looked startled. "I think he must be in the garden, or, um…upstairs."

"Pa, you must keep an eye on him. He's probably up to no good."

Ben went outside but was soon back. "He's not there," he said. He went upstairs and returned with Jonny tucked under his arm.

"What's he been up to now?" Florrie looked stern.

Ben placed Jonny down on the floor, where he stood with his finger in his mouth.

"He was in my room rifling through my bedside cupboard," he told her.

"What were you looking for, Jonny?" she asked. "You know that's Grandpa's room."

"Choccy."

"Grandpa doesn't eat chocolate in bed!" Florrie exclaimed.

"He does," her son answered, solemnly.

Ben looked embarrassed. "Only sometimes."

He and his grandson stood before Florrie, looking distinctly guilty.

CHAPTER THIRTEEN

BEN GOES MISSING

THE LAST TWO WEEKS OF the term proved challenging for everyone. Florrie became increasingly tired, and Sarah became fretful because her routine had changed. Ben had to spend a lot of time soothing her and rocking her in his arms. Jonny became naughty, as he knew his mother wasn't there, and Stephen was stressed, as he had to organise interviews to appoint a new teacher for the autumn term. Christopher was the happiest—he loved going to school with his parents.

Finally, it was the end of term, and Florrie and Stephen arrived home with their son.

"I think we're all glad that's over!" exclaimed Stephen as Ben put the kettle on the range.

Florrie sat down and kicked off her shoes. "I did enjoy it, but it was exhausting!" She put her arm round Christopher, who was standing beside her waiting for a cookie from the tin on the table. "You've been so good," she said. "And you remembered to call me Mrs Faircross."

"You're Mummy now," said Christopher, still eyeing the tin.

"Yes, I'm Mummy now." Florrie reached in and got out a cookie, which she gave to him.

He ran off, and shortly after, Jonny came for his. "I been good too," he said, looking at his mother with wide open eyes.

Florrie looked at her father. "Has he?" she asked.

Ben stroked his beard. "Now, let me see. I think, on the whole, yes."

Florrie gave her youngest a cookie, and he ran off to join his brother. She closed her eyes and gratefully drank her tea, thinking about how they would spend the summer holidays.

She and Stephen had discussed whether to visit Stephen's parents in Plymouth, and they received a letter a few days later from his mother asking if they would be coming. Florrie was concerned that it might be too much for his mother to cope with them all, but her husband reassured her that his parents were very keen that they all come.

"Father hasn't been too well," he said as he read the letter. "He has a bed downstairs now." He looked concerned. "I think we should all go."

"What about Pa?" asked Florrie. "Do you think he'll mind being left?"

"We'll ask him," replied Stephen.

At supper that evening, they put the question to Ben.

"You must go," he replied without hesitation. "I shall be fine. A little peace and quiet won't come amiss."

Florrie set about packing the cases, and the little family set off the next day. Ben waved to them as the full motor pulled away down the lane.

Charles was waiting for his mother. She was getting ready for a short trip away. Eventually she came downstairs, pulling on her gloves.

She kissed Sapphire goodbye while Charles went to fetch her case.

"Have a lovely time, Mummy," said Sapphire. "I wish I was coming."

Lucinda had told them that she was staying with a friend. Sapphire was unable to leave the gallery and was expecting a consignment of artworks from Amanda and Lionel. She reluctantly waved her mother goodbye.

When her visitors arrived the following day, Sapphire helped Amanda unload the motor, and they began to take the items straight to the gallery.

"How are things there?" Lionel asked Charles as they watched them go. "No more incidents, I hope. Fancy that man turning up like that. You should have had him arrested."

"I think the police had put the wind up him," replied Charles. "He said they had been to see him."

"Poor Sapphire! She must have been scared."

"She did the right thing sending for me. I've never run so fast in my life! I must say he was surprised to see me."

"Charlotte Elizabeth did well."

"Yes, we explained to her afterwards that she had been a great help to Mummy."

As the two men relaxed in the conservatory with their drinks, Charles suggested they drive over to see Ben the following morning. "Florrie and the family have gone to Stephen's parents in Plymouth, so he'll be on his own. The girls will be busy at the gallery, so we have the day to ourselves."

Lionel welcomed the idea. "We could take a picnic basket and some beers." Pleased with this suggestion, Charles went to find Mrs Harris to make the arrangements.

The next day, Sapphire announced that she and Amanda were going to be rearranging the gallery, and she would take Charlotte Elizabeth with them.

Charles grinned at Lionel. "We have some plans too," he said. He collected the picnic basket, and they jumped into Lionel's motor. "I expect Pa will be surprised to see us. It will be good to take him out for the day," said Charles as they set off.

They chattered good-naturedly as they drove along. Charles and his half-brother had always got along well; their friendship had begun early, when they were introduced to each other as young boys. During the war years they had been forced apart but had met up again and had been able to support each other before their marriages.

The motor swept up the lane and stopped outside Forge Cottage. Charles was excited as he got out to greet his pa. He was surprised to find the door locked. He rattled the handle a few times. Lionel arrived carrying the picnic basket and the two men looked at each other, puzzled. They knocked loudly, but there was no answer.

"He must have gone out," said Charles, stepping back and looking round.

They found the key under the flowerpot and let themselves in. Charles called out Ben's name as they entered. He scanned the room. Everything in the kitchen looked neat and tidy, and there was no sign of anyone having been there that morning. The table was bare, the chairs neatly pushed in on each side. Lionel felt the top of the range.

"It's cold," he said, sounding surprised.

"Surely he would have lit the range," said Charles. "It is the first thing he does every morning."

Lionel peeked into the parlour, came back, and shook his head. They both went up the stairs and peered into Ben's bedroom. The bed was made and showed no sign of having been slept in.

"Where the devil has he gone?" said Lionel, sounding exasperated.

They returned to the kitchen.

"We'd better go over to see if he's at Aunty Millie's," suggested Charles. "Perhaps he's staying there."

They walked down the lane to the village. When they arrived at the shop, they found Millie busy behind the counter.

"Hello! What brings you over here?"

"We've come to see Pa," said Charles. "Do you know where he is?"

Millie looked mystified. "Isn't he at home?"

"No, we've just been there."

"He didn't tell me he was going away. Perhaps he's just gone for a walk or caught the bus into Kingsbridge."

Still puzzled, the two men thanked her and said they would return to Forge Cottage and wait for him. They walked slowly back.

"Perhaps he has gone for a walk," suggested Charles. "I know some of his favourites." The brothers turned into the path that led through the wood beside the stream. "Pa told me he and Ma did their courting along here," he said, with a smile.

After half an hour or so, they emerged into the lane again. There had been no sign of Ben. As they walked back to Forge Cottage, Lionel suddenly stopped and turned to his half-brother.

"When did you take my mother to the station?" he asked.

"Yesterday morning. Why?"

"I was just wondering."

Charles frowned.

"Are you thinking what I'm thinking?" Lionel asked.

"You think he—they—might have gone away together?"

"Yes."

The two men fell silent, then Charles said, "I wasn't expecting this. He's been coming to see Lucinda quite often. Do you think they've planned a holiday together?"

"It looks like it. Whatever it is, Pa obviously wants to keep the arrangement a secret."

"Yes." Charles looked slightly embarrassed. After a short pause he said, "Do you mind, Lionel?"

"No, not at all. If they want to find some happiness together, good luck to them."

Charles agreed. "If Pa doesn't want anyone to know, we must respect that."

Lionel nodded. "What we think we know stays with us."

The two brothers shook hands.

CHAPTER FOURTEEN

TWO WIDOWS

S TEPHEN AND FLORRIE WERE WARMLY welcomed when they arrived at his parents' home in Plymouth. Florrie carried Sarah inside while Stephen dealt with the luggage. She handed Sarah to Stephen's mother, Jenny, who took her to where her husband was seated in his bed in the corner of their sitting room.

"Look at her, Jim," she whispered.

Stephen's father leant over and touched the child's head, and Jenny gently put her into her grandfather's arms. Stephen came in with the cases to take upstairs, and Christopher and Jonny came running in behind him.

"Boys, steady down!" instructed their mother, looking nervously at Mr Faircross.

They stopped and stood side by side, staring at their grandfather.

"Hello, you two," he greeted them. "Now let me see… which one is which? You're Jonny and you're Christopher!" He looked at them each in turn with a twinkle in his eye.

They fell into fits of laughter.

"No, no," exclaimed Christopher. "*I'm* Christopher!"

Jenny hastily retrieved Sarah, and the boys tumbled onto the bed, still laughing. Their grandfather hugged them both.

"Why are you in bed?" asked Jonny.

"Because I'm a bit poorly, young man."

Stephen came downstairs. "Don't crowd round Grandad," he told them.

"Gwandad not well," said Jonny, seriously.

"How are you, Dad?" asked Stephen.

"Not so bad, thanks, son. I feel better for seeing you all."

Florrie lifted the boys off the bed. "Granny has a surprise for you in the kitchen," she said. They shot out through the door, and she turned to her father-in-law. "I hope we're not going to be too much for you."

"Not at all," Jim replied. "I've been looking forward to your visit. Now, Stephen, how are things at your school?"

Florrie left them to chat together. She went to see Jenny and took Sarah from her. The boys both had lollipops. "I hope you said thank you," Florrie said.

They both nodded as she shooed them out of the kitchen into the small garden at the back.

"How *is* Dad?" she asked.

"He's not at all well," answered Jenny. "The doctor says there is little he can do for him now." She put her hand on Florrie's arm. "I'm so glad you all came."

Stephen took his family out most days during their stay, while Jenny stayed with his father. On one such trip, they sat high up on the green beside the lighthouse, called 'The Hoe'. They had a good view out to sea, and the boys loved watching the ships making their way in and out of Devonport dockyard.

"I wish Dad was with us," said Stephen as a tall, masted vessel sailed past. "He knows all about these ships. He would bring me here when I was a boy and tell me about them. I've even seen submarines going into the dockyard."

Christopher listened to his father as he pointed out the passing boats. Later that evening, his grandfather told him about the dockyard at Devonport, where he used to work, and showed him some old photographs of ships.

"They've just made Plymouth into a city," he said proudly as he closed the album.

"What's a city?" asked Christopher.

"It's bigger than a town and usually has a cathedral—a big important church."

Jim continued telling his grandson about his memories of the old days. Christopher would ask him questions, and they continued to enjoy each other's company.

Jonny hung around his granny, hoping for treats. Jenny said he was a little poppet.

The family visited one of the local beaches tucked away in a little bay. It had rock pools for the boys to explore, and they ran about excitedly with their buckets and spades looking for crabs. Florrie spread out a blanket over the sandy shingle, and Sarah lay on it waving her arms and staring at the sky. Florrie settled down with a book to read while Stephen played with the boys. Jenny had packed sandwiches for them with flasks of tea, and later they enjoyed their picnic together.

On the last day of their visit, Stephen was helping Florrie get packed up and ready to leave. He loaded the motor with their luggage and then returned to say his farewells to his parents.

"Thank you, Mum, for looking after us," he said, giving her a hug. "I know the boys have had a wonderful time, and it's been a good break for Florrie."

"She told me all about her spell of teaching," replied Jenny. "Don't let her work too hard, Stephen."

"We've appointed a new teacher now. Christopher will be starting school next year, so that will lighten her load."

"Little Jonny is a bit of a handful," said Jenny. "He's very sweet, and he knows it!"

Florrie had gone to fetch the boys to say their goodbyes to their grandad, and he was having a joke with their names again.

"Grandpa keeps on getting us muddled up!" Christopher laughed.

"Goodbye, boys," Jim said as he embraced them both, looking visibly upset.

Florrie brought Sarah to his bedside. He took her in his arms and kissed her gently.

"Goodbye, little one," he said. "Remember your grandad."

Florrie fought back her tears. "She will, Dad. I'll make sure of that."

It was a difficult parting, and Florrie and Stephen spoke little on the return journey. The boys soon fell asleep in the back seat of the motor as they made their way home.

Charles had finished his morning rounds and was on his way to see Donald. He sometimes met with him at this time of day to discuss some of the patients and have a coffee. Caroline answered the door.

"I'm so glad you're here," she said, looking anxious. "I'm worried. Donald's feeling unwell and is pretending there's nothing the matter."

"That's very typical of a doctor," remarked Charles. "I'll see what I can do."

He went through to where his friend was sitting in his chair by the window. "Hello, Donald. Caroline says you're feeling a bit under the weather."

"Oh, tush! Just a bit of old age creeping on. I'll be fine."

As Charles talked about some of his patients, he could see Donald was gripping the arms of his chair, and his face looked strained. Finally, Charles got up, took out his pocket watch, and held the doctor's wrist. After a few moments, he let go and sat down again.

"You must know what this is," he said to the older man. "What do you want to do?"

"I've had these attacks before, and they usually pass. This one's a bit worse. I really don't want to worry Caroline."

"She's already worried."

"Well, what do you suggest, Doctor?" asked Donald, managing a faint smile.

Charles mentioned some medication he thought would be suitable for heart conditions and said he would bring it round. He saw how tired the man was looking, so he took his leave.

Charles went back to his surgery to make up the prescription, and that afternoon he returned and saw that his friend and colleague was no better. Caroline came in with a jug of fresh water and placed it on the table. She glanced anxiously at Charles. Donald managed to swallow the tablets, and Charles sat with him for a while. The older doctor had closed his eyes, so Charles left the room and spoke to Caroline in hushed tones.

"I think you realise he's in a bad way," he said.

"Yes. Should he go to hospital?"

"I strongly advise you not to move him. Send for me any time. The tablets should help a little and give him a comfortable night. I'll come back first thing in the morning. If he's no better then, it might be as well to contact Harriette and Dorothy."

Charles returned to Acacia House in a sombre mood. He was very fond of his colleague and felt frustrated he couldn't do more for him. He hoped he might see an improvement the following morning.

He was woken next day by Mrs Harris tapping loudly on his and Sapphire's bedroom door.

"Doctor! Wake up! There's an urgent message for you."

Charles sat straight up in bed. "Coming! Thank you!" He was often alerted in this way.

Getting up quickly, he put on his dressing gown and went downstairs.

"This note was delivered this morning," the housekeeper said, handing him a small, folded piece of paper.

He quickly read it. "Oh, no," he muttered. He raced back upstairs.

"Sapphire!" he said, shaking her gently. "Sapphire, wake up!"

His wife moaned and turned over. "What is it?" she mumbled.

"Donald died last night."

Her eyes opened, and she sat up quickly, staring at him. "Oh, Charles!" She placed her hand on his arm. "The poor man!"

"When I saw him yesterday, he was in a bad way, but I didn't know it would be this quick." He brushed his hand across his forehead. "I wish I could have done more for him."

Sapphire could see her husband was distressed. "I'm sure you did your best, darling. You were not to know. You've often said to me doctors don't—can't—know everything."

Charles grasped her hand. "I shall miss him, Sapphire. He was such a great friend to me. I owe him everything."

He dressed quickly, as did his wife, and they set off to the Baileys' house straightaway. Caroline was quite calm, as if she had prepared herself for this for some time. She led them through to where Donald sat peacefully in his chair, a blanket round his knees.

"This is just as I found him this morning," she explained. "I kissed him goodnight last night, then went to bed. I wanted to sit with him, but he insisted I lie down and have a good night's sleep. I wish I had stayed."

Charles examined the doctor briefly and pronounced him dead.

"I wish the girls had been here," went on Caroline. "They will be very upset. It's all been so sudden. He's had these turns before, but yesterday he allowed me to tell you. I should have told you before."

"It wouldn't have made much difference," replied Charles, reassuringly. "He was probably self-medicating."

"I'm so very sorry," said Sapphire, putting her arm round Caroline. "If there's anything we can do, let us know."

"Thank you," replied Caroline. "That's very kind." She turned to Charles. "We have two lovely daughters, but Donald saw you as a son, Charles. He often told me how pleased he was that his patients were in such good hands."

"He was a very good friend." Charles was fighting back his emotions. "I am enormously grateful for all the did for me. He was a fine example to follow."

He turned away as he put his stethoscope back in his bag, tears welling up in his eyes. "I'll write out the certificate and bring it round later," he managed to say. "I'll help you make the necessary arrangements."

"Thank you, Charles. I'll contact the girls."

Most of the village turned out to pay their respects to Doctor Bailey on the day of his funeral. They lined the little High Street that led to the church at the top of the hill. Charles and Billy had been asked to be pallbearers. Sapphire had offered Acacia House as a venue for the wake, and Caroline had gratefully accepted, her own house being smaller. The mourners filled the rooms—Doctor Bailey had been well known and well loved.

Ben had been back for two weeks now and was relieved none of the family seemed to have noticed his absence. Lucinda had travelled on to complete her shopping trip in London and was still away. He had offered to look after the children while Florrie and Stephen attended the funeral. They returned home full of sadness, and Florrie reminisced how fortunate Charles was to have been taken on by Doctor Bailey.

"He was sponsored by someone, but we still don't know who," she said.

"I think it might have been Billy," said Ben. "He was in a position financially to do so."

"If so, that was extremely generous of him," added Florrie.

It was near the end of the summer holidays, and Stephen was preparing to go back to school. "I love the beginning of the new term," he told Florrie cheerfully. "The school smells of polish after the cleaners have been, and everything is fresh, waiting for the children to return."

Florrie stood at the gate and waved him off on his first day, then returned to her chores. Ben had gone out, and she decided to tidy his room. He wasn't good at putting his clothes away, so she began to sort out those that needed washing. She was emptying the pockets of a pair of trousers when she found a piece of paper inside. She unfolded it and saw it was a short, scribbled note. On it was written "Love You xx."

She thrust it back quickly, as if it had burned her fingers, and could feel her face getting hot. What did it mean? Who had written it? Her thoughts spun round and round in her head. She had seen that it wasn't a child's handwriting, and Charlotte Elizabeth was the only grandchild who had begun writing her letters. She could think of only one person—Lucinda.

She decided to keep her discovery to herself and continued with her work for the rest of the day, but her thoughts kept returning to the note. Stephen came home with his news about the school, and this helped her to forget for a while. He told her he was happy with the new teacher.

She was always pleased when it was time to put the kettle on and welcome Stephen home. Each day followed the next in much the same way until one afternoon a telegram arrived. Stephen had just returned home. The banging on the door alarmed them both as they drank their tea at the kitchen table together. Florrie looked surprised and went to see who it was. When she opened the door, a young boy on a bicycle thrust a yellow envelope into her hand and pedalled off. She handed it to Stephen, and his hand trembled slightly as he took it from her. She watched as his face went pale as he read it. When he looked up at her she knew what he was about to say.

"My father died earlier today."

Florrie put her arms around him. "He was a lovely man," she said, with tears in her eyes.

Stephen stood up quickly, full of nervous energy. He said he would have to leave straightaway to drive down to Plymouth, but he would have to sort out things at the school first.

"I'll have to see Mr Fraser and ask him to manage my absence. It might mean sending my class home. I must go and see Mother—she must be devastated. I suppose she has contacted my sister, but Scotland's a long way away, and I don't know if she can come all that way."

He sat slumped at the table, holding his head. Florrie could see he was not coping. She tried to calm him down. "Mr Fraser will know what to do," she said reassuringly. "And Jenny will be managing. She must have known this was going to happen. I'll pack your case, and then you can set off later."

"Will you tell the boys?" he asked. "I know Christopher will be very upset."

Florrie assured him she would, and Stephen left to see his chairman of governors. When he returned, Florrie saw him off on his drive to Plymouth.

"Please give Jenny my deepest sympathy," she said. "We shall always have lovely memories of Jim."

Stephen arrived back later the next day and told Ben and Florrie the funeral was to be the following Tuesday at Jenny's local church. Ben said he would look after the boys at home, and it was decided Florrie would take Sarah with her.

CHAPTER FIFTEEN

FAMILY UPSET

JENNY HAD ALWAYS BEEN A practical, optimistic person, and Florrie was relieved to see she appeared to be coping well when they arrived the day before the funeral. The sitting room had been put back to how it had been before Jim's illness, his bed having been removed. His book of ships was on the table, and Jenny picked it up.

"I know Jim wanted Christopher to have this," she said, giving it to her son. Stephen thanked her as he took it. "He so enjoyed your visit," she went on. "He talked about nothing else afterwards, and it made him very happy."

"Is my sister coming to the funeral?" Stephen asked.

"No, she said it was too far to come." Jenny looked somewhat tight-lipped.

"There's the expense as well, I suppose," commented Stephen. "That husband of hers holds the purse strings."

"She sent a letter." She went to find it.

Stephen read it through, then passed it to Florrie without comment. She saw that it was full of excuses, as if his sister's life was more important than her father's. She couldn`t imagine treating her own pa like that. She handed the letter back.

"I expect Rosa and Hilda will come," she said.

Rosa had lodged with Stephen's parents when she began nursing in Plymouth, and Jenny had taken in Hilda when her stepson had been abusive towards her.

"Yes, Rosa came round a few times to visit Jim. She hasn't forgotten us. Hilda still comes to the mothers' meeting at the church every week."

Florrie gave Ben's apologies, saying he was looking after the boys. "I'm not sure what to do about Sarah," she said. "I think I'll have to sit at the back of the church in case she cries."

The following day, Florrie and Stephen met up with Rosa and Hilda, and after the funeral service walked up the path to the church hall, where drinks and sandwiches were spread out on two trestle tables. It was a simple affair, but well attended by Jenny's many church friends and a few of Jim's retired colleagues from the dockyard. The vicar sailed round in his flowing vestments welcoming everyone, shaking hands, and offering words of comfort.

Florrie found a quiet corner with Sarah asleep in her arms.

Rosa came and sat beside her, peering at her young niece. "She's growing fast."

"Yes, and thankfully no more mishaps," Florrie said, holding her daughter close.

"And how is Pa?"

"Rosa, I want to tell you something."

She described to her sister how she had found the note in their father's pocket. "I wasn't snooping around," she added quickly. "I was only doing his laundry."

Rosa pursed her lips when she was told what was written on it. Then she said, "It can only be from one person, Lucinda."

"That's what I thought."

"Has he been seeing her?"

"He goes to visit Charlotte Elizabeth every week on the bus. I suppose he sees Lucinda when he's there."

"I think you ought to ask Charles. He must know if something's going on. I hope not. Ma hasn't been in her grave a year. I would like to ask Pa the details about what happened with Lucinda all those years ago. We've never been told the whole story."

"Do you think we should?" asked Florrie cautiously, her eyes open wide.

"Yes. It was obviously an affair after he had married. If he takes up with her again, it could cause a scandal. Think of Stephen's position at school."

Florrie looked serious. "If he is having an affair, he's keeping it very quiet."

"These things have a habit of coming out into the open. What if someone else had found that note? Have you told Stephen?"

"No, you're the first. I must say I felt very shocked when I found it, then I thought Pa deserved a little happiness."

"He's got to realise the consequences of his actions. If he is sleeping with her, I shall be very angry."

"I'll speak to Charles. We mustn't jump to conclusions. I'll write to let you know what he says."

Rosa nodded, but still looked concerned. Florrie got up to find Stephen. It was time to go.

It was two weeks after the funeral before Florrie saw Charles. He had brought Charlotte Elizabeth over to see her grandfather, and they were reading stories together in the parlour.

"Come and see the new trees in the orchard," said Florrie to her brother. They walked down the garden together. When she had shown him the trees Ben had planted for his grandchildren, she suggested they sit on the bench.

"Charles, I wanted to ask you something. Do you think Pa is having an affair with Lucinda?"

Her brother looked at her warily. "What makes you think that?"

"I found a note in his pocket." She told him what it said.

"I think they have grown close," he said cautiously, looking into the distance.

They sat in silence for a few moments listening to the pigeons cooing in the surrounding trees.

"Are they often alone together?" Florrie persisted.

"He goes up to her sitting room sometimes."

"But why would she put a note in his pocket?"

Charles leant back and surveyed the cottage where he had grown up. A thin wisp of smoke curled out of one of the chimney pots, and he watched as it dissipated into nothing. He turned to look at Florrie.

"Keep this to yourself, but I think they both met up to go away together at the beginning of the holidays. Lionel and I came to see Pa to take him out for a picnic, but he wasn't here."

"When we went to Plymouth?"

"Yes."

Florrie sat quietly after being told this. "Where did they go?"

"I have no idea. All I know is that if Pa wants to spend time with her discreetly, he has every right to do so."

His sister nodded. "I agree, but I'm afraid Rosa doesn't. She feels very angry about it and wants to ask him the details of his affair with Lucinda when he was married to Ma."

Charles raised his eyebrows at this. "When did you tell her about the note?"

"When I saw her at Jim's funeral."

Charles looked serious. "I think it will upset Pa. He would have told us if he had wanted us to know. Do you think you can talk Rosa round?"

"I'll try."

They got up, and Charles gave his sister a reassuring smile. As they walked down the path towards the cottage door, Charlotte Elizabeth ran out to meet them. "Gandy's planted a tree for me!" she exclaimed joyfully. "He's going to show me where it is!"

Ben hurried after her, looking pleased.

When her guests had left, Florrie waited until Ben took the boys up to bed and then followed Stephen into the parlour and closed the door. She told him about finding the note in her father's pocket. Stephen looked intrigued.

"When was this?"

"Several weeks ago. I felt very upset at the time, and perhaps I should have told you sooner, but I didn't know what to do about it."

"Have you told your brother and sister?"

"Yes. I told Charles this afternoon, when we were in the garden."

"What do they think?"

"We all think he's having an affair with Lucinda." She related how Charles and Lionel had found him missing. "It was when we went to Plymouth at the beginning of the holidays."

Florrie then told him what little she knew about Ben's affair with Lucinda. Her husband listened intently.

"I've always wondered about the relationship regarding him and Lionel," he said. "But I have never liked to ask."

"You must think we are a dreadful family."

"Not at all. I try not to judge, especially where affairs of the heart are concerned."

"What am I to do, Stephen?"

"I can't decide for you," he replied. "But I think you should consider talking to your father and telling him you accidentally found the note."

"Yes, I'll do that. I think that would be best." She put her arms round her husband and gave him a kiss.

Florrie felt relieved now she had told her brother and husband about her concerns. She wondered if she was making a fuss about nothing, but she had been surprised at Rosa's reaction. Was she causing trouble for the family?

The next day, after breakfast, Florrie put Sarah down for her rest and told the boys to play in the garden. Then she sat down and poured another cup of tea. Ben was sitting in his chair, reading the newspaper. Florrie took a sip and said, "Pa, I've something to tell you."

Ben put his paper down. "What is it, love?" he asked, looking up.

Florrie took a deep breath and then proceeded to tell him about her find.

Ben looked taken aback. "I suppose you want to know who wrote it?"

"Not if you don't want to discuss it. It's none of my business, but it has upset me."

"I'm sorry if it has. Have you told anyone else?"

"Rosa knows, and Charles, and I've told Stephen as well."

Florrie explained how Charles knew he had gone away with someone and how he and Lionel had guessed it was with Lucinda. She told him how angry Rosa was when told.

Ben looked away. "I didn't want to hurt any of you. We were trying to be discreet."

"Rosa was afraid that it would cause a scandal if it got out."

"Yes, I can see that."

They sat in uncomfortable silence. Then Ben asked, "What do you feel about it, Florrie?"

"I think you deserve a little happiness, Pa, but you need to think how it might affect the family."

"Yes, I've been very selfish."

"I know you loved Ma, but have you always loved Lucinda? You have never told us what happened all those years ago. We feel we would like to know. Then we can begin to understand."

She looked at her father and saw that there were tears in his eyes.

"Don't get upset, Pa. Please."

He wiped his eyes and sat up. "I'd better tell you the whole story."

Ben went on to relate how he and Sophie had lost a child, and he had made the decision to finish blacksmithing for good.

"My sister had married Sophie's cousin Frank, who had been living with us. He had some money, and they decided to set up a guest house business in Salcombe. They rented a large house belonging to the estate of Lucinda's husband, Sir Ralph."

"Lucinda was Lady Lucinda then?"

"Yes, she was."

He continued telling her that Frank had asked for help to get the house ready for their visitors, so he and Sophie had left Forge Cottage for a while to join him. Lady Lucinda had offered him a job as a groom on the estate.

"I had always wanted to work with horses. I loved the job, but it put me in contact with Lucinda, as she rode out every morning. I'm afraid that's when it happened. We just formed a sudden passionate attraction for each other. She was very unhappy in her marriage. I can offer no excuse for my behaviour—what I did was unforgivable."

"When did Ma find out?"

"Lucinda became pregnant and went to live with her brother. When I found out, Sophie and I returned to Forge Cottage, and that's when I told her."

"And then what happened?"

"She was heartbroken. I told her how sorry I was, and I promised to be faithful. It took a long time to repair the damage, and shortly afterwards, Charles was born. Lionel was born later the same year. I didn't want to abandon him, and Sophie agreed I could keep up some contact with him. After Lucinda remarried, her husband adopted Lionel, and I was banned from visiting. Eventually Lionel was allowed to come and visit his half-brother and sisters from time to time."

"Yes, I remember his coming. We played with him in the lane."

"Sophie found it difficult to accept his visits at first, but she did so to enable Charles to have a brother."

"Ma was very forgiving."

"Yes, she was."

Ben looked forlorn. "I'm sorry, Florrie. I'm sorry for all of it. I won't go away with Lucinda again, I promise."

"I don't see why you can't continue to have a loving friendship," she replied. "And I'm sure Charles will feel the same."

"I'll speak to Charles and go and see Rosa. You don't need to do anything."

Florrie gave her father a hug.

"I didn't tell you all this before because I was afraid you would judge me," he said. "I wanted my children to look up to me."

"We do. We all love you very much."

Ben nodded and smiled.

CHAPTER SIXTEEN

UNFORGIVING

BEN TOOK THE FIRST OPPORTUNITY to visit Rosa. He didn't announce his decision beforehand in case she refused to see him. On the way he had plenty of time to think. He was glad he had told Florrie the truth about his past relationship with Lucinda, but that was Florrie, she was already 'on side' and had accepted his friendship. But now he had to face Rosa. He knew his youngest daughter always voiced her own mind and had set ideas. He recalled when she had got involved with politics many years before and had attended a rally in Exeter. They had not agreed then. Ironically enough, that was when he'd bumped into Lucinda after many years of separation. How was he going to convince Rosa that he had always loved her mother, but also had feelings for another woman? He knew he could never justify his affair, but now he felt he had the right to some happiness. He turned his dilemma over and over in his mind as the journey progressed.

When he got to Plymouth station, he caught the bus to her house and walked slowly up the street. He could feel a lump inside his chest, as if all his remorse was back again.

When he knocked on the door, Danny answered.

"Ben! Is everything all right? What's happened?" He looked worried.

"Nothing's wrong," Ben replied. "I just need to speak to Rosa about something."

"Come in," said Danny, looking relieved. "I'll go and get her."

Rosa came through from the kitchen and stopped when she saw her father. "Hello, Pa," she said cautiously. Digger jumped up, remembering him, and Rosa took his collar, led him into the kitchen, and closed the door.

Ben kissed her cheek, and she showed him into their small sitting room. He sat down.

"I think you know why I'm here," he said. "I want to try to explain things."

Rosa looked uncomfortable but listened to her father while he related to her all about his love affair with Lucinda before she was born.

Rosa fidgeted and looked upset. "It's funny how you grow up with something and never question it," she began. "Lionel was just there in our lives, and we accepted his visits as being normal, and I never wanted to question anything. Now you've told me what really happened, I see it all differently. Poor Ma! She must have been devastated."

Ben avoided eye contact.

"What's going on now? Between you and Lucinda? Are you lovers?" Rosa demanded.

Ben was taken aback by her tone. "We have developed a friendship," he replied, calmly.

"Ma hasn't been dead a year!" declared his daughter in a loud voice, standing up. "Whatever are you thinking?"

Ben winced and tried to explain that Sophie had forgiven him and had accepted Lionel into their family. "I loved and cared for her until the day she died. Her passing left a huge hole in my life. I didn't want to go on without her. Since then, I have tried to love and care for my family, but I still felt lonely. You all have your partners, your lives and children, and I felt I needed someone too."

Rosa gave him a hard look. "Going away with Lucinda was a betrayal to the memory of my mother."

"I'm sorry you see it that way, my love. I wouldn't have done it if I felt the same, and I think Sophie would not have felt that way either. She's gone now, and I must live my life without her. I have a loving friendship with Lucinda, and it has helped me rebuild my life."

"That's just selfish, Pa."

"Maybe it is, but it doesn't change the loving memories I have of your mother and my love for my family."

"I still think it's the wrong thing to do. That woman has a hold on you. She has seduced you twice now. She—"

Ben stood up and interrupted her. "You're wrong, Rosa. It's not like that!"

They both looked angrily at each other. Finally, Ben said, "I had hoped that I could convince you that the love Lucinda and I have for each other is something special and need not affect any of my children's lives."

"You're wrong there, Pa, *very* wrong. What are people to say when it all comes out? It will cause a scandal!"

Ben could see his daughter was getting worked up. He put out his arms, wanting to embrace her, but she backed away and held the door open.

"Please leave! I don't want to see you again until you can promise me you won't be seeing that woman again."

"Rosa, please!"

She stood resolutely, waiting for him to go. He sighed and left, wishing he had never come.

Travelling back to Forge Cottage, Ben was thoroughly miserable, his face forlorn. When he came through the door, Florrie looked at him. She had been chopping vegetables, and she put down her knife and got up to put her arms round her father. He gave a weak smile and slumped into his chair. He told her what had happened.

"She'll come round, Pa. Don't upset yourself. You know she's always had strong opinions. I'm sure this will all blow over."

"I hope so, Florrie. I hope so."

The omnibus was late, and Ben stood at the stop in the lane in Clayden waiting. He felt little joy at his impending visit to Acacia House, knowing he would have to speak to his son and then tell Lucinda the family all knew about their assignation. He stood staring up the road. *Where was that dratted bus?* He felt irritable and not in the best of tempers.

Finally, it arrived; he put his hand out, and it drew to a halt. It was a short ride to Kingsbridge, where he usually caught another bus to Modbury. He knew he would miss it, as this one was late, and it meant waiting another half hour. More time to turn things over in his mind. He sighed heavily.

On arrival, he walked the short distance to the surgery and rang the bell. Mrs Harris answered and ushered him in. She told him Sapphire was at the gallery and Charles was out on a call, so he would have to speak to his son another time. When Charlotte Elizabeth ran towards him, he felt joy return to his heart. They spent an enjoyable hour together in the sitting room, reading her favourite books and then playing with Nipper.

"I need to see your granny now," he said, getting up. His granddaughter pulled a face, but it was time for her tea.

He climbed the stairs to Lucinda's sitting room and knocked on the door. On hearing her answer, he went in.

Lucinda was sitting reading. She closed her book as Ben entered and smiled broadly.

"Hello, Ben. You're a little later today."

He explained why and then sat beside her.

"I'm afraid the cat is out of the bag," he said.

She looked at him, seeming confused.

"Our little holiday. All my family seem to know about it."

Lucinda's jaw dropped slightly. "However did they find out?"

Ben proceeded to explain about the note and how it had caused some consternation within his family.

Lucinda looked grave. "Oh, dear."

"To be honest, Lucinda, why are we being so secretive anyway? Surely there's absolutely nothing wrong in two single people forming an attachment."

"Except when they have a past such as ours."

Ben got up, went over to the window, and looked out. It had begun to rain, and the leaves on the trees were dripping onto the grass. A blackbird was hopping across the lawn, stopping now and again to look for worms. He swung round and faced Lucinda.

"I don't really care what anyone thinks of us. Let the tongues wag, and when they see we aren't bothered, they'll look for something else to gabble about."

Lucinda began to laugh. "Good for you, Ben! You never have taken any nonsense from anybody."

Ben was trying to get the boys dressed. "Keep still!" he said sternly, as Jonny wriggled about.

Florrie could hear him getting exasperated. *He's been very edgy recently,* she thought as she changed Sarah. *And I think I know why.* She put the baby down and went into the boys' bedroom.

"Jonny! Behave!" she said sharply. Seeing his mother, Jonny complied. "It's all right, Pa, I'll take over," she said, putting a hand on his shoulder. Ben went downstairs, and a few moments later, she heard the latch on the kitchen door close as he went out for his morning walk.

He returned for lunch, and they sat down to their bread and cheese. The boys looked at their grandpa warily. Florrie had given them both a good talking to that morning. Ben said nothing as he cut the cheese up, and Florrie gave everyone a slice of bread.

"Don't want it!" declared Jonny, and Christopher stared at him, wide-eyed.

"You'll eat what you're damn well given!" shouted Ben. Everyone froze. He had never raised his voice like that before at the boys.

"Pa," said Florrie gently. She turned to her sons. "Please be good boys and eat your bread and cheese."

Jonny looked scared and began to cry. Ben got up from his chair and went to him. "Don't cry, Jonny. Grandpa didn't mean to upset you." The child turned away from him and put his arms up towards his mother.

Ben picked him up and hugged him. "My, you're getting to be a big boy! Too big to cry at your grumpy old grandpa. Are we friends again?" he asked, tickling his tummy. Jonny stopped crying and nodded. Ben put him down, and they all resumed their meal.

Afterwards, when the boys had gone out to play, Florrie said, "Pa, what made you so angry? Is it this trouble with Rosa?"

Ben began clearing the table. "Yes."

"Oh, Pa, please don't worry! I'm sure she'll come round."

"I'm sorry I made little Jonny cry."

Florrie gave her father a hug. "Don't worry about that. It won't hurt them to see that you have feelings. They'll have forgotten about it by now."

Ben took the dishes out to the scullery. "I think I can hear that daughter of yours wanting her next meal," he called out.

September had come. Slowly each day was visibly shorter, and the leaves on the trees were changing colour. Ben remembered that he needed to plant the next fruit tree, and it was Rosa's cherry. He asked Stephen to take him to a tree nursery just outside Kingsbridge, where he chose a morello. On their return, he tipped it into the hole he had dug earlier and covered the bare roots with soil. He firmed the earth round the base of the tree with his boot and then went to fetch the watering can. The water supply to the cottage was obtained by a pump in the scullery.

When he walked through the kitchen, the boys were sitting at the table, waiting for their lunch. Florrie was seeing to Sarah. Ben winked at Jonny as he went by. He and his youngest grandson would be spending more time together after Christmas, as Christopher was to begin school. They had a close bond despite Jonny being mischievous, and one child would be easier for Ben to manage. At times, he found it hard to cope with the two of them.

He went back to the orchard and watered his tree, then returned for lunch.

"You've planted Rosa's tree, then?" asked Florrie as he came in.

"Yes, and with a heavy heart," he replied.

Nothing had been heard from Rosa about their falling out. Florrie had written her usual newsy letter, and Rosa had replied without mentioning it.

Ben returned to the orchard in the afternoon. He cleared up some dead branches that were lying about and built a bonfire. All the time, he kept thinking of Rosa. Her reaction had brought back memories of his relationship with Sophie after he had told her about his affair. She had been silently angry with him for weeks afterwards. At least his daughter had shouted at him and told him exactly how she felt. He never knew what Sophie was thinking. What was he to do? He needed Lucinda in his life. He knew she had a hold on him. He loved her so much, but he also loved his Rosa. Did he really have to choose?

Christopher and Jonny came running out, and he allowed then to watch as he lit the dried grass he had stuffed under some smaller twigs. The boys ran round excitedly, finding more twigs for him to throw on. The fire blazed upwards, licking hungrily round the larger branches and gleefully crackling as they devoured them.

Soon, the flames were reaching for the sky. Ben pulled his grandsons back by their arms as the fire took hold, and they stood and watched, their faces warmed by the ferocity of it.

"Many years ago, we had a fire here," Ben told them. "It burned the old forge down." He did not mention that his nephew Billy had been responsible. The forge fire had not been extinguished properly, and Billy had been playing around with it and had accidentally caught the roof on fire. "Fire can be dangerous," he added.

"Fire's very hot," stated Jonny seriously.

"Yes, we have to be very careful with it."

They waited until the flames began to die down, having consumed most of the wood. A few charred branches remained, and Ben poked them with a stick, causing showers of sparks. He made sure it was all out, throwing earth over the embers, and then took the boys inside. Florrie complained they smelt of burning ash and would have to have baths.

CHAPTER SEVENTEEN

ROSA'S DILEMMA

ROSA WAS WAITING FOR THE nurse to take away the bedpan before she stepped forward to change her patient's dressings. She removed the bandages to reveal the sores on the elderly woman's leg. The patient winced with pain.

"We'll make this more comfortable for you, Mrs Whitehead," she said.

"Thank you, sister, you're very kind."

Rosa smiled and continued to clean the wound and administer new dressings. Mrs Whitehead leant back in her bed and relaxed, closing her eyes in relief.

"There, is that better?" asked Rosa as she replaced the bed covers.

"Oh, yes, thank you."

Rosa hadn't told her father, but she had recently been promoted to ward sister. Her joy had been thwarted by the fact that she strongly suspected that she was pregnant. It had annoyed her that this was happening just as she was progressing in her career. She hadn't even told Danny she was expecting. He had been impressed she'd worked hard to become a sister and had told her how proud he was. Now all this business about her pa and Lucinda added to her troubled feelings.

She went about her ward duties, checking on the nurses and finding she got impatient with them if they failed to live up to her standards. Her father's visit had upset her, and she had regretted telling him to go.

When she talked to Danny about it, he had expressed the opinion that she needed to let her pa live his own life.

Rosa's feelings made her feel uncomfortable, so she was glad when her shift ended, and she was able to leave. As she sat on the bus home, she realised that Danny was probably right, but she still felt her father's friendship with Lucinda was happening too soon. Tears welled up in her eyes as she remembered her mother's illness and death. How she missed her, unable to share with her the news of her promotion and her pregnancy.

The shift had been a late one, and she didn't get home until after eight o'clock. As always, Hilda had kept her evening meal hot for her, and Hilda carefully lifted it out of the oven and placed it on the table while Rosa changed out of her uniform.

Danny was reading the newspaper when she came in. He folded it away, ready to chat to his wife as she ate her meal. They exchanged news of their working day, and when Rosa had finished her meal, she waited for Hilda to come and join them.

"I have something to tell you," she said, looking steadily at them both. "I think I'm expecting."

Hilda jumped up and hugged her. "Oh, how lovely!" she exclaimed.

Danny sat open-mouthed for a few minutes. He looked stunned. "Rosa, are you sure? I mean, how long? This is wonderful!" He got up to embrace his wife, putting his arms round her middle, lifting her up, and spinning her round.

"Steady on!" Rosa laughed.

"Danny! Be careful with her," said Hilda, her hands clasping her face.

Danny put his wife down gently.

"It's early days, but I think the due date will be about February," Rosa said, smiling with relief now that she had told them. Danny and Hilda exchanged joyful looks. "I shall have to leave nursing soon, or they'll realise I'm married," she added seriously.

"Oh, love, just when you've been promoted," Hilda commiserated.

"Well, that's life," Rosa said, resigned.

The following week, she decided to see Matron to submit her resignation. She knew she had to give a month's notice, and she didn't want to be working when her pregnancy started to show. She went to Matron's office and knocked on the door. When told to enter, she found the woman sitting behind a desk covered in paperwork.

"Yes, sister? You wished to see me?"

Her manner was always brisk, and it slightly unnerved Rosa.

"Yes, Matron. I regret to say I shall be leaving."

The woman looked up with a surprised look on her face.

"I'm going to get married."

"Close the door, sister."

Rosa turned and did what she was asked, wondering why this had been requested.

"Sit down, please."

She began to feel apprehensive.

"This is very sudden. You have only recently received promotion to ward sister."

Rosa looked down, unable to make eye contact. She did not reply. Matron's eyes narrowed slightly as she scrutinised her.

"I want to marry and have a family," stated Rosa, looking up and hoping to prevent any more questioning.

There was a short pause before Matron leant forward in her chair. "Sister Browne, are you pregnant?" she asked gently.

Rosa was stunned. She nodded and felt herself reddening. She had no wish to lie to the matron, whom she respected.

"I see." The matron continued to fasten her look on her. She leant back. "Well, Sister Browne, you aren't the first nurse to sit before me having succumbed to the charms of the opposite sex. I'm glad you have decided to marry, but I shall be very sorry to let you go. You have been an excellent nurse, and I had high hopes for you as a ward sister. The nursing profession is losing a good practitioner in you."

"Thank you, Matron. I'm sorry to be leaving, I've been very happy here."

Matron gave her a kind smile. "Perhaps one day nurses will be able to continue their careers when they marry, but we have to live with the rules as they are, I'm afraid."

They discussed Rosa's leaving date, and Matron sighed as she declared she would now have to find a replacement.

When Rosa returned home that evening, she was in a sombre mood. She had hated having to pretend she was not married and deceive Matron. Danny saw she was down and asked her what was wrong. She revealed her concerns, and he listened as she told him what had happened that day.

He took hold of her hand. "Rosa, you don't need to feel guilty. What you did has helped us have a better life. The rules are very unfair to women. They serve no purpose. Sometimes we need to stand up for common sense."

Rosa nodded, managing to smile.

"We have our child to look forward to," Danny added, encouragingly.

Rosa wrote to her family, telling them the news. Florrie answered first, saying how pleased they all were. She said that Ben sent his love. Rosa bit her lip when she read it. She still felt angry with her father but didn't know what to do. She regretted their argument but wasn't prepared to back down about his friendship with Lucinda.

When Rosa told her colleagues she was getting married, they congratulated her enthusiastically, and again she felt uncomfortable not being able to tell the truth. She explained that she was going away to be married, and it was to be a quiet wedding. One or two of the girls exchanged glances. They must have guessed that she was having to marry.

Rosa hadn't expected to become pregnant at this time. She knew Danny had always been keen to start a family, but she'd wanted to delay it as long as possible. They had discussed it when they had married, and he had gone along with her wishes. Now she had to face the fact that she had to give up her nursing career, which meant everything to her.

During this time, Danny tried to cheer her. On her last day, the nurses gave her a sendoff, and someone had made a cake, which they all shared. They presented her with a gift, a set of table mats with roses on them. She told them all about Danny—how she had nursed him at her local hospital and how he had regained some sight by having an operation. She thanked them sincerely and told them she would miss them all.

Before she left, Matron asked her into her office. "Well, Sister. Your last day. As I said before, I'm very sorry to see you go. Please keep in touch, I would like to know how you get on. There are lots of opportunities for nurses to do private work, which you might consider. Meanwhile, take care of yourself, and I hope all goes well." She gave Rosa a kind smile and reached into her desk drawer, taking out a small package. Handing it over, she said, "A little something for the baby. Goodbye, Rosa. I wish you all the best."

By this time, tears were streaming down Rosa's face. She shook the woman's hand. "Thank you, Matron, for being so understanding. You've been very kind."

When Rosa got home, Hilda welcomed her as she came through the door. She put her arms round her daughter-in-law. "I expect it's been a difficult day," she said.

CHAPTER EIGHTEEN

A PROPOSITION

CHARLES HAD ATTENDED SEVERAL CONFERENCES on childhood illnesses at one of the London hospitals, pursuing his interest in the development of immunisation. He had heard that American research and development was far ahead of what was happening in England. After one of the lectures, he asked the professor why this was so. He wanted to know when the vaccines for certain diseases would be available, especially diphtheria. He was told that Britain needed hospitals and doctors to begin trials for this to happen, and they needed some form of liaison with the medical authorities in America. In short, the whole thing lacked any proper incentive from the government.

"We need to send representatives over there to verify results and arrange with the drug companies to send us supplies. Our scientists have been trying to catch up, but it's taking time for us to be able to manufacture the vaccines. Also, our health system is run on private lines mainly and is not fully regulated or coordinated," the professor said.

"Time means children's lives," commented Charles.

"Exactly. It would be quicker to buy in the vaccines for now."

Later, the professor found Charles at the bar and bought him a drink. "You seem very interested in what we were talking about earlier," he said, handing him his whisky and soda. "Would you consider going to America to do some research for us?"

Charles did not hesitate. "Yes, I think I would."

"There's a very good children's hospital in Philadelphia. They've been researching the whooping cough vaccine. I'll contact them and see if I can get you a placement. Would a year be suitable?"

Charles nodded. "I'm very keen to get these vaccine programmes introduced over here. I shall have to arrange for a locum at my practice, but yes, I'm very interested."

The man took Charles's details and said he would contact him as soon as he heard anything. Charles was very excited about this possible proposition and on the journey home mulled over in his mind what it would mean in real terms. He wondered if he could obtain sponsorship, or would the hospital give him a salary? How would Sapphire and Lucinda react? What about his daughter? What about his patients? He had a lot to consider, but he knew it was all worth pursuing.

Charles had to pick his moment in telling Sapphire about his conversation with the professor. He had been back several days before he broached the subject.

"A year!"

"Yes," he replied, trying to sound calm.

"But what about us? Your family? Are we all to be uprooted, or will it be just you?"

"That's what we need to discuss." He looked at his wife with pleading eyes. "I've wanted so much to get involved with this aspect of medicine, especially after what happened to our daughter. These vaccines are saving hundreds of children's lives. A little sacrifice from us might help to bring the vaccines over here."

"You call it a little sacrifice?" Sapphire appeared unconvinced.

"We all need to talk about this," continued Charles. "I wanted to put it to you first, Sapphire. Please think it over. I realise there are many implications to consider."

The next day, Charles asked his mother-in-law to join them for afternoon tea. He was off duty and had spent the morning writing notes about what needed to be done if he went on a year's sabbatical. Lucinda came in just as her daughter was pouring out the tea. Sapphire handed her a cup and offered her a shortbread. Lucinda took it and sat down.

"I sense something in the air," she said, eyeing them both.

Sapphire and Charles glanced at each other.

"You're right, Lucinda. Nothing much gets past you!"

She smiled. "Out with it, then."

He told her what he had told Sapphire the day before.

Lucinda put her cup down. "I see."

"I realise it will mean a lot of upheaval."

"Will it mean your going, or all of us?"

"That's what I want to discuss."

She turned to her daughter. "Do you want to go, darling?"

"Yes. I've thought it over, and I think I should like to. It sounds exciting, an opportunity not to be missed."

Lucinda nodded. "For my part, I would rather stay here. That leaves Charlotte Elizabeth."

"I think the best thing to do is to ask her. She always knows her own mind. She comes with us to America or stays here with you. Would you mind looking after her, Mummy?"

"No, we spend a lot of time together as it is."

"Either way, it's a big ask for a little girl," said Charles.

There was a feeling of uncertainty at Acacia House for the next few days. Charles had not yet received a formal invitation from the professor. Nothing was said to Charlotte Elizabeth, and her routines stayed much the same. In the mornings she would spend time with her grandmother, doing a few lessons that Lucinda had asked Florrie to prepare for her. After lunch she would go to the gallery with her mother or help Mrs Harris in the kitchen. When her father was free, he would take her out for walks or trips to local places that interested her. Sometimes he took her to Forge Cottage to see her Gandy and Aunty Florrie.

They arrived there one afternoon, and Christopher and Jonny ran out to greet them. They flung their arms round Charlotte Elizabeth as they came in.

"Steady on, boys!" Charles said, laughing.

Ben joined them and wrapped his arms round his granddaughter. "Hello, my best girl!"

She took his hand, and they went into the parlour. Charles produced a child's reading book.

"Florrie, Pa, Charlotte Elizabeth wants to read to you."

They listened attentively as the girl slowly read the first page of the story and then looked up in triumph. Everyone clapped, and Florrie nodded in approval and said she was reading very well.

"Lucinda has done a good job," she told Charles.

She gave the children each a cookie from a jar on the dresser, and they ran outside. When they'd gone, Charles produced a letter from his pocket.

"This arrived yesterday," he began, and then went on to explain that he was being offered a sabbatical year in America to study childhood illnesses. Florrie and Ben looked astounded.

"It's at the Children's Hospital in Philadelphia."

"Where's that?" asked Ben.

"It's a city in Pennsylvania, south of New York."

"Why there?" asked Florrie. "Couldn't you do your research over here?"

"America is at the forefront of developing vaccines for childhood illnesses. I want to know why we can't introduce them over here."

"Are you all going?" asked Florrie, looking perturbed.

"No, Sapphire and I will go, but Lucinda says she doesn't want to leave. We asked Charlotte Elizabeth, and she said she wanted to stay here with her grandmother."

Ben breathed a sigh of relief.

"What about the gallery?" asked Florrie.

"Sapphire says that Caroline Bailey will run it. She says she welcomes having something to do since losing Donald."

"This *is* a surprise." Ben spoke slowly. "You'll miss out on a year of your daughter's life. Are you sure about it?"

"It's something I've been wanting to do. The diphtheria vaccine is up and running in America, saving thousands of children's lives. If we can get it over here, it will do the same—just think of that."

"You'll both find it hard, though, leaving your little girl behind."

"Yes, of course we shall. We have talked it over with her and explained everything. She said she wants to help the children here get better, like she did."

Ben smiled.

"Lucinda has made another suggestion," went on Charles. "She says if Amanda agrees, she might relocate to Richmond for some of the time and help look after her when she has the baby. Charlotte Elizabeth has always loved seeing Amanda, and there will be lots of interesting places she can go to in London."

"It sounds as if all is settled, then," said Ben.

"When will you be going?" asked Florrie.

"In January," her brother replied.

"A few weeks' time, then."

"You'll miss seeing Rosa's baby."

"Unless it's early, yes."

Charles got up to collect Charlotte Elizabeth, and when he'd gone, Florrie looked at her father. "What do you think about all that?"

"Too much gadding about these days. Let's hope it will do some good," he said.

When Stephen came home from school, Florrie told him about Charles's visit.

"I think it's very commendable of Charles to want to do this," he replied. "It will be an upheaval for his family, though."

After supper, they found an atlas, and Stephen indicated where Philadelphia was on the map of America. Florrie peered at where his finger was pointing.

"It's in Pennsylvania," explained Stephen. "I'm afraid I know little about it other than it was one of the first states in America and was where the Quakers settled, led by William Penn."

"Oh, I've heard about him when I was at school!" exclaimed Florrie. "He wanted to establish a free state over there."

"I'll see what else I can find out," said Stephen. "I'll pop into the library in Kingsbridge. I expect Charles will get some information too if they are to live there. I suspect it's a lot different now from the time of William Penn."

"It all sounds rather exciting," commented Florrie, closing the atlas.

CHAPTER NINETEEN
PREPARATIONS

At Acacia House, Charles had begun putting arrangements in place. As his new appointment was to start in the New Year, he needed to find a locum quickly. He set about advertising for one straightaway. He and Sapphire had decided that the new doctor would be invited to live in, and their housekeeper was informed about the changes. She raised her eyebrows at the proposition but listened attentively.

Mrs Harris had a full-time job at the surgery, and her daughter would often help when needed. Susan was in her final year at school and would be fifteen in a few months' time. She was sometimes required to keep Charlotte Elizabeth company, and the two got along well together. Mr Harris came to see to the fires each morning during the winter months before he went to work. Charles realised that the Harris family were dependent on their jobs to supplement their income. He wanted to sort out the different arrangements and what this would mean for their salaries.

He had several applicants for his replacement, and two weeks before Christmas, after shortlisting them, he was about to conduct the interviews.

"It's always difficult whether to go for a newly qualified doctor with the latest knowledge, or a more experienced one," he commented one evening as the family sat together.

"I know which I prefer," said Lucinda. "The latter, as I think they would know the best way to treat their patients."

"He'll have to be someone you're happy to have live here."

"I'll have a nice young one then!" answered his mother-in-law.

"There's one, I think, *would* be suitable," said Charles, sifting through the paperwork on his lap. "Yes, here it is." He found the letter of application.

"How old is he?"

"He's sixty. He retired from a very busy practice in Exeter and wants to come to a country village. He's widowed and says he would like to live here while he looks for a suitable property."

"He sounds as if he would be good company for you, Mummy," remarked Sapphire.

Lucinda gave her daughter a quizzical look but said nothing.

Charles concluded the interviews and made his choice. It was the the older applicant, Dr Ian Burns, and he invited him to move in the following week and accompany him on his rounds before his departure date.

The new doctor arrived with two large suitcases, and Mrs Harris showed him his accommodation. Sapphire had given him one of the larger guest rooms and had furnished it so it could also be used as a sitting room, if required. She and her mother were looking forward to meeting him at dinner, and he joined them for drinks beforehand. He was of middling height, a little overweight, with red bushy eyebrows and a red beard. He was good-looking for his age and had a charming smile, which he used to good effect as Charles introduced his wife and mother.

"Good evening, ladies," he said, giving a small bow. "What a lovely house you have here." He had a soft Scottish accent, and his blue eyes twinkled in a kindly manner.

"I hope you've settled in and are happy with your room," said Sapphire.

"Very much so, it's very comfortable."

"You're welcome to join the family downstairs whenever you wish," she added.

"Well, that's most generous of you, but I'll be sure not to make a nuisance of me self." Again, his eyes twinkled. "I understand you have a wee child?"

"Yes, Charlotte Elizabeth. She'll be staying here with my mother."

"I have two bonny granddaughters myself," said Dr Burns. "But I don't see much of them. They live in Scotland."

"I'll hope you'll be happy with us," said Lucinda, smiling sweetly.

"I'm sure I will." He smiled back. "I'm not much trouble."

Ben and Florrie were preparing for Christmas. They always made the same arrangements following the family traditions, and it was to be no different now they had lost Sophie. It would be their first Christmas together at Forge Cottage without her.

Ben put on his coat and boots and said he was going to the farm to order a bird for their Christmas dinner.

"Will you be able to deal with it?" he asked his daughter. "Your mother could never bring herself to."

"I'll give it a go if you tell me what to do," Florrie replied bravely. "Stephen and I would always get ours ready cleaned and prepared from the butchers in Kingsbridge."

Florrie was chopping nuts for the cake. When her father had gone, she put down her knife and reminisced. She remembered her father had told her that they got a lot of their basic food from the farm years ago.

Life was so different then, she mused. *The old ways prevailed in the village for a long time.*

How lucky they were to have the shop close by now, where they were able to buy milk and other fresh produce. *How ever did my ma manage without it?* she wondered. She knew her mother had worked hard curing meat and making pies and still found time to educate her three children.

She picked up her knife to resume her task and turned her thoughts to who was going to be at the Christmas meal. It would just be Aunty Millie and Uncle Harry this year, as Agnes and her husband Ted were going to his family. *That will be seven altogether, and Sarah of course.* She peered across at the child asleep in her cot in the corner of the kitchen. Thank goodness she had reached her first Christmas with no more episodes of heart trouble.

That evening Florrie persuaded Stephen to help with the home-made crackers they always had beside their plates with their Christmas dinner. She told him about the times past when she helped her mother roll them up in coloured paper and write out the jokes to tuck inside. Instead of gifts they would put coins in some and buttons in others, which always caused a great deal of merriment on Christmas day when they were pulled open.

After Christmas, the weather changed and there was a cold wind and flurries of snow, so Ben put off going to Acacia House. He waited until Florrie and Stephen and the children had left for their usual visit to Plymouth, and then ventured out when the weather improved a little.

He waited a while at the bus stop in the village, but the bus was late again, and when he arrived, he was very cold. Mrs Harris welcomed him into the kitchen and made a pot of tea. She informed him that the family were out. "I don't think they knew you were coming," she told him. "I think they're out shopping."

Ben had brought Charlotte Elizabeth her Christmas present, which he left on the table. He had chosen some reading books that he knew they would enjoy together. After chatting to Mrs Harris for a while, he got up to catch his bus home.

"You'll not wait then?" she asked.

"No, I'll see Charlotte Elizabeth next week, unless they come over to Forge Cottage before then. They may not have time before they leave."

"They'll want to say goodbye to you," replied Mrs Harris good-naturedly as she showed himout.

CHAPTER TWENTY

THE VOYAGE

Ben did not return to Acacia House before Charles and Sapphire left for America, as they arrived at Forge Cottage the next day, saying they were sorry to have missed him. Charlotte Elizabeth was not with them.

"We don't want to make it difficult for her," said Charles. "We're trying to keep her routines normal until we go."

"When is it you sail?"

"The end of the week."

"I won't be coming to see you off," Ben told his son. "That's why I came over yesterday. I would rather say goodbye here. I hope you don't mind."

Charles put a hand on his shoulder. "I do understand. Keep an eye on things for me. Lucinda and Charlotte Elizabeth will need lots of support."

"Yes, of course I will," replied Ben. "I'll visit as often as I can. Has your new locum settled in?"

"Yes, he seems very nice and has a good manner with the patients. I think I've left them in good hands."

Charles told his father that Billy would be taking them to the docks at Southampton to board their liner. "It will take five days to cross," he added. "I'll send a wire as soon as we land."

Ben held on to Charles's hand as he said goodbye. "I admire you doing this, son. I know it won't be easy leaving your daughter. I'll take care of her, don't worry."

Charles hugged him. "Thank you, Pa. See you in December."

Ben then embraced Sapphire. "This is a wonderful opportunity for both of you. Enjoy it!"

When they had left, Ben sat in his chair. He didn't feel very well and kept sneezing. He went to bed early and slept soundly.

On the day of departure, Billy drove Lucinda and her granddaughter to Southampton together with Charles and Sapphire. He and Charles had taken the two large trunks the week before and had them checked in. They set off very early that morning and had arrived in good time. The Cunard first-class departure lounge was busy, but they found a quiet corner where they could say their goodbyes.

Charlotte Elizabeth was dressed in a coat with a fur collar and cuffs, and she wore a little felt hat. She was a pretty child and attracted some attention. An American woman nearby drooled over her, saying to Sapphire, "My, what a lovely little girl you have there! What's your name, honey?"

The girl was uncharacteristically quiet. Sapphire smiled. "This is my daughter, Charlotte Elizabeth."

"Are you all going to the States?"

"No, just myself and my husband."

The woman turned to Charlotte Elizabeth again. "Well, I hope you go there one day, honey. It's a wonderful place!"

A steward began reading out names for boarding. There was a general stir and murmuring, and the woman and her companion stood listening, ready to move if their names were called. Charlotte Elizabeth looked rather bewildered, realising something was happening. She held Lucinda's hand tightly.

"That's us," said Charles as he heard their names. He gathered up his daughter in his arms. "Goodbye, my best girl. Daddy loves you lots." He kissed her, then embraced his mother-in-law. "Thank you so much for letting us go, Lucinda. Take care."

Sapphire then kissed her daughter. "I'll write to you, darling. Be a good girl. I'll bring you back some presents."

Charlotte Elizabeth hugged her tightly. "Goodbye, Mummy." Tears appeared in Sapphire's eyes, and she turned away quickly as she picked up her bag. She kissed her mother. "Goodbye, Mummy. Take care of her!" Her voice choked with emotion.

They said their farewells to Billy and then joined the other passengers surging towards the exit. "Bye, Mummy! Bye, Daddy!" called out a high-pitched voice, hardly audible over the crowd.

"Bon voyage!" Lucinda waved frantically as Charles and Sapphire disappeared through the departures doorway without looking round. Billy put his arm round Lucinda's shoulders. "They'll be fine," he said.

Charles had booked berths on the Cunard Line's *Mauretania,* and they would be arriving in New York harbour at the end of five days. Built in 1906, the *Mauretania* had achieved the fastest crossing to New York, winning the prestigious Blue Riband award for several years. She was at that time the largest ship in the world. Her boilers had recently been converted to oil firing, which had slowed her current crossing time down.

Charles and Sapphire were shown to their cabin by a steward, who unlocked the door and led them into a small panelled sitting room. It was comfortably furnished with an upholstered fitted seat, a coffee table, a desk, and a padded armchair. Elegant drapes hung at the windows, as their suite was above the waterline. The steward opened the door to the bedroom and stood aside, allowing Sapphire to look round. She smiled in approval, and after assuring them both he was "at their service," he withdrew.

Sapphire opened the two polished wooden doors of the closet, revealing a set of drawers with brass fittings and two full length mirrors, one either side. Adjacent to the bedroom was their own bathroom with luxury brass fittings and fluffy white towels. She came out of the bedroom and found Charles peering out of the window.

He turned with an anxious look in his eyes. "Have I done the right thing, Sapphire?"

She put her arms round him. "Definitely, darling. It's going to be a marvellous adventure!"

"I hope so."

"I can't wait to explore the rest of the ship," she said enthusiastically. "Mummy would love all this opulence."

"This is the less expensive end of the first-class accommodation," explained Charles. "I believe the better ones have a whole suite of rooms."

"Oh, to be rich!" exclaimed Sapphire, flinging herself onto the shiny eiderdown covering the bed. Charles lay down beside her. "Sorry, darling. You married the wrong man for that."

"I'm not sorry," she said, putting her arms round his neck again. "You'll do for me."

He began kissing her gently, gaining comfort from all his doubts.

Later, they made their way to the first-class dining saloon for luncheon. The large room they entered was divided into an upper and lower dining space, and the crowning feature of the room was the vast plasterwork dome in the centre, painted in white and gold and decorated with the signs of the zodiac. They both looked up in awe of their surroundings.

A middle-aged man had followed them in, escorting his plump wife. She had very blonde hair, and her face was heavily made up. "Quite something, ain't it?" he said to them in a strong American accent. "This your first voyage?"

"Yes," answered Charles. He introduced himself and Sapphire.

"Maddox Grant," the man replied, holding out his hand for Charles to shake. "And this here is Esme."

His wife gave a warm smile. "Maddox and I have made the crossing several times since he retired. We just *love* England."

"If you want any help, just ask us," Maddox said, reassuringly. "She's a big ship, and you're gonna get lost at least once." He grinned broadly at them.

"Thank you," replied Sapphire. "That's very kind."

They had reached an empty table, and the man hesitated. "If you'd like to join me and my wife, we would be happy to share, but I quite understand if you folks want to be alone together."

Sapphire looked encouragingly at Charles.

"Thank you very much," he replied. "We would be delighted."

Maddox proved to be a good conversationalist. He had a relaxed manner and was endowed with the self-assurance of a self-made businessman. He was very interested in Charles's reasons for coming to America. He got out his wallet and produced a business card.

"What you're doing is very commendable," he stated as he handed it to Charles. "If I can help in any way to get those medicines to England, you let me know."

After luncheon, Charles and Sapphire returned to their cabin to unpack, only to find the steward had already been there.

"Maddox and his wife are very charming," said Sapphire, as she sunk into one of the easy chairs. "He seemed very keen to help you."

"I think many Americans are very generous and willing to help each other."

"Esme and I have arranged to meet up in the hairdressing salon tomorrow morning. Is that all right, darling?"

"Yes, of course. As long as she doesn't persuade you to have your hair dyed blonde."

Sapphire laughed and threw a cushion at him.

Everything she saw on board took her breath away. The ship had undergone a major refit two years previously, and no expense had been spared for her interior refurbishments. After dinner that evening, they mingled with the other passengers in one of the saloons, and when Charles returned to Sapphire's table with their drinks, he had a broad grin on his face.

"I've just made the acquaintance of a doctor," he said as he put the glasses down.

"You mean, out of hundreds of passengers, you've found another doctor?" Sapphire exclaimed incredulously.

He nodded and laughed. "Afraid so."

Their time on board passed by quickly. Sapphire said she was loving every minute of it. She told Charles she was writing a journal to share with her mother when she returned at the end of the year.

After lunch each day, they would go up to the Verandah Café for afternoon tea and join some of the friends they had made. It could be accessed from the deck in good weather and was enclosed, with a large skylight letting in the natural light. It had been redecorated in a style based on the Orangery at Hampton Court Palace. Comfortable wicker chairs were placed round small tables covered in white cloths, and potted plants were placed throughout the room. The walls were fitted with ornamental trellises, and the roof was supported with Ionic pillars. Sapphire would often look round to admire it all as she sipped her tea.

The weather was too cold to go up on deck, but they could watch the waves from their window in their suite. Sapphire had not comprehended the vastness of the ocean, and it took her breath away. Miles and miles of grey swirling waves topped by an equally grey sky. She would sit at the window looking out and wondering what Charlotte Elizabeth was doing while her husband scribbled his notes. After two days she began to feel rather down and told Charles she was missing home, her daughter, and her mother.

"Those feelings will pass, darling," he replied. "It's very natural to be like that."

Sapphire smiled. *Charles has a very good bedside manner,* she thought to herself.

Sailing into New York was an experience Sapphire and Charles would never forget. They had wrapped themselves up warmly and were standing on deck with the other passengers who were also braving the chill to see the sights. Sapphire was wearing a coat with a fur collar and a cloche hat, and Charles was in a long overcoat, a scarf tied securely round his neck, and a homburg hat. It was windy, and they both were holding their headgear.

The huge ship always made a magnificent entrance into the harbour with her four splendid funnels sending out plumes of smoke. She was guided by several smaller pilot boats ensuring that she berthed safely.

"Look! Look!" said Sapphire excitedly, pointing to the Statue of Liberty as it came into view. "It's so big," she exclaimed.

The *Mauritania* sailed majestically past and once she had moored at the dock, the passengers began to disembark. The ship had been very full, but first-class travellers were allowed to leave before those who were in second class and steerage. Charles and Sapphire went through customs and were then interrogated by a uniformed man in a peaked cap at immigration.

"How long is your stay?" he asked sternly.

"A year."

He held out an outstretched hand. "Passport and visas."

Charles produced the documents together with his letter of appointment from the hospital in Philadelphia. The man studied them carefully. "This your wife?" he asked, glancing at Sapphire.

"Yes."

He took her documents.

"Have you read the regulations regarding entry to the United States?"

"We have."

"Please sign here."

Charles signed the form.

"Welcome to America, Doc."

Charles suppressed a smile and thanked him, and they went to locate their luggage. A porter was found, and he took their trunks to load on the train. When he held out his hand, Charles fumbled to find some coins. He had exchanged money on the boat and hoped he had given the right amount. He had heard that tipping was mandatory in America.

They had to wait a while before boarding their train to Philadelphia, so they found a restaurant at the station. Sapphire sat down at their table and sighed. "I'm exhausted!"

After their meal, they felt more relaxed. Sapphire looked round as Charles sorted out the tip. The room was noisy with chatter and cigarette smoke. Everyone seemed to be talking loudly. Their waiter was a black American who smiled broadly, showing his white teeth as Charles placed some money in his hand.

They left to board their train, walking along the platform looking at the numbers displayed on the side of each carriage. Charles kept glancing at the ticket he was holding, making sure they did not get into the wrong one. Eventually they spotted the right one and settled into their small but well-equipped compartment. Shortly afterwards a steward knocked on the door to see if they wanted anything. They asked for tea, and after drinking it, got ready for bed and climbed into their bunks.

Sapphire was just dropping off when Charles suddenly exclaimed, "Damn!"

She sat up. "Whatever's the matter?"

"I forgot to send a wire home to say we've arrived."

"Do it tomorrow," she said, snuggling under the blankets again. "You should be able to at one of the stops."

The train rattled on, whining loudly from time to time.

CHAPTER TWENTY-ONE

BEN'S ILLNESS

FLORRIE, STEPHEN, AND THE CHILDREN returned early from Plymouth because there was a forecast of snow, and Stephen had concerns about getting back to school on time.

When they entered the cottage, Florrie sensed something was wrong. The range had gone out, and the table had not been cleared. Stephen followed her in carrying two large suitcases.

"Ben!" his daughter called. Still holding Sarah, she went into the parlour and looked round. Nothing seemed untoward. She returned to the kitchen and placed Sarah in her cot. Stephen was still unpacking the motor, so she went upstairs. Opening the door, she peered into Ben's room and saw him in bed. She could see he wasn't well as he lay there. His face looked red, and his hair was tousled. As she placed a hand on his forehead he stirred and moaned, hardly recognising her.

"Stephen," she called down the stairs. "Pa's not well!"

He ran upstairs and looked at his father-in-law.

"He seems very poorly," he said. "I'll get Agnes to phone the surgery."

Florrie was very worried as she could see her father was running a temperature. When Stephen returned, she told him Ben seemed worse. They kept the children away, and she sat with him until Dr Forster arrived.

After the doctor had examined him, he turned to Florrie. "It's pneumonia. He must have caught a chill."

Florrie gasped. "He will be all right, won't he?"

"With careful nursing, probably. He's a strong man, and he should recover. If he shows signs of getting worse, send for me; otherwise, I'll return in a few days to see how he's progressing."

Florrie nodded and told him she had been a nurse in the war. "It's a while ago, but I think I remember what to do."

When the doctor had left, Florrie asked Stephen to tell Millie. "I shall need some help when you go back to school. I can't manage nursing Pa and looking after the children."

"At least you'll have Christopher off your hands," he said as he left. "He's getting very excited about starting school."

Florrie gave a half smile. She had almost forgotten it was an exciting time for her eldest son, but all she could think of now was her father. Would he recover? Whatever would she do without him?

Stephen returned with Millie. She looked very anxious and went up to her brother's room to see him. "Is there nothing the doctor can do for him?" she asked when she came downstairs.

Florrie shook her head. "No, we must keep him cool and get him to drink water."

Millie suggested that she would help nurse Ben during the day and let Florrie get on with her work. "Someone will need to sit with him at night to begin with. We'll take it in turns. Don't worry, Florrie—I'm sure he'll recover."

Stephen took the boys for a walk before getting them their tea. Florrie dealt with Sarah, then lay down to rest as she was to sit with Ben that night.

That night the time dragged on as she continually mopped Ben's head with a cold compress and attempted to give him sips of water. He was very restless as he tossed and turned in the bed. At eight the next morning, Millie arrived. Florrie was almost nodding off as her aunt came into Ben's bedroom.

"Oh, Millie! Bless you!" she exclaimed as she suddenly came to and saw her.

"Stephen's doing breakfast," Millie announced. "I'll sit with Ben while you see to Sarah. Then you can go to bed and get some sleep."

"But what about Jonny and Sarah?" Florrie looked distraught.

"Agnes is going to have them for the day."

Relief flooded over Florrie as she went downstairs to see her husband and son off to school. Stephen had got Christopher dressed and ready, and he was standing by the door with his satchel over his shoulder and holding his shoe bag, looking anxious.

Florrie gave him a hug. "Have a lovely time, darling. Daddy will make sure you're all right."

She glanced at Stephen as he came out of the parlour holding his briefcase.

"How's Pa?" he asked.

"He's sleeping." He nodded. "Time to go!" he said, kissing Florrie quickly and taking Christopher by the hand as he hurried out of the door.

Florrie felt overwhelmed, not knowing what to do first, as she felt so tired. She gave Sarah her breakfast and let Jonny play with his toys on the floor. The door opened and Agnes's beaming face appeared.

"Hello, Florrie!" she said.

Doctor Forster called in at the end of the week and said Ben was making slow progress but still had a way to go. Florrie sat at the table when he had gone, resting her head on her arm, her hair flopping over her brow. She felt so tired all the time; sitting up with Ben every other night was exhausting. Agnes had continued to have Jonny and Sarah, much to her relief, and Millie was taking turns doing nights and days when needed. She got up and attended to her chores quickly before going upstairs to be with her father, thankful it was Friday, and she would have Stephen to help her at the weekend.

By lunchtime Ben was awake, and she managed to get him to sit up, propped up by pillows. She had prepared some soup, and she carefully and slowly fed him with a spoon. When he had finished, she wiped his chin with a cloth, and he leaned back into the pillows.

"Thank you," he whispered weakly.

Florrie was so grateful she had nursing experience, as it gave her confidence she was doing the right things for her father. In the war she had volunteered as a nurse at her brother's hospital in Portsmouth caring for wounded servicemen. She realised that had been over ten years ago.

Stephen volunteered to sit with Ben that night and give her a break. On the Saturday morning, he allowed Christpher and Jonny to see their grandpa, instructing them that they would need to be very quiet. Both boys tentatively entered Ben's bedroom and stood staring at him.

"I've been to school," announced Christopher proudly. "I've made lots of friends."

"That's good," said his grandfather weakly.

Jonny said nothing, but standing on tiptoe placed his favourite soft toy on the pillow.

Ben smiled. "Thank you."

"Come on, you two," said Stephen, steering them out of the bedroom. "Grandpa needs to sleep."

After the doctor's next visit the following week, Ben began to improve. Florrie and Millie no longer needed to sit up with him at night, and after one more week he was helped downstairs.

Florrie was overjoyed to have him with her in the kitchen and chatted away as he sat in his chair by the range with a rug round his knees. One morning she said she needed to go to the shop, and he assured her that he would be fine left alone for a short while. She wrapped up Sarah warmly in the pram and pushed it through the door. Jonny followed, trying to persuade her to buy him sweeties.

"Let him have some!" called out her father. "He's been a good boy."

"Oh, Pa!" Florrie answered as they left.

When she returned, she showed her father a letter.

"I picked up the post from Agnes. There's one with a Plymouth postmark." She tore it open and read it quickly. "It's from Hilda, Rosa's had the twins! Two identical boys." She passed it over to Ben.

Dear Florrie and Stephen,

You will be pleased to hear that our Rosa had the twins yesterday evening, two healthy-looking boys. We are finding it hard to tell them apart! Danny is thrilled and glad Rosa got through safely. They have come early. We shall be kept very busy from now on. Stan has let Danny have a few days off.

Love to you all,

Hilda

Ben put the letter down.

"Two more grandsons," exclaimed Florrie. "I'm glad she's all right. I wonder what they will call them?"

Ben handed it back. "I'm glad they were delivered safely," was all he said.

Florrie was pleased when Ben was well enough to take a short turn round the garden or a stroll up and down the lane. He would find his stick and say, "Come on, Jonny," and off they would go, Florrie making sure he wrapped up warmly and wore his scarf.

A few days later, Florrie came in from the garden, looking flustered. She found her husband polishing his shoes in the scullery.

"Can you come outside a minute? I want to show you something."

Stephen put down the shoe, got his boots on, and followed her out to the garden. They went down to the orchard, and Florrie pointed to a pile of earth. Stephen peered down to see what it was. One of the newly planted fruit trees had been uprooted.

"I think it's Rosa's," said Florrie.

"How could that have happened?" asked Stephen. "Do you think a fox or badger is responsible?"

Jonny had followed them out. "Grandpa did it," he said. "He was cwoss."

Stephen looked at Florrie incredulously. "Why would he have done that?"

"He said he was upset that Hilda's letter made no mention of him. I think he feels Rosa has cut him off completely."

"She wouldn't do that, surely. It was just an oversight of Hilda's."

"He's been very down lately. It must be the effects of his illness, he's not fully recovered yet. Even Lucinda hasn't bothered to contact him."

They went back inside.

"Where's Ben now?" asked Stephen.

"Upstairs resting," replied Florrie.

"We won't mention this. Can you write to Rosa? Try and sort this out. Meanwhile, I'll get a spade and replant it. I'm sure it will survive."

Stephen put on his coat and went back outside to find a spade.

Florrie wrote a letter to Rosa and another to Lucinda. It wasn't long before she heard back from Lucinda.

My dear Florrie,

I am so sorry to hear about Ben's illness, I had no idea. Brian made no mention of it to me, I have no idea why, but he has been very busy with our new doctor. I am so relieved to hear that Ben is recovering. Now Charles and Sapphire are gone I do not have the motor, but I do hope to see him again soon. The weather has been horribly cold, and my hands have been full with my granddaughter.

I am so sorry about this rift with Rosa, and I do hope it heals over. I feel I am to blame. I value Ben's friendship very much, but I have never wanted it to get between him and his family. Meanwhile, please tell him I shall write to him. My very best wishes and love,
Lucinda

Two weeks later Ben was feeling stronger, and on the Saturday morning decided to take the short walk to the village shop. He said he would collect the post. The weather was better, and the sun was coming out from time to time. He took his stick and strolled down the lane. There were a few snowdrops under the hedgerows, and a robin was singing nearby, its pure notes filling the fresh air. It filled Ben with joy, and he began to quicken his step. On reaching the post office he found Agnes filling her postbag.

"Hello, Uncle! You're just in time—I was about to set off." She handed him some letters and the daily newspaper. "Lovely news about Rosa's twins," she said enthusiastically. "I expect you're longing to see them."

Ben gave a faint smile and took the post from her. He stood and watched as she pedalled off on her bicycle and then began to walk slowly home. When he turned the corner of the lane, he could see a motor parked outside Forge Cottage, one he did not recognise. Intrigued as to who it was visiting, he opened the gate and went in through the door. In front of him, sitting in his chair, was Rosa. She was holding two beautiful babies, one in each arm, and on seeing her father her face lit up as she said, "Hello, Pa. Come and meet the twins."

"Rosa!" Florrie watched as Ben put his arms out and gave his daughter a hug.

"We drove up early this morning to surprise you," Danny said, looking pleased.

"It was a surprise," added Florrie. "They arrived just after you had left."

"It's wonderful to see you," exclaimed Ben, his eyes shining. He stood back to admire his new grandsons. "Quite an armful, aren't they?" He laughed.

Carefully, he took one baby from Rosa and held him close. "Have they got names yet?"

"Alan and Albert," Danny replied proudly. "We chose them because I thought they would look good on a garage sign. Stan's made me a partner, and I hope to own my own garage one day."

"Well done, Danny," said Ben. "You certainly have the future all sorted!" He turned his attention back to the tiny baby he was holding. "Which one is this, then?"

"Um, Alan, I think," said Rosa. "Look on his neck, Pa. There should be a small mark."

Ben carefully moved the shawl to one side and nodded. "Hello, Alan," he said, kissing him gently on the forehead. Danny took the baby from Ben, allowing him to pick up Albert.

"And hello, Albert," he said, kissing him also.

Rosa got up and insisted Ben sit in his chair while he held Albert.

"Are you feeling better, Pa? We had no idea you were so ill. Poor Florrie has had her hands full, I know."

"I'm still a bit weak," he replied. "Any exercise tires me out."

"Aunty Millie came in every day," said Florrie." She's been such a help."

"We'll pop in to see her and Uncle Harry before we go," said Rosa. She bent down and kissed her father on the cheek. "Sorry," she whispered in his ear.

Ben clasped her hand and squeezed it. "All forgotten," he replied quietly.

Stephen had been out with his boys and returned shortly before lunch. Christopher and Jonny burst into the kitchen and stopped short when they saw there were visitors. Stephen followed, and they were all introduced to the new additions. Jonny was particularly interested and kept staring at the two babies. He studied Alan and then went over to look at Albert.

"They're twins," explained his father. "They look alike, don't they?"

Florrie ushered them all into the parlour so she could get the lunch ready. "What a house full," she exclaimed.

As they went, Rosa suddenly announced, "I think I'll see how my cherry tree is doing."

Ben looked alarmed.

"I think you'll find it's doing very well." Stephen, looked intently at his father-in-law. "I'll take Rosa down to the orchard. I looked at it the other day, and it seemed to be fine."

They both went outside, followed by Danny, and Florrie gave her father a broad smile.

After lunch, Rosa and Ben had a quiet chat while the babies slept. Stephen, Florrie, and Danny took the boys out for a short walk up the lane.

"Florrie came to see me when they were visiting Jenny after Christmas," said Rosa. "She told me I was being too hard on you. I said I was upset about losing Ma and agreed I shouldn't have spoken to you like I did."

"It was a mistake for me and Lucinda to go away in secret," replied Ben. "We booked separate rooms at the hotel. We just wanted a holiday together."

Rosa looked contrite. "I was jumping to conclusions, then. I agree with Florrie and Charles—you *do* deserve some happiness. Ma has been dead a whole year now. How I wish she could have lived to see my twins."

"Florrie felt the same when she had Sarah."

"How is Sarah doing?"

"Very well," Ben said. "She should be able to live a normal life, although Charles recommends she has regular checkups."

The others returned, and after tea and cake, Danny said they should be getting back. "We'll call in at the shop on the way," he added.

After they had left, Florrie calmed down her excited boys.

"I'm glad I don't have identical twins at my school," commented Stephen. "Could cause some confusion!"

"It's been an exciting day," said Ben as he went upstairs for a rest.

CHAPTER TWENTY–TWO

THE NEW DOCTOR

Dr Burns was in the surgery attending to the mother and baby clinic, which took place one afternoon a week.

"Next!" he called. He did not bother to get up from his seat to usher in the next patient, but the villagers were getting used to his eccentricities.

"Well, he *is* Scottish," whispered a young woman when eyebrows were first raised.

Dr Burns welcomed each mother with the same greeting. "That's a bonny wee bairn you have there!" She would beam as the child was gently lowered into the dish of the weighing scales. "Mm," he would say to each mother while he fiddled with the weights. "Thriving! Keep it up, dear. Breast is best."

The mothers loved him and would rarely miss the clinic, and word had reached Lucinda that he was becoming very popular. Dr Forster told her he would soon be out of job.

"Nonsense," she'd said. "They just want to get a look at him. Things will go back to normal, you'll see."

Lucinda wanted to keep arrangements at Acacia House on a friendly but formal basis to begin with. Before Sapphire and Charles left, she used to join them for their meal after evening surgery. They would meet for drinks shortly before and share news of their day, then convene in the dining room, and Mrs Harris would serve their meal. Charlotte Elizabeth had her tea in the breakfast room earlier.

Lucinda discussed the matter with Mrs Harris. "Now Charlotte Elizabeth is getting older, I think she should start having dinner. We could have it earlier in the evening in the breakfast room. It would save you laying up the dining room every day."

Mrs Harris nodded in agreement.

"That would be better for me, I must say, ma'am. But what about the doctor?"

"He can have his later, after evening surgery. I hope it will help you finish sooner. You can always leave the pots until the next morning."

"Thank you, ma'am, I do appreciate that. Sometimes Mr Harris does get a bit fed up waiting for his supper. He could have it without me, but we do like to sit down together."

"We'll see how things go," suggested Lucinda. "There may be times when I ask friends round for a meal from time to time. Perhaps that could be at the weekends, when your daughter could help. I'd like to ask Dr Burns for Sunday lunch, which we'll have as usual in the dining room. Is that acceptable to you? Please say if it isn't. We need to establish some routines that we're all happy with."

"That all sounds fine to me, Mrs Wells. I'm sure my Susan would welcome some extra work. Young miss Charlotte Elizabeth is growing up fast now, isn't she?"

"Yes. I'd like to spend as much time as possible with her while her parents are away."

"I'll ask the doctor if he has any dietary requirements," Mrs Harris suggested. "I hope he doesn't want haggis every night. I've already bought a packet of porridge oats."

Dr Burns was very easy-going and said he was happy with whatever Lucinda had arranged. He'd stood looking at her with his twinkling blue eyes while she outlined her suggestions, which she found disconcerting. She had assured him he would be welcome to come to the sitting room whenever he liked, and then asked him to come to lunch on Sundays.

"That's most kind of you," he replied, bowing slightly.

Charlotte Elizabeth was very excited when her grandmother told her she could join her for dinner every evening, as it would mean a later bedtime. She insisted on wearing her best frock 'like Mummy does' and Lucinda gladly agreed.

It still worried Lucinda that her granddaughter had no friends of her own age. She decided to discuss the matter with Caroline Bailey, so she wrote a note asking her to Sunday lunch. *Then I won't have to entertain Dr Burns on my own,* she thought.

Caroline sent a reply accepting the invitation and spoke to Lucinda after church on Sunday morning.

"How is the new doctor settling in?" she asked, putting on her gloves after handing in her hymnbook.

"Oh, very well. The patients love him."

"I shall look forward to meeting him. I'll see you a little later."

After saying goodbye to her friend, Lucinda took Charlotte Elizabeth's hand, and they walked back home down the hill together.

"How did we know Mummy and Daddy got to America?" the girl suddenly asked. Lucinda had already told her they had arrived safely.

"Daddy sent a wire."

"What's a wire?"

"It's a message that comes through a cable under the Atlantic Ocean between here and America. It's sent by something called Morse code. Every letter of the alphabet has several beeps, and someone taps it out one end and someone else writes it down at the other. Then they send it in a little yellow envelope to who it is addressed to."

"Did we get a little yellow envelope?"

"Yes, I have it at home."

"Can I have it?"

"Of course."

Charlotte Elizabeth let go of her grandmother's hand and skipped down the pathway the rest of the way home.

Lucinda let her granddaughter keep the telegram announcing Charles and Sapphire's safe arrival in New York. Charlotte Elizabeth said she was going to keep it in her box of 'special things'. She began writing little telegrams to her dolls on small pieces of paper and asked her grandmother to find her some yellow paper when they went shopping.

Lucinda was rearranging the flowers on the dining room table when Mrs Harris came in with a jug of water.

"Whisky!" exclaimed Lucinda. "Have we got enough whisky? I wonder what he prefers. I understand the Scots are very particular about their blend of whisky."

Mrs Harris smiled reassuringly. "We'll have to ask the doctor, then."

Lucinda went into the sitting room to check the drinks on the sideboard. She knew Charles often had a whisky and soda after evening surgery and hoped there would be some left. She found the bottle half full. It looked a good blend, and she breathed a sigh of relief.

Mrs Harris ushered in Doctor Burns. He was dressed in his kilt and had a tweed jacket on. "Good morning to you, Mrs Wells," he said. "This is grand, asking me to lunch. Very much appreciated."

He turned to Charlotte Elizabeth, who was sitting on the rug by the fire. "Is this your wee grandchild?" He bent down to her and held out his hand. "How do you do, young lady?"

Charlotte Elizabeth stared at him.

"Do I look funny?" he asked. "This is what men wear in Scotland. It's called a kilt, and every family has its own pattern, called tartan."

The girl smiled, then glanced at her grandmother for reassurance.

"What would you like to drink, Dr Burns?" asked Lucinda.

"A whisky, please, if you have it."

She poured him one. "Soda?"

"Och, no. Neat will do fine."

Lucinda poured herself a sherry and gave her granddaughter a glass of lemonade. Mrs Harris showed Caroline in, and Lucinda introduced her.

"This is Mrs Bailey. She and her late husband used to live here. He was the doctor before my son-in-law."

Dr Burns bowed politely. "Very pleased to meet you," he said, offering his hand. "And my condolences on your loss."

"Thank you, Dr Burns. I understand you've made quite an impact in the village."

"Is that so?" His eyes had that familiar twinkle.

Lucinda handed Caroline a sherry, and soon after, Mrs Harris announced dinner was ready.

During the meal, Dr Burns told them a little more about himself. He said he had lost his wife five years before from cancer, and that he had two daughters, one living in Edinburgh and the other in Dunedin in New Zealand.

"Goodness," said Lucinda. "That's a long way away."

"Do you get to see them?" asked Caroline.

"I go up to Edinburgh by train to see my two granddaughters, but I've never been to New Zealand."

"Would you like to go?"

"Yes, very much so. Maybe I'll go when I finish here."

He continued to entertain Lucinda and Caroline, who both listened to him with great interest. The dinner lasted longer than usual, but finally they adjourned to the sitting room, and Charlotte Elizabeth went up to her room to play. Lucinda offered the doctor another whisky.

"Thank you. Just one more, then," he replied. "If I have too many it will blur my speech, and then you'll never understand me." He took his drink from her and downed it quickly.

"I'll be leaving you ladies, if you'll excuse me," he said. "I'm off for a wee stroll this afternoon. Thank you again for a lovely meal and your wonderful company." He wished them good afternoon and left.

"Well," said Caroline, her eyes shining. "What a charmer."

"He's certainly very good company," replied Lucinda.

They looked at each other and collapsed into girlish giggles.

Lucinda didn't see much of Dr Burns the following week. He had his breakfast early and remained in his room in the evenings. Mr Harris had included Dr Burns's room when he came every morning to do the fires and had laid it ready to be lit in the afternoons. He made sure all the coal scuttles were full as the weather continued to be cold.

When bringing Lucinda her afternoon tea one day, Mrs Harris said, "I was talking to one of the mums down at the butcher's. She's just had her next one and has had trouble with feeding."

Lucinda perked up. Mrs Harris often brought her snippets of gossip after she had been shopping.

"She said she went to Dr Burns's clinic, and he was very helpful and gave her a couple of packets of this new dried baby milk, Cow and Gate it's called, I believe. She says it's worked wonders, and her little one is doing very well on it."

"Really?" responded Lucinda. "That's interesting. I haven't heard of that before."

"There's packets of it in the surgery," added Mrs Harris, her hands on her hips. "Clutters the place up when I'm cleaning."

Lucinda wondered where it had come from and made a mental note to ask Dr Burns when she next saw him.

In the excitement of the Sunday lunch, Lucinda had forgotten to seek Caroline's advice about Charlotte Elizabeth's lack of friends. She invited her for coffee the following Wednesday morning, when the gallery was closed for the day.

"How are things going?" asked Lucinda once they were settled by the warm fire in her comfortable sitting room.

"It's very quiet," Caroline said. "No one comes in this cold weather. I'm thinking of closing in the afternoons—Sapphire said I could please myself about the opening hours."

"That makes sense. You'll have to put a sign in the window."

"Yes, I will do."

Lucinda voiced her worries about her granddaughter. "I have no means of transport and it's too cold to wait for the bus, so I can't take her over to see her cousins. She really needs friends of her own age."

Caroline frowned. "The children at the nursery are all too young for her now. She should be starting school soon."

"Sapphire won't let her go to school unless it's private one. It's such a shame Molly had to leave. She was a lovely little girl. I'm spending as much time as I can with her, and her reading is coming along well. She tends to want to be very grown up and emulate her mother. She insists on dressing for dinner!"

"Oh, bless her."

They drank their coffee, and Lucinda offered a shortbread.

"Is this Scottish shortbread? Speaking of which, how is Dr Burns?" Caroline asked, giving her friend a knowing look.

"I hardly see him in the week. He tends to keep himself to himself." She told Caroline about the powdered baby milk. "I imagine he gives it away. I wonder where he gets it from."

The following Sunday, Lucinda promised Mrs Harris they would finish the meal earlier so she could get home at a reasonable time. "I'm very grateful to you cooking the Sunday lunch for us," she said. "Why don't you cook extra and take some home to have with your family afterwards?"

Mrs Harris raised her eyebrows. "Oh, ma'am, could I? That would save me having to do another one."

After another enjoyable meal, Dr Burns finished his second whisky and, putting his glass down, stood hesitating. "I wonder if I could join you this afternoon?" he asked tentatively. "It's blowing a hoolie out there, and I don't fancy getting soaked."

Charlotte Elizabeth burst out laughing.

"You'll get used to my funny words, lassie," he said to her.

"Of course you're welcome to stay," said Lucinda.

"Is that a game of draughts I see over there?" He eyed a pile of board games and puzzles on the bookshelf.

Charlotte Elizabeth jumped up and went over to fetch the box. She opened it up quickly and put out the counters. "White or black?" she asked.

"Och, I don't mind. You choose."

As they played, Lucinda noticed how at ease Dr Burns was with her grandchild. After two games, Charlotte Elizabeth said, "Dr Burns isn't very good at draughts, Grandma. He keeps on losing."

The doctor smiled broadly and winked at Lucinda. "One more, and we'll see if I can do better."

This time he won, and Charlotte Elizabeth pouted and packed up the game. She got out a puzzle, and they spent the rest of the afternoon on it.

Mrs Harris had left the tea things together with plate of sandwiches before she had gone home, so Lucinda could serve it herself. As she handed Doctor Burns his cup of tea, she said, "I wanted to ask you about this baby milk you've been giving out."

The doctor explained that he had introduced it as he always worried about those babies who couldn't fight off early infections because they were undernourished. He added that he was against it being used by mothers just for convenience.

"Where do you get it from? Do the shops have it?" enquired Lucinda.

"Yes, it's available, but not everywhere. It *is* expensive for poorer families."

Lucinda explained that her son-in-law was very interested in child welfare, and she was sure he would want to continue the practice.

"I'm chair of the village nursery," she continued. "We could distribute the milk there to the mothers who need it. If we get in a supply, it can be kept in one of the cupboards at the church hall. You could write out a prescription, and the mother could then hand it in and collect her packets."

Dr Burns looked impressed. "Well, that sounds as if it would work very well. I congratulate you, Mrs Wells. You're a true entrepreneur!"

"We would just need to know where to get the supplies from."

"I ordered a consignment, and it came by train. I collected it from Kingsbridge Station."

"From now on, please allow us to purchase the supplies."

"If you wish. I'm fine with that," replied Dr Burns, picking up a sandwich.

CHAPTER TWENTY–FOUR

CHARLOTTE ELIZABETH'S BIRTHDAY

LUCINDA ASKED CAROLINE TO COME to lunch every Sunday. She enjoyed her friend's company and told her it couldn't be much fun for her, dining alone every day, especially at weekends. Dr Burns continued to join them and would often stay on during the afternoon to play games with Charlotte Elizabeth. The occasions had a family feel about them, which Lucinda appreciated.

The weather was improving, and soon it would be March and Charlotte Elizabeth's fifth birthday. Her parents had left gifts and messages behind, which Lucinda had carefully hidden away. Now she had to make the arrangements for the party. All the cousins were to be invited.

She and Caroline were discussing it over coffee one morning. "I'll ask Mrs Harris's daughter Susan to come and help. She knows all the children by now. We need to think of some entertainment," said Lucinda.

"Dorothy could play the piano, and we could have party games like musical bumps and musical chairs," suggested Caroline.

"What a good idea. And what about 'pass the parcel' and 'pin the tail on the donkey'?"

"The children are all very young, but I think they could manage those. The older ones could help the little ones."

Lucinda scribbled down the ideas in her pocketbook.

"What are you giving Charlotte Elizabeth?" asked Caroline. "And what can I give her?"

"She's learning to read—early, I know. She would love a storybook. I'm going to give her some jewellery, a locket and chain."

"She's a lucky little girl."

They continued to discuss what to provide for the tea. "Mrs Harris has kindly offered to make the birthday cake, with pink icing, of course," said Lucinda.

"You'd better warn Dr Burns that the house will be full of children that day," Caroline observed.

On the day of the party all Charlotte Elizabeth's cousins arrived and soon the house was full of excited children. The party games were a success, if a bit disorganised at times. The grownups were kept entertained watching their offspring having fun. Afterwards all the children paraded into the dining room, and Charlotte Elizabeth opened her presents and blew out the candles on her cake. She loved being the centre of attention, and Lucinda noticed how happy she was.

When all her guests had finally gone, the girl curled up beside her grandmother on the sofa and put her thumb in her mouth.

"Have you enjoyed your birthday, darling?" asked Lucinda, putting her arm round her.

Her granddaughter removed her thumb and nodded. "I wish Mummy and Daddy were here," she said plaintively.

"I know," replied Lucinda, holding her close. "I think they're probably wishing the same."

There was a knock on the sitting room door, and it opened slowly. "Is it safe to come in now?" asked Dr Burns. He was holding a small package in his hand.

"Yes, all clear," replied Lucinda.

He came over and handed Charlotte Elizabeth her present. "Just a little something," he muttered. "Happy Birthday."

She sat up and opened it. Inside was a little tartan hat. It was shaped like a beret with a bobble in the middle.

"It's called a Tammie," explained Dr Burns. "Another funny Scottish word for you to learn."

Lionel and Amanda had sent their present by post, and it arrived the following morning. Amanda had had given Charlotte Elizabeth some crayons and drawing books, as she knew her niece loved drawing. She'd enclosed a letter telling Lucinda her confinement was only a month away. She wanted to firm up arrangements for Lucinda and Charlotte Elizabeth's visit.

Lucinda had to inform Dr Burns that she would be leaving for several weeks. That afternoon, she asked him to join her and her granddaughter in the sitting room before evening surgery.

"First of all, thank you for your present," she began when he arrived. "Charlotte Elizabeth is delighted with it, aren't you, darling?" She turned to the girl, who was drawing at the table with her new crayons.

"Yes. I'm going to wear it to church!"

"Where did you get it from?" asked Lucinda. "I've never seen one before."

"I wrote asking my daughter to send it. It arrived earlier this week. It's a Burns tartan."

"Well, you'll look very special in that," Lucinda told her granddaughter. Turning to Dr Burns, she said, "I need to discuss with you the arrangements for our departure at the end of the month. I think my son-in-law mentioned it to you. We're going to stay with my son in Richmond, London. His wife is expecting, and the baby is due then. We shall be gone a few weeks. Mrs Harris will still be here, so I hope you'll manage all right."

"Och, I'll be fine," he replied. "I hope all goes well."

He left to take early evening surgery, and Lucinda continued to make notes for all the arrangements she needed to make. She was kept busy for the next few days and was sorting out Charlotte Elizabeth's clothes to pack one morning when Caroline arrived unexpectedly. Lucinda hurried downstairs to greet her friend.

"How nice to see you. Is everything all right at the gallery?"

"Yes, I haven't come about that." She sat down, seeming agitated, fussing with her gloves and handbag. "Yesterday, Dr Burns came into the gallery."

"Did he buy anything?"

"No. He had a good look round, though." She hesitated. "He asked me out to dinner."

Lucinda was startled. "What did you say?" she asked, her voice wavering slightly.

"I accepted."

There was a short silence.

"Well, what a surprise!" said Lucinda.

"Lucinda," began Caroline. "I don't want this to come between us. I had no idea he was going to ask me out. Do you mind me accepting?"

"Of course I don't mind! He's a lovely man, and I'm glad for you."

"I wasn't sure whether to accept. Donald has only been gone six months."

"It's two friends having dinner, you shouldn't feel guilty about that."

"Thank you, Lucinda. I must admit I felt very awkward telling you."

"You go and enjoy your evening. There's absolutely no reason why you shouldn't."

Caroline stood up and, looking relieved, came over and kissed her friend goodbye. When she'd gone, Lucinda sighed. She went over to her desk and began a letter to Ben, asking him when he was going to resume his visits.

CHAPTER TWENTY–FIVE
AMANDA'S CONFINEMENT

UCINDA WAS HELPING CHARLOTTE ELIZABETH pack her cases for their move to Richmond. There were clothes and toys strewn round her room, on chairs, and on the bed. Lucinda thought to herself that the child had too many things. Her mother was always buying her new outfits, and she had received a lot of gifts on her birthday.

Charlotte Elizabeth was busy putting her dolls into an empty case.

"No, darling, you can't take *all* your dolls, just some of them," Lucinda remonstrated. Her granddaughter had amassed quite a collection, and each doll had a name.

"It's hard to choose some and leave the others behind," Charlotte Elizabeth stated firmly. "They will be *very* upset."

Lucinda sighed. "I'm sure Mrs Harris will take care of them," she suggested.

"No, they need me. *I'm* their mummy."

Lucinda gave in. "All right, you can take them all."

Charlotte Elizabeth gave a self-satisfied smile and continued placing the dolls in her case. Lucinda began to pick up some clothes and sort them into piles. It would be nice for the girl to go on some outings and visits while they were in London and show off her wardrobe. There were few places to be taken locally, just invitations to tea with Sapphire's friends, or weekly visits to church.

It was a busy time, and Lucinda was hard-pressed to remember everything that needed to be arranged. She had sunk into a chair one afternoon, holding her head, when Mrs Harris brought in her tea.

"Oh, Mrs Harris," she exclaimed. "I do hope I haven't forgotten anything."

The woman put down the tray. "Have you made lists, ma'am? I always find them useful."

"Yes, but what if I've forgotten to put everything that needs doing on them?"

"Have you got them there?"

Lucinda handed over several pieces of paper, and Mrs Harris scanned them carefully. "I can do some of this," she said, looking up. "You don't need to worry about any of the domestic arrangements. Just leave it to me."

She sat next to her employer and began discussing the items. Borrowing Lucinda's pencil, she ticked some of them. "That leaves you with the packing and travel arrangements," she said as she returned the lists. "I'm sure Dr Forster and Dr Burns can sort out the surgery side of things. That's what you pay them for."

Lucinda thanked her. "You're a treasure, Mrs Harris!"

Caroline came to see Lucinda before they left and was shown upstairs to her friend's sitting room. As she entered, Lucinda could see excitement in her eyes. She knew exactly what it was about.

"Hello, Caroline. Tell me how it went, then," she asked enthusiastically as her friend sat down.

Caroline's eyes shone as she described her experience. "We went to a very nice country hotel in Ermington. Ian told me a little more about himself. I'm sure he won't mind my telling you. His daughter in Scotland is having marriage problems—in fact, her husband has left her. He's very upset about it. She has two daughters, six and eight years old. He wants them to come and visit him with a view to joining him here. Just think, they could be friends with Charlotte Elizabeth!"

"That would solve a problem," replied Lucinda calmly. "Are you going to see Dr Burns—Ian—again?" It occurred to her that she might well be seeing less of her friend if she was going to go off on jaunts with the doctor.

"He hasn't asked me, but I wondered if you would both come to lunch this Sunday?"

"That would be lovely," answered Lucinda, feeling a little more cheerful. "I shall look forward to it. I'm sure Mrs Harris will welcome an afternoon off."

She met up with Caroline the following Sunday after church. Caroline's house was a short walk down the hill, and they went straight there. Dr Burns joined them a little later.

Caroline bustled round looking after her guests and then disappeared to see to the dinner, leaving Lucinda and Charlotte Elizabeth to converse with the doctor.

"I expect Caroline told you my two granddaughters might be coming to visit," Dr Burns said.

He's calling her Caroline, is he? Lucinda thought to herself. *Am I to remain Mrs Wells, I wonder?*

"Yes. I expect you would love to see them again."

Dr Burns's eyes twinkled. He looked at Charlotte Elizabeth. "Your wee granddaughter reminds me of them, especially the youngest one."

"All little girls are the same at that age." Lucinda smiled demurely.

Caroline came back and ushered them into her small dining room. They sat themselves down, and Caroline lifted the dishes carefully onto the table.

"Please help yourselves. It's probably not up to your standards, Lucinda. I've cooked it myself."

"I'm sure we shall all enjoy it," said Dr Burns, tucking his napkin under his chin. Charlotte Elizabeth couldn't take her eyes off him.

Paddington Station was very busy, and Lucinda held her granddaughter's hand tightly as she walked briskly along the platform. The porter had to break into a run as he pushed the luggage trolley behind them. Finally, Lucinda caught sight of Lionel at the gate and breathed a sigh of relief.

"Oh, darling, I'm so glad you're here," she said as they embraced.

Lionel smiled broadly and then bent down and kissed his niece lightly on the cheek.

"Hello, Uncle Lionel," she said shyly.

He scooped her up and carried her the rest of the way to where his motor was parked. The porter unloaded the cases, and they set off for Richmond.

"Aren't the roads getting busy now," observed Lucinda as they drove along. "The streets are so crowded and noisy after life in our quiet village."

Charlotte Elizabeth peered out of the window, staring wide-eyed at the omnibuses and motorcars driving past. "Look, Granny!" she exclaimed, pointing to an open-top omnibus going by. "All the people will get wet if it rains."

"I don't think they go up on the top deck if the weather is bad," replied Lionel. "They will need umbrellas if they do."

"Can I go on one?"

"Yes, we'll do lots of exciting things while we're here," promised Lucinda affectionately, patting her granddaughter's knee.

Lionel's motor scrunched up the short drive to his home, and Charlotte Elizabeth jumped out quickly as her aunt came down the steps to greet them.

Amanda embraced her warmly. "Hello, darling. How lovely to see you again!"

Lucinda emerged and gave her daughter-in-law a hug.

"Aunt Amanda's got a very fat tummy," announced Charlotte Elizabeth.

Lionel was getting the cases out from the back of the car. He burst out laughing.

Amanda took her niece's hand, and they went inside. "I'm so glad you're here," she said, turning round to Lucinda. "I really appreciate your coming."

"My pleasure, and Charlotte Elizabeth has been really looking forward to her visit, haven't you, darling?"

The girl nodded happily.

They took off their coats and settled into the comfortable sofas in Amanda's sitting room.

"Have you heard any more from Charles and Sapphire?" asked Lionel as he dispensed drinks.

"Nothing yet. I expect they will write, but goodness knows how long a letter will take to arrive."

"And has the new doctor settled in?"

"Yes, he's very popular with the patients." *And with my friend,* Lucinda thought.

A week later, Amanda went into labour. Lucinda sat with her until the doctor arrived with a nurse. She carefully explained what was happening to Charlotte Elizabeth, who listened wide-eyed.

"You must amuse yourself quietly for a while," Lucinda instructed. "Uncle Lionel and I will be very busy." She was glad her granddaughter had packed her dolls.

Lucinda ensured everything was taken care of—Lionel had prepared carefully for his wife's confinement. Later that afternoon, she was delivered of a fine healthy daughter. Lionel came in to see them, his face full of concern for his wife.

"Darling, how are you?"

"We have our little girl!" exclaimed Amanda. "Oh, Lionel! I never thought this day would come!"

Lionel put his arm round her and kissed her. "We've waited a long time. Well done, my love. She is beautiful, isn't she?"

Lionel carefully gathered her into his arms. "Do you think she'll have red hair?" he asked, looking at the little screwed-up face.

Lionel and Amanda decided to call their new daughter Edith.

"You've still got some congestion there," said Dr Forster, wrapping his stethoscope up and placing it back it the case. "It's going to take time getting better."

"I want to go to London to see my new granddaughter," pleaded Ben.

"Not yet, I'm afraid," replied the doctor. "You don't want to spread any infection. Best to wait a week or two."

Ben sighed. He was disappointed. Jonny was standing beside him, watching the doctor avidly with his big brown eyes. The doctor ruffled his hair and smiled at him.

"Jolly little fellow, isn't he?" he remarked.

"And a lot of trouble most of the time," said Ben. "Wears me out."

The doctor left, and Florrie returned from the shop, where she'd gone with Sarah.

"I'm still housebound," Ben told her. "Dr Forster won't let me go anywhere until after Easter."

"Let's hope the weather's better then," replied Florrie. "You don't want to get another chill."

Ben looked doleful. "I expect that other fellow will be there to see Edith," he grumbled, referring to her other grandfather, David.

"Oh, do cheer up, Pa. You're a puddle of gloom."

"Puddle of gloom, puddle of gloom," chanted Jonny, dancing round the kitchen until Ben grabbed him and pretended to growl like a bear, making his grandson laugh uncontrollably.

CHAPTER TWENTY-SIX
SCHOOL FOR CHARLOTTE ELIZABETH

AFTER EASTER BEN WAS MUCH improved, and Florrie allowed him to go to Richmond to see little Edith. She packed his case, and Stephen took him to the station the following Saturday. They had written beforehand, and Amanda had replied, inviting him to stay a week.

Ben was welcomed by all when he finally arrived, especially Charlotte Elizabeth. He delivered the presents for the baby that Florrie and Millie had sent, and then Amanda brought her little girl for him to see.

Ben took her in his arms, and his eyes watered as he looked at her. "What a treasure!" he whispered. "She's very beautiful."

He sat for some time holding her, until Charlotte Elizabeth approached, trying to get his attention. He gently returned Edith to her mother and then allowed himself to be led away to join Charlotte Elizabeth's dolls' tea party.

After dinner that evening, Lucinda had a moment to speak to Ben. "I hear all is well between you and Rosa," she said. "Florrie wrote and told me. I'm so relieved, and you must be proud of your two new little grandsons."

"I'm lucky to have all these wonderful grandchildren," he replied.

"I hope you'll be able to continue your visits to us when we get back, now the weather is improving. We've missed you."

At the end of the week, Ben returned home. Lucinda was staying on until arrangements were made for her replacement. She had realised that Amanda would need some live-in help, as she and Charlotte Elizabeth couldn't stay indefinitely.

She suggested to Amanda that Mrs Harris's daughter, Susan, might be the ideal person to employ to help with Edith. "She's very good with children, and she has a sweet personality," she explained. "She's just left school, as she's fifteen now. Would you like me to write and ask Mrs Harris what she thinks?"

Amanda was very enthusiastic. "I'd like to have someone we know, rather than a stranger," she said. "I'm sure Lionel will agree."

A reply arrived saying that Susan was very keen to accept the offer, and Lucinda wrote suggesting that Mrs Harris come to Richmond with her daughter as soon as they were able. They arrived two days later, and once Amanda had conducted a short interview with the girl and her mother, all was settled.

Lucinda announced that she and Charlotte Elizabeth would now be leaving, and they would be accompanying Mrs Harris on her journey home. As they travelled back on the train, Lucinda asked about the gallery.

"I think Mrs Bailey's there every day. Dr Burns goes over to her house on his weekends off and some evenings. I must admit, ma'am, I haven't been overworked with meals. It's given me time to do a bit of spring cleaning, and I think you'll find your apartment spotless." She gave a satisfied smile.

"Thank you. I know you like to keep busy, but you deserve some time off."

On her return, Lucinda noticed a difference in Dr Burns. Always a confident man, he now sounded positively jaunty, whistling his Highland tunes as he came downstairs to go to work in the surgery.

Lucinda had decided to take Charlotte Elizabeth on a short holiday to the seaside. Her granddaughter was very excited when told, and she decided that her dolls would have to stay at home this time as she "couldn't possibly look after them all while on holiday."

"Why don't you take your favourite one?" asked Lucinda. "Then she can tell the others all about it when we come home."

Charlotte Elizabeth clasped her hands together, and her eyes shone. "Yes, I'll do that," she exclaimed. "I can't wait!"

Lucinda had selected a small seaside town with a sandy beach and overhanging cliffs. They lodged with an elderly couple who let out rooms for holidaymakers and provided meals.

Lucinda and Charlotte Elizabeth ventured down to the beach on the first morning of the holiday carrying bags full of towels and rugs. The girl immediately removed her shoes and socks and ran towards the sea.

"Come on, Granny," she called out as she entered the shallow water. "It's not very deep."

Lucinda took off her canvas shoes and joined her, carefully placing her feet along the edge of the waves. She held her granddaughter's hand as they paddled along together.

The sea sparkled, and Lucinda breathed in the pure sea air. She recalled the week she and Ben had stayed at this same resort and marvelled at the fuss it had caused. When Sophie was alive, she had felt very much on the edge of Ben's life, and she had hoped that they would become closer now that they were both widowed. She realised that Ben had an expanding family and would want to spend time with his grandchildren. Her best friend was preoccupied with the doctor, and Lucinda was left wondering what was going to happen when Charlotte Elizabeth went to school.

She felt a tugging on her arm. "Granny, what are you thinking about?" Charlotte Elizabeth said, looking up at her anxiously.

"Oh, nothing, darling. Look, there are some donkeys." She pointed further down the beach. "Would you like a ride?"

Back home, Charlotte Elizabeth had just tipped her bucketful of seashells onto the floor in the conservatory.

"Oh darling, don't do that in here."

"But Granny, I'm showing them to my dolls," the girl replied. "They want to know all about my holiday." The dolls were all sitting in a row in front of her, with one sitting in front. "Arabella is telling them all about it."

Lucinda smiled and allowed the child to have her way. What did a little mess matter?

At breakfast the next day, Charlotte Elizabeth was banging her boiled egg with a teaspoon when she said, "Why don't we see Dr Burns anymore? I liked playing games with him."

"He's rather busy, I think," replied Lucinda, buttering her toast.

"But he wasn't busy before when he had dinner with us."

"He's got a friend, and he goes there for some of his meals."

"But *we're* his friends."

"I'll ask him to lunch on Sunday, then."

"And Aunty Caroline too?"

"Yes, and Aunty Caroline too."

The girls resumed eating her egg, and Mrs Harris came in with the post. "There's one from America," she declared as Lucinda took the bundle from her.

Lucinda's hands shook slightly as she opened the letter in the blue envelope with an American stamp. It was several pages long, and she avidly read all her daughter's news.

Dear Mummy,

How are you? And how is that daughter of mine? I miss you both, but I try to keep busy. Life is so very different here.

We have settled into our new home now. It's called an apartment and consists of a sitting room, bedroom, kitchen, and bathroom. There's also a small study for Charles. We are five floors up, and the view over the city is amazing, almost like being in an aeroplane!

I've made some friends amongst the wives of Charles's colleagues. They are so very kind and welcoming, but life here needs getting used to. The buildings are huge, and everyone lives in apartments. There are many more automobiles, and the roads are very busy and noisy. There are lots of black people too, and some segregation, which Charles and I hate. We are hoping to go to somewhere called South Street and hear a jazz band play. There's a very good art gallery, which I've visited, and there are plenty of theatres and some very good restaurants. We eat out nearly every evening, as everyone does here. The portions are huge! I can't really go far on my own, just the city centre, as there's a lot of crime in some of the neighbourhoods. It's a totally different world, but I'm finding it very exciting.

Please tell Charlotte Elizabeth Daddy and I miss her very much. Did her birthday party go well? I thought of her all day and felt so upset I couldn't share it with her. Did she like her presents? Give her a big hug and kiss from me and Daddy.

I trust Amanda is recovering well, I'm longing to know what she had, and I hope your letter arrives soon. I shall love hearing news of the family. I do get dreadfully homesick sometimes, but I'm glad I came. It has been such an interesting experience being here.

Charles is working very hard, and I have a lot of spare time. The other wives invite me to different events, coffee mornings, and afternoon tea. Charles and I have been to a few cocktail parties. It's such fun meeting new people. Everyone is interested in my art gallery, and of course I told them all about the art theft!

I will write again soon. My love to everyone, Charles sends his.

Sapphire xxxx

Lucinda put down the letter and sighed. She was relieved that Sapphire was enjoying her stay, but it made her realise how much she herself missed city life. She couldn't remember the last time she had been to a concert or a party.

Lucinda read parts of the letter to Charlotte Elizabeth after breakfast. She seemed unperturbed by it and carried on playing with Nipper.

"That cat's getting rather fat," commented Lucinda.

"He likes his food, like Dr Burns," replied her granddaughter.

Lucinda suppressed a smile.

Charlotte Elizabeth put her head to one side. "I don't think Nipper's very well, Granny. He doesn't let me cuddle him, and he keeps hiding in corners."

"We'll get Uncle Billy to take a look at him."

The girl nodded and continued playing with her ball of string. Nipper cuffed it with his paw a few times, then walked off, his tail in the air.

"Charlotte Elizabeth, I have something to ask you," began Lucinda. "Would you like to go to school?"

Her granddaughter looked animated. "Oh, yes!"

"We need to talk to Mummy and Daddy about it."

"When will they be back? I want to see them." She suddenly looked sad.

"Not until before Christmas, darling, a few months yet. I think I will write to them before that and ask if you can start school after the summer holidays. Aunty Dorothy says there's one in Kingsbridge that might be suitable, but we would have to get you there each day. Would you like that?"

Charlotte Elizabeth clapped her hands together. "Oh, please let me go there, Granny!"

"It depends what Mummy and Daddy say."

Lucinda answered her daughter's letter straightaway, telling her about the school and asking if she could enrol Charlotte Elizabeth there if it proved to be suitable. *She's missing you, and I think it will help her through these last months,* she wrote.

She placed the letter on the table in the hallway ready to post and picked up the telephone receiver to arrange for Billy to come over to see Nipper.

When Billy arrived next day, Charlotte Elizabeth carried her pet in and handed him over to her uncle. After examining him, he released the wriggling cat, who ran off. Charlotte Elizabeth immediately followed. Billy closed his bag, and Lucinda could see he was smiling broadly.

"There's nothing much wrong with that cat except he's a she and expecting kittens very shortly."

Lucinda put her hand to her mouth. "No!" she exclaimed and burst out laughing.

Her granddaughter returned, holding the bundle of fur in her arms. "Is he all right, Uncle Billy?" she asked anxiously.

"Absolutely fine, but I must tell you, my love, that you have a girl cat, and she is expecting."

Charlotte Elizabeth looked perplexed.

"Nipper isn't a boy," added her grandmother.

"What's *expecting* mean?"

"She's going to have kittens."

Charlotte Elizabeth put the cat down.

"The kittens are in her tummy," explained Billy. "When they have finished growing, they will be born."

"When will that be?" the girl asked, looking wide-eyed.

"Very soon, I think. Probably in a week or a few days."

"I'm so excited," she exclaimed. "I can't wait! I'm going to tell Mrs Harris." She ran off, leaving Billy and Lucinda laughing.

When they had composed themselves, Lucinda said, "Billy, there's something I wanted to ask you and Dorothy." She went on to explain about the school in Kingsbridge that she was considering for her grand-daughter. "You see, it would be difficult getting her there each day, as I have no transport while Charles and Sapphire are away. I wondered if she could stay with you in the week. I could then collect her and bring her home on the bus at the weekend. It would only be this term. I know it's a big ask, but she's missing her parents, and it would help to distract her if she went to school."

"I have no objections," Billy said, "but I'll have to ask Dorothy. I'm sure we could come to some arrangement."

"I would be so grateful to you both. She's not got a place yet—I'm waiting to hear from her parents. Where are you thinking of sending young Frankie?"

Billy and Dorothy's eldest was slightly younger than his cousin.

"Dorothy and I are happy for him to go to Stephen's school. He can walk there on his own when he's older. He's a robust little fellow, and I think he'll be happy there. I certainly don't want him to go away, as I did."

Billy had been given the opportunity to go to a private school by his grandmother. Sophie had secretly contacted her after the rector had died. Millie had been treated badly by the parents of Billy's father. They had refused to help her and had sent their son away, leaving Ben to bring up his sister's illegitimate child. Eventually Milly had agreed, and Billy had been enrolled at his father's old school in Exeter.

"Weren't you happy at your school?"

"Not at first, but I braved it out as everyone said how lucky I was to be there, and my grandmama was paying the fees. It was a very good school, but there was still a certain amount of rough and tumble."

"I'm sorry you had a bad time of it."

"It wasn't too bad—nothing compared with what we went through in the war—so I don't worry about it."

Charlotte Elizabeth arrived back breathless.

"What did Mrs Harris say?" asked Lucinda.

"She said 'oh, no'," answered her granddaughter. "Isn't it exciting?"

Three weeks later, Lucinda received her reply. Sapphire agreed that her mother could choose a suitable school for Charlotte Elizabeth and hoped she would settle happily. This time, she had included a simple letter for her daughter to read, with Lucinda's help.

Lucinda wanted to see the school by herself and had asked Dr Forster if he would take her there to attend an interview. Mrs Harris had agreed to have Charlotte Elizabeth. The kittens had been born, and the girl was very preoccupied with them.

After Dr Forster had dropped her off, Lucinda found the large Victorian villa situated in one of the side roads off Fore Street. By the side of the porch was a brass plaque on the wall, which was inscribed *Academy for Young Ladies, Proprietor Miss Langdale.* She mounted the steps leading up to the door and rang an old-fashioned iron bell pull. It was answered by a young lady dressed from head to toe in black, who showed her in.

Lucinda entered a spacious hallway, and she could hear the distant chatter of girls in one of the rooms. She was taken upstairs to Miss Langdale's study. As she entered, she saw a mahogany desk in one corner with two large windows behind, flooding the room with light. The walls were papered with a flowery design, and there were several ferns in pots on pedestals. Lucinda looked around, admiring what she saw. A smart middle-aged woman came towards her with her arm outstretched, indicating for Lucinda to sit in one of the comfortable armchairs in front of the desk. The woman sat down opposite her.

"Mrs Wells, how *very* nice to meet you. I'm Miss Langdale," she said. She was wearing a stylish black mid-length dress with broad pleats down the front, and she had a long row of pearls hanging round her neck. Her fashionable low-heeled shoes were fastened with buttons.

"Can I offer you some refreshment, coffee or tea?" Miss Langdale asked.

"Coffee would be very acceptable, thank you."

She asked the young lady who had shown Lucinda in to bring some coffee and then turned her attention to her visitor. "I understand you are looking for a place for your grandchild"—she glanced at a letter she had in her hand—"Charlotte Elizabeth."

"Yes, that's correct. Her parents, my son-in-law and daughter, are in America on a protracted visit, so I'm acting on their behalf." Lucinda then described some details about her family and home life.

"It sounds as if your granddaughter would welcome some friends."

"Very much so. She has too much adult company."

Miss Langdale gave an understanding smile. "We have some delightful young ladies here. There are never more than about twenty in all, and we teach them in two groups, upper class and lower class, according to age."

She suggested they take a short tour of the school, and when they had finished their coffee, she got up to escort Lucinda round the establishment. She walked confidently in front, and Lucinda followed dutifully behind. She was shown two classrooms in the upstairs rooms.

Downstairs there was a communal room and a music room with a baby grand piano.

"I like my young ladies to have some musical training," explained Miss Langdale. "I used to be a professional singer myself, so I take these lessons. We give piano lessons if desired, which would be extra."

Lucinda was impressed.

They came to the end of the hallway. "The kitchen is at the back." Miss Langdale indicated a closed door at the end, from which emanated a delicious smell of cooked food. "And the offices are in outhouses in the yard." She opened the door and led Lucinda outside. "It's all kept scrupulously clean. We pride ourselves on never having had an outbreak of illness."

The women toured the small garden, a grassy area surrounded by trees and partly paved, where the young ladies had their exercise. They then returned to Miss Langdale's sitting room upstairs, where Lucinda asked about the curriculum.

"The three R's, of course," replied Miss Langdale. "But alson elocution, music, and art. We employ an art tutor once a week to teach the older pupils the rudiments of drawing. I prefer to let the younger girls have free expression when it comes to art."

"My granddaughter is, in my opinion, quite talented in art, so she will enjoy that," responded Lucinda. "Her mother owns an art gallery."

Now, it was Miss Langdale's turn to look impressed.

"I would like to reserve a place for Charlotte Elizabeth. I think she would very much enjoy coming here."

"Of course, Mrs Wells, that can be arranged. I would request that we meet her beforehand just to see if she would 'fit in,' as it were."

She handed Lucinda a copy of the school prospectus. They then planned for Charlotte Elizabeth's visit, and Lucinda gave her thanks and left.

When she arrived back home, she told her granddaughter all about her visit to the school. The girl listened, but her attention was full of the kittens.

"She's had five," she exclaimed. "There are two tabby cats, a black-and-white one like Nipper, and two black ones. Nipper doesn't like anyone to touch them yet, but Mrs Harris said she would later. They're so lovely, Granny. Can we keep them?"

"I don't think we can have the surgery overrun with cats, darling. We'll find good homes for them all."

Charlotte Elizabeth looked disappointed.

"Perhaps Aunty Caroline will have one," suggested her grandmother.

Charlotte Elizabeth was so preoccupied with the kittens that she almost forgot about her impending visit to the school. The day of the visit Charlotte Elizabeth held her grandmother's hand tightly as they walked the short way to the Academy, having been given a lift from Dr Forster.

"Here we are," said Lucinda, trying to sound cheerful as they reached the doorway. She felt anxious for her little protégé, knowing it was a big step for her to take.

They were shown inside and entered Miss Langdale's room. She was very welcoming. "Hello, Charlotte Elizabeth, it's lovely to meet you," she said, bending slightly to address the child. "We'll show you round the school," she added briskly, straightening up.

They followed her elegant figure as she strode off to a classroom where several young girls of Charlotte Elizabeth's age were working at their lesson. They were all wearing smart black pinafores over their dresses together with black tights and shoes. They looked up and studied the visitors with interest.

"This is the first class," announced Miss Langdale. "We have eight students in here. They are taught by our resident teacher, Miss Davies."

The teacher smiled at Charlotte Elizabeth. "Has the child had any schooling?" she asked when informed that the girl was to be her new pupil.

Lucinda explained that her granddaughter had begun to read and knew her letters. Miss Davies looked impressed. "That sounds very promising," she said.

Charlotte Elizabeth surveyed the many faces in front of her and held her grandmother's hand more tightly. The young students eyed her with interest.

Miss Langdale continued to show Lucinda and Charlotte Elizabeth round the rest of the school, then they returned to her study.

"Do you think you would like to come here?" Lucinda asked.

Charlotte Elizabeth nodded enthusiastically.

After giving more information about the school, Miss Langdale saw them out. "I think your granddaughter should be very happy here, Mrs Wells," she said, standing at the doorway. "We like to think of ourselves as one big family."

Lucinda led Charlotte Elizabeth down the steps of the Academy and towards Fore Street. "Come along," she said. "We need to buy you some black shoes."

Back home, she told the child about the arrangements for her to attend the school each day. "Aunty Dorothy will take and collect you, and you'll stay with her and come home at weekends until Mummy and Daddy come back."

Charlotte Elizabeth was very excited and ran off to tell Mrs Harris all about it.

Lucinda sat back in her chair and closed her eyes. She was thankful that she had found a suitable school, Miss Langdale had been very pleasant. Perhaps now she could have some rest. It had been quite demanding looking after her granddaughter. It was still eight months before Sapphire and Charles were to return.

CHAPTER TWENTY-SEVEN
CHARLOTTE ELIZABETH BEGINS SCHOOL

IN THE FIRST WEEK OF September, Dorothy and Charlotte Elizabeth made their way to the Young Ladies' Academy. As it was near the veterinary practice, they were easily able to walk there.

Charlotte Elizabeth looked at her new shiny black shoes as they hurried along. They made a nice hollow sound on the pavement, which made her feel important. Under her coat she was wearing a new black pinafore over a plain grey dress, the uniform of the school. Her aunt had plaited her hair and tied the pigtails up over her head, telling her she looked very grown up. She was carrying a small bag that contained a box with pencils, an eraser, and a pencil sharpener inside. She also had a pair of plimsolls that she was to wear indoors.

She had found it difficult to eat any breakfast that morning, having had to get up earlier than usual. Even now, her stomach felt in a tight knot as she walked briskly along beside Aunty Dorothy. They turned the corner, and the school came into view. Several pupils were being delivered at the door and were waving their parents goodbye. A motorcar roared away, having dropped off two little girls.

Charlotte Elizabeth walked the final few yards along the street holding her aunt's hand, and they mounted the steps to the entrance. Miss Langford was standing just inside, smiling broadly and wishing 'good morning' to the girls as they passed. Dorothy had a quick word about the arrangements for collecting her niece, then turned to her.

"Goodbye, dear. Have a lovely day!" She bent down and kissed her, and then went quickly down the steps.

Miss Langdale took her new pupil by the hand. "Good morning, Charlotte Elizabeth. Come this way." She showed her where to hang her coat and waited while she changed her shoes. They then went upstairs to the schoolroom. The class of young girls were sitting in pairs at shared desks, and they all regarded the new girl intently as she entered. Charlotte Elizabeth's eyes met their stares boldly.

Miss Davies gave her a kind smile and welcomed her. She turned to her pupils. "This is Charlotte Elizabeth, come to join our class. Wish her good morning, please, everyone."

"Good morning, Charlotte Elizabeth," chanted the girls.

Charlotte Elizabeth did not drop her gaze, replying "Good morning" in a clear voice. She was shown to her place and found herself next to a pretty girl with short fair hair. Looking round at the other girls, she noticed that many of them had short hairstyles with partings at the side.

"What's your name?" asked the girl. "Mine's Elsie."

Charlotte Elizabeth told her.

"That's a long name. Can I call you Lizzie?"

"All right."

Miss Allen tapped her desk with a ruler. "Silence, please, girls, for registration." She began to read out the names, and each girl replied "Present!"

She finally closed the register and told them to get out their English exercise books. She got up and handed Charlotte Elizabeth hers. "Write your name on the front," she instructed, indicating the place with her finger. "Do you have some pencils?"

Charlotte Elizabeth fumbled in her school bag and drew out her pencil box. The lesson had begun.

At recess, the other girls crowded round Charlotte Elizabeth. "Her name's Lizzie," said her new friend.

Charlotte Elizabeth found it rather overwhelming but held her nerve. She answered all their questions and felt she was accepted.

They were in the small garden and some of the girls were playing with handballs and others had skipping ropes. Others were practising handstands against the wall. Charlotte Elizabeth kept with Elsie.

"We have different lessons in the afternoons," Elsie told her. "Things like art and music and elocution."

"What's that?"

"Teaching us to talk nicely."

Charlotte Elizabeth was perplexed. It had never occurred to her that she might not be speaking properly.

The lesson happened to be singing that day. After lunch, the girls sat round the piano in the music room, and Miss Langdale presided. "Now, girls, we shall sing this scale." She played a series of ascending chords, and the girls followed, singing each note.

Charlotte Elizabeth loved every minute of the lesson and sang as lustily as she could. After a while, Miss Langdale stopped playing and looked at her.

"Charlotte Elizabeth, can you come out here?"

She got up and went to the piano.

"Sing that again, by yourself."

Charlotte Elizabeth sang the scale she had just learnt.

Miss Langdale looked at her seriously. "You have a very good voice, child. Would you like singing lessons?"

Charlotte Elizabeth nodded enthusiastically.

"I'll speak to your grandmother." She turned to the class. "We'll now sing 'Bobby Shafto,'" she instructed.

At the end of the day Dorothy was waiting outside, and Charlotte Elizabeth bounded down the steps towards her.

"Did you have a good day, dear?" her aunt asked, putting her arm round her shoulders and hugging her.

"Oo, yes," exclaimed Charlotte Elizabeth. "The first lesson was a bit hard, but my friend Elsie helped me. Then we had to do sums, which were quite easy, and after lunch we had singing, and we learnt some songs."

She proceeded to sing one of them in her clear voice as they walked along.

"If you like, we can do some music at home," suggested Dorothy. "I can play the piano for you, and I can teach you how to read music."

Charlotte Elizabeth looked up at her aunt and gave her a dazzling smile.

By the end of the week Charlotte Elizabeth was enjoying school immensely but was looking forward to going home for the weekend. When her grandmother arrived on Friday afternoon to collect her, she greeted her enthusiastically. After answering Lucinda's questions about how her week had been she said, "Miss Langdale wants me to have singing lessons. *Please,* can I?"

"I'll have to ask your parents, darling. It's not up to me."

Charlotte Elizabeth pouted. "But I want them *now*. It will be ages before Mummy sends a letter."

"All right, I'll pay for them to begin with. I think Mummy will probably agree."

Back home at Acacia House, Lucinda tucked a very tired little girl into bed and kissed her goodnight. She was just about to leave when a voice said, "Can I have my hair cut, Granny?"

Lucinda gave a short laugh and closed the door. She certainly could not agree to that request.

CHAPTER TWENTY-EIGHT

SIX MONTHS LATER

BEN WAS READING HIS NEWSPAPER, as he did every morning. "There's a lot of trouble in America," he said.

Florrie was darning socks and looked up.

"The stock market in New York has crashed," he went on. "There's been a run on the banks—it's chaos."

"What does that mean?" asked Florrie.

Ben turned the page over and read on for a moment. "It means there's no money to go round, or to put it simply, the dollar will be inflated."

He explained to his daughter as best he could what had happened. The share prices on the New York Stock Exchange had collapsed. This had been the result of too much speculation, and debts were mounting, caused by easy credit. There had been crowds queuing to withdraw their money from the banks in all the cities.

"So, all the money is devalued?" asked Florrie, looking wide-eyed. She got up and came to read the newspaper over Ben's shoulder. "I wonder if this will affect Charles and Sapphire?"

"It's bound to," Ben said. "It's affecting all the cities over there."

The door suddenly opened, and Millie appeared, holding a folded newspaper in her hand. "Have you heard what's happened?" she asked, waving it in the air.

"Yes, we've just been reading about it," replied Ben.

"Harry says it's really serious," Millie went on. "We think it's bound to affect Tom."

Ben shook his head. "I don't really understand why this has happened so suddenly. But I do think it is going to have serious repercussions."

Millie sat down at the table. "I hope it doesn't mean Tom will lose his job, or any savings if he has any. I know they've bought a house over there. He deals in motors now as well as fixing them. He's done so well. Oh, Ben, I am worried!"

"I'm sure he and Louise will be all right. They may lose money, but I'm sure he can build his business up again after all this has blown over."

Millie looked a little happier at her brother's reassurances. "I hope you're right."

Lucinda was in her sitting room reading. Her days were now quiet, and she had few interruptions. Sometimes she felt they were too quiet. Charlotte Elizabeth was at school and Dr Burns was at Caroline's a lot of the time, so she had the place to herself.

She was alerted by a quick knock on her door and Mrs Harris burst in.

"A telegram, Mrs Wells," she announced breathlessly, handing it over.

Lucinda sat up quickly and tore it open. She read it and then said, "No reply."

Mrs Harris left to dismiss the telegraph boy but returned quickly and asked if everything was all right.

"It's from Charles. They're coming back early." Lucinda looked shocked as she studied the short message, her hand on her throat.

"When will that be?"

"He doesn't say. I suppose it will be a week or so. It just says they will be returning as soon as possible because of the Wall Street stock market crash."

"It's been all over the papers, ma'am," announced her housekeeper.

Lucinda had not seen a newspaper recently. She had cancelled them when Charles and Sapphire had left. She asked Mrs Harris to buy her a newspaper so she could see what was going on in America. Mrs Harris left and soon returned with several. Lucinda scanned them all, but none mentioned Philadelphia specifically, only stating that all the big cities were affected. She realised that October 24, 1929, would be a date to remember.

She decided not to tell Charlotte Elizabeth of her parents' impending return. The child had settled well at her school and at her Aunt Dorothy's during the week. This was bound to excite her, and Lucinda wanted the term to finish normally if possible.

Each day, the papers were full of worse news, and Lucinda began to realise how serious it all was. It must have had some impact on Charles's work at the hospital if he was having to return. She had written to Lionel, and he replied that he, too, had received a telegram.

When Ben arrived for his visit during the week, Lucinda told him the news.

"I'm not at all surprised," he said. "I've been reading all about it. It sounds like chaos."

He told her that Millie had been round, worried about Tom. He said it was as if a dark cloud has settled over America and was moving towards them.

It was early Saturday afternoon ten days later when Charles and Sapphire arrived by taxicab. Charles had sent a telegram as soon as their ship had berthed at Southampton, and Lucinda had told her granddaughter that morning of their expected arrival.

Charlotte Elizabeth's eyes opened wide, and her mouth dropped open. "Mummy and Daddy are coming home *today*?" she asked in disbelief.

Lucinda smiled broadly. "Yes, darling. They've decided to come home early."

Charlotte Elizabeth danced round the room in a frenzy of excitement and afterwards looked out of the window every few minutes. Eventually Lucinda heard her scream and knew that Charles and Sapphire had arrived.

They both hurried outside, and everyone hugged each other, laughing with joy and relief. Lucinda ushered her daughter and granddaughter inside, leaving Charles to assist the cabbie with unloading all the cases. Charlotte Elizabeth clung to her mother, her arms wrapped tightly round her neck.

Sapphire looked at her daughter. "Who is this beautiful young lady?" she asked. "She is *so* grown up!"

Eventually, Charlotte Elizabeth released her, and they sat down together.

"Oh, Mummy, I have so much to tell you," announced Sapphire.

Charles joined them and embraced his daughter. "My lovely girl," he exclaimed, kissing her.

Lucinda asked them both if they'd had a good journey.

"Not too bad," replied Charles, looking grim.

"It was *awful,*" interrupted Sapphire. "We had to come second class—all the firsts had gone when we tried to book our tickets. All the well-off people are leaving. I can't tell you what it's been like since the crash."

"What crash?" asked Charlotte Elizabeth, looking anxious.

"Not a real crash," Charles said quickly. "It means all the banks have lost a lot of money."

"Have we lost a lot of money too?" asked his daughter.

"No, darling, our money is safe."

"Is it?" asked Lucinda. "I was talking to Ben, and he thinks it will affect us over here."

"We'll just have to see. No good worrying at this stage," answered Charles calmly.

"What's happening over there?" asked Lucinda.

"Complete panic. There was a stampede on the banks when the stock exchange collapsed. People were queuing and rushing into the shops before all the prices rose. There's going to be a lot of hardship and un-employment. The hospital advised us to return home and terminated my contract. No one really knows what's going to happen. The dollar has lost a lot of value—food will be very expensive."

"What a shame you couldn't finish your research."

Charles smiled reassuringly at his mother-in-law. "I think I've learnt a lot during my time there. I now need to persuade our health authorities to bring the vaccines over here."

"What are we going to tell Dr Burns?" Lucinda went on. "He was expecting to leave at the end of the year."

"I'll keep him on," replied Charles. "I shall have to write up my notes, and I need to go to London a few times. How has he been, by the way?"

Lucinda pursed her lips and smothered a smile. "Busy," she said. She told Charles about the powdered baby milk, and he was very impressed.

Charlotte Elizabeth suddenly blurted out, "Dr Burns is in love with Aunty Caroline."

Charles raised his eyebrows and looked at Lucinda, who was trying not to laugh. Sapphire gasped, putting a hand to her mouth. "Mummy, what's all this about? Do I sense romance in the air?"

"He's asked her out a few times, that's all," said Lucinda. "He spends some of his time over at her house."

"Does he indeed?" said Charles.

"He's not very good at draughts."

Charlotte Elizabeth's comment caused some laughter, and Lucinda hastily explained that he had often spent Sunday afternoons playing games with them. The girl then took her mother by the hand to see the kittens, and Lucinda continued to give Charles news of the surgery.

"It's good to be back home," he said. "I've missed you and Charlotte Elizabeth more than I thought I would. I'm glad I went, though. It has been very interesting. America is far ahead of us in all the fields of medicine. There's certainly more money for research—well, at least there was."

"Have you thought about how to use all this research?"

"I'm going to write and publish a scientific paper. It's important the medical authorities here know about these advances in medicine. Then they can lobby the government for funding, although now is perhaps not the right time for this."

"What will be in this paper?" enquired Lucinda.

Charles proceeded to tell her all about the discoveries that had been made, such as penicillin, insulin, and vitamins, and how they had dramatically reduced many common diseases and chronic conditions, especially in children.

"Do you know that something called an 'iron lung' has just been invented for patients with polio, which will save their lives?" he added.

Lucinda looked impressed.

He continued to describe other treatments to his somewhat overwhelmed mother-in-law, who nodded in agreement as if she understood all he was telling her. "You have obviously used your time in America to great advantage," she said.

"I'm so grateful you enabled me to go, Lucinda. You've been a great help with Charlotte Elizabeth and thank you for finding her a school."

"She's settled in very well. I was very impressed with the school when I was shown round. The principal, Miss Langdale, offers singing lessons, so I've paid for those as extras. In fact, there's a little production at the end of the term, and Charlotte Elizabeth has been given the star role."

Charles laughed. "That doesn't surprise me. She loves any kind of attention. I'll look forward to seeing her perform."

"We'll ask Ben to come too. He'll love it."

Sapphire, Charles, and Ben were all sitting together in the second row of the church hall in Kingsbridge. Lucinda was to join them later, after helping Charlotte Elizabeth get ready backstage. There was a friendly hum of chatter filling the hall, signalling the audience's anticipation.

Sapphire had been trying to keep her daughter calm in the days running up to her school production. Charlotte Elizabeth had been beside herself with excitement. She had been rehearsing after school with Miss Langdale, as well as having her usual singing lessons.

The lights suddenly dimmed, and the pianist began playing the introduction to the performance of *Cinderella*. Lucinda arrived and slid quickly into her seat. Sapphire glanced at her mother, her eyes bright with excitement. The red velvet curtains parted, revealing a sad looking Charlotte Elizabeth leaning on her broom. Sapphire gasped as her daughter began her first song alone on the stage. She was filled with joy at seeing her perform so confidently under the bright lights.

At the end of the performance she clapped loudly as the little girls lined up to take their final bow. She could hear Charles beside her calling "Bravo!" The little play had been an enormous success, and the proud parents were vociferous in showing their appreciation.

After the performance, Sapphire went to find her daughter in the room behind the stage, which was full of excited and noisy little girls.

"Darling, you were magnificent!" Sapphire stretched out her arms to embrace Charlotte Elizabeth, and the girl's eyes shone with pleasure.

Miss Langdale came hurrying over. "Your daughter is *so* talented. She has a wonderful voice, Mrs Wells. We must continue to train it so it can achieve its full potential," she gushed, clasping her hands together.

Sapphire beamed. "I'm very proud of her," she replied, hugging her daughter.

On the way home, Charlotte Elizabeth sang some of her songs again. She then made an announcement. "When I grow up, I want to be an *actress*!"

The car lurched slightly as Charles regained control of his driving. Ben put his arm around his granddaughter. "That sounds a wonderful idea," he said, his eyes twinkling.

CHAPTER TWENTY-NINE
NEW OPPORTUNITIES

During the following weeks, Charles worked on his notes and wrote articles that he hoped would be published in *The Lancet,* a medical journal for doctors. Charlotte Elizabeth was now living back at home, and Sapphire would drive her into school each day before going to the gallery. Lucinda hardly saw either of them and was grateful for Ben's visits.

He came one day towards the end of November. Sitting in Lucinda's warm sitting room, he looked concerned.

"I'm not sure I can continue coming during the winter months. It's too cold waiting for the bus. I'm not getting any younger."

"I do understand," she replied. "You don't see Charlotte Elizabeth when you come, so you could wait until the weekend and get Stephen to bring you."

Ben looked pleased at the idea. "It's good to get away," he said. "The cottage can be quite noisy at weekends, especially when the boys squabble."

"Even when they have a headmaster for a father?" asked Lucinda, raising an eyebrow.

"It's Jonny most of the time. Christopher is the quieter of the two and has taken to school well. He reminds me very much of Charles at that age."

"Perhaps Jonny will calm down when he starts school."

"I hope so. He's very excitable and has a great sense of fun. I really don't know who he takes after."

Ben paused to reflect on what he had just said. He remembered that he had been an excitable child, but although his mother had tolerated his behaviour, his father did not, and he would often receive punishment. His father had been too hard on him. He had beaten him for quite small misdemeanours, and Ben had grown up fearing him.

"Not yourself at that age?" Lucinda looked at him with amusement. Ben looked up, startled.

"No, my father wouldn't have stood for any nonsense. He was quite strict. Fathers were in those days."

"My father spoilt me—I was his little darling," said Lucinda, putting her head to one side as she remembered those times. "I grew up to be rather self-centred and foolish."

"I'm sure you're being too hard on yourself."

"I certainly had to learn from my mistakes."

"As did I."

They both sat in silence, knowing each other's thoughts.

There was a knock on the door of her apartment, and Mrs Harris appeared. She informed Lucinda that Mrs Bailey had arrived. Ben got up to take his leave, but Lucinda held up her hand. "Please don't go yet, Ben."

He sat down again as Caroline was shown in.

"I'm sorry if I'm intruding," she began, settling down.

Lucinda reassured her that was not the case and asked Mrs Harris to bring the tea.

"I wanted to tell you that Ian's daughter's coming for Christmas with her two girls," began Caroline. "They're staying with me, and Ian will be coming to us on Christmas day. I wanted to tell you the arrangements." She appeared slightly nervous.

"I'm so pleased that his family are coming, he must have been missing them," Lucinda responded. "Do you know what he's planning to do when he leaves us at the end of the year?"

"He wants to retire here and find a property. He likes Devon and says it's a lot warmer than Scotland. He's hoping his daughter will move down here. He wants me to meet her and the girls." Caroline gave a nervous laugh.

"I'm sure they'll find you to be a wonderful friend, as you have been to me and Sophie and Ben," Lucinda responded graciously, reaching out and touching Caroline's hand. "Where will he live when he leaves? If it's a problem, he can stay on here as a paying guest until he finds a house."

"That's very kind of you, Lucinda."

After tea, Ben announced that he needed to catch his bus and left. As he travelled home, he thought about Caroline. He recalled how Sophie had first met her at Billy's grandmother's house, and Caroline had asked his wife to make some clothes for her two stepdaughters. This had helped their finances at a time of hardship. Sophie and Caroline had remained close friends after that. He remembered he had felt somewhat uneasy about his wife's 'posh friend'. How ridiculous he had been to think she might have looked down on him because he was a blacksmith.

The bus rumbled to a stop and Ben got out and walked up the lane, hoping his two grandsons would be in bed when he got home.

Caroline and Lucinda had remained chatting after Ben had left. After a pause in their conversation, Caroline suddenly said, "Do you think it's wrong of me to have this friendship with Ian?"

"Why would you think that? Of course I don't."

"It's all happened so quickly. I'm sure eyebrows are being raised in the village. People expect a high level of respectability from a doctor's wife."

"It doesn't mean you have to turn into a nun! It's been over a year now since Donald died, and you've had your time of mourning. Now you must get on with your life. Have you spoken to Dorothy and Harriette?"

"No, I have to admit, I haven't."

"I should tell them about Ian. If your family are happy and his daughter is too, there is no reason for you not to pursue your friendship."

"I have a feeling he may propose. I don't know what I would say."

"You'll know when it happens. He's too sensible to do anything quickly."

Caroline nodded. "Thank you, Lucinda. You're just the right person I need to share this with. Please don't say anything about what I told you."

"Of course not. It all sounds rather exciting, so enjoy it!"

Caroline gave a cautious smile and got up to go.

As Lucinda did not see Dr Burns much, she wrote him a note and left it in the surgery. She had invited him to bring his family to visit Acacia House to meet everyone on Boxing Day. The following morning, he knocked on her door and told her he was delighted to accept her invitation and was looking forward to it.

Ben, Stephen, and Florrie arrived on Christmas day with their three children, and Billy brought his family over in the afternoon. The conservatory at Acacia House resounded with the sound of excited children as Christopher and Jonny chased their cousins. Charlotte Elizabeth had decided to stay with her mother in the sitting room with the other adults. Eventually, little Phoebe ran in and clung to her mother. Three boisterous boys were too much for her.

"I remember being overwhelmed as a child at Forge Cottage when Billy, Charles, and Lionel were there rushing around," said Dorothy, laughing as she gathered her daughter up into her lap for a cuddle.

Billy got up to see what was happening, and the adults could hear him giving the boys a good talking to.

"I bet anything that's Jonny's fault," remarked Ben. "He's a little tearaway."

Stephen looked helplessly at his wife.

"They're just excited, it's Christmas," said Charles.

The following day was a quieter one for Lucinda, and she looked forward to receiving her guests. Caroline had insisted on bringing a basket of sandwiches and a cake, and Sapphire offered to do the teas. Mrs Harris was having a well-deserved day off.

Dr Burns's two granddaughters soon made friends with Charlotte Elizabeth, and they spent a happy afternoon playing with her dolls. Lucinda could see that Caroline and Ian were growing very close. He would constantly look at her with his smiling blue eyes. Sapphire served tea and passed round the sandwiches.

"How is the house-hunting going?" Lucinda asked Eleanor, Dr Burns's daughter.

"We've decided to settle down here to be near Dad, but it's quite the wrong time of year to look for a property," she replied. "It's a lovely part of the world, and we shall love being near the sea. It didn't take long for him to talk us into it!"

"It will be so nice to have you here," said Sapphire, picking up the teapot. "More tea, anyone?"

Dr Burns held out his cup, looking pleased with himself.

"They're going to publish my article!" Charles held up the letter he had just read.

Sapphire and Lucinda looked at each other. They were fussing round Charlotte Elizabeth, as it was the morning of her first day of term.

"What article was that?" asked Sapphire, buttoning up her daughter's coat.

"The one in *The Lancet*," he replied excitedly. "It will be read by hundreds of doctors."

"I'm so pleased," said Lucinda.

Charles continued enthusiastically, "I hope it produces some interest. I want to do as much as I can to bring an awareness of all the research going on in America. We need a cohesive health system here. It's too fragmented, and many GPs are not using up-to-date treatments for their patients, especially children."

"Whatever the treatment is, it is of little use if many patients cannot afford it," pointed out Lucinda. "We need insurance that covers everyone. All these health schemes and savings clubs are all very well, but there are too many different systems. Everyone should have good medical care."

Charles nodded in agreement, but their conversation was cut short by Sapphire saying it was time to take Charlotte Elizabeth to school. Charles suddenly realised that it was an important morning for his daughter and kissed her goodbye, saying he hoped she'd have a good day. He then returned to his surgery to begin morning appointments. He felt excited and restless, wondering what he could do to promote his ideas. He ushered in his first patient, a woman who had a chronic chest condition, and he knew she did not have the three shillings and sixpence required for the consultation. He often had to ask his patients to pay what they could when they could, and most of them did their best to pay something. His well-off patients were given no such leeway, and Charles would often charge more when he was required to give extra attention.

"Good morning, Doctor," the elderly woman greeted him. "So nice to have you back. What's happened to that lovely Dr Burns?"

Charles smiled to himself. "He's left us now, Mrs Hughes. I believe he's going to retire."

"Oh, that's a shame," she replied, clutching her handbag. "We were just getting used to him."

Well, you've got me back now, thought Charles. "How's your chest been?" he asked as he got up to examine her.

He worked his way through his list of patients, most expressing their pleasure at having him back. As the last one left, he gave a sigh of relief and leant back in his chair.

He heard the door bang and realised Sapphire had returned home. Jumping up, he went to join her for their morning coffee.

"I want to ask you something," he said, pouring himself a cup from the tray Mrs Harris had left in the sitting room.

"Be quick then," replied his wife. "I'm just off to open the gallery."

"If I applied for a permanent research placement in one of the London hospitals, how would you feel about that?"

Sapphire stood still, staring at him. "I don't know. What would it mean?" she asked cautiously.

"It would probably mean relocating to London."

Sapphire looked stunned as they sat in silence for a few moments. "I'll have to have a long think about that," she said.

"I've loved general practice, but I feel compelled to do more. I sensed that more than ever this morning."

Sapphire nodded. "It would mean giving up the gallery, and I wonder what Mummy would say."

"I'll speak to her today. I wanted to ask you first."

"I don't mind living in London, but I wouldn't want to give up the gallery completely. I must admit it is a bit boring sitting in there all day waiting for customers. We would also have to find Charlotte Elizabeth a suitable school."

"There's a lot to think about, and I haven't got a placement yet," said Charles, swallowing down his coffee. "I'm off to do my rounds." He got up and hurried out, leaving his bemused wife behind.

Lucinda was shocked when Charles told her about his plans. She put her hand on her chest to calm herself. "This is a surprise," she managed to say. "And yet I knew your trip to America might unsettle you."

"I won't apply for anything yet," said Charles hurriedly. "I just want you to think about it and let me know your feelings."

"It will mean moving away from your father and sisters. For me, it would be lovely to be nearer to Amanda and Lionel. I do love living here, although I know Sapphire can become restless and would probably like to live in London again. Oh, there are so many considerations!"

"I think we had better leave any discussions for a few days and then all talk about it when we have had time to think about the implications," suggested Charles.

Lucinda agreed. When her son-in-law had left, she stood and looked out of the window of her apartment onto the garden. Would she be able to leave Acacia House, where she had been so happy after Samuel's death? Would she be able to leave her friends in the village, especially Caroline? Would she be able to leave Ben?

CHAPTER THIRTY

LEAVING

UCINDA DECIDED TO TALK ABOUT her concerns regarding the move to Caroline, and she wrote a short note inviting her to afternoon tea. When her friend arrived, Lucinda had second thoughts. Caroline was positively animated, and Lucinda had a good idea why.

The women kissed affectionally, and as she sat down, Caroline said, "I've something to tell you. Ian has proposed—he asked me yesterday. I was surprised it was so soon after his daughter left. I knew something was afoot as he looked so nervous, unlike him, but I was still taken unawares. Oh, Lucinda, I said yes!"

She paused for breath, and Lucinda could see how excited she was. Before she was able to reply, Caroline continued.

"I realise it's only just over a year since Donald's death, but I couldn't bring myself to refuse, and he's widowed too. Just think, I shall have another daughter and two granddaughters. Apparently, Eleanor is pleased for him to remarry, he assured me of that. I did what you suggested and spoke to Dorothy and Harriette, and both want me to be happy, the dear girls."

She paused, and Lucinda was finally able to speak. "Many congratulations. Ian is a lovely man, and I'm sure he will take good care of you."

"I seem to be making a habit of marrying Scottish doctors!"

"They must make good husbands." Lucinda laughed.

"All we need to do now is look for a new home. It would be lovely to stay in the village and remain near you."

Lucinda took this opportunity to tell Caroline about Charles's proposition. "Nothing's decided yet. I don't think Charles will want us to move if Sapphire and I are unhappy about it, but I can see he is really wanting to go, and I don't want to stand in his way."

Caroline looked upset. "This is a surprise. What a difficult decision to make," she said. "What does Sapphire think about it?"

"I haven't asked her yet."

"I shall be so very sorry if you leave, but you must do what you think is best. You'll be near your son."

"Yes, that is helping to convince me we should go."

"What about Sapphire's gallery? I don't think I shall be able to help anymore."

"That I don't know. There's lots we need to discuss."

"And we shall lose you on the nursery committee. You'll be greatly missed there."

Before she got up to leave, Caroline said, "We're keeping our engagement quiet for the time being. I'm going to choose a ring next time we go to Exeter, whenever that will be. I wonder what the village will think when we make our announcement—tongues are bound to wag."

"I think you'll be very surprised. You and Ian are much loved, and people will be very pleased for you."

Before dinner that evening, Lucinda, Charles, and Sapphire discussed what a move would mean, and Charles asked Lucinda to tell him what she thought about it.

"I think you should apply," she responded. "It's something I know you really want to do, and I'm going to support you in that. Of course, I'll be sorry to leave my friends, and I do like living here, but as long as I am with my family, I shall be happy. I shall miss Ben's visits, but he's told me it's a difficult journey for him now, and I don't know how much longer he'll be able to do it."

"Sapphire and I have discussed it," Charles said, looking at his wife. "She, too, is happy to move to London, but we wanted to see what you had decided. So, if we are all in agreement, I shall go ahead and apply for a position." He got up and gave his wife and mother-in-law drinks, thanking them as he did so.

"Oh, Mummy. I'm so glad you want to come with us. I wasn't sure what you would decide to do."

Lucinda lifted her drink. "To our new beginning!"

They raised their glasses together.

"All we need to do now is sell the house," said Charles.

Lucinda placed her drink carefully on the table in front of her. "I think I may know a buyer," she said. The other two looked at her, intrigued. "I'll have to ask you both to keep this quiet, but Caroline came to see me today, and Ian has proposed, and she has accepted."

"Oh, good for her," exclaimed Sapphire.

"She told me they were looking for a property in the village for them all to live in. I think Acacia House might be just the place."

"I would love them to live here," declared Sapphire. "But what about the surgery?"

"I've had some discussions with Brian," replied Charles. "He certainly cannot afford to buy Acacia House, but he is happy to relocate to his house and buy my practice if we decide to move."

"Well, that was easy, wasn't it?" said Sapphire. "All seems to be settled. I still need to decide about my gallery, though."

"And we need to talk to Charlotte Elizabeth. It will mean moving schools," added Charles.

"And Mrs Harris. I hope she can stay on and look after Caroline's new family. I can't imagine she would want to move with us to London," said Sapphire, looking concerned.

"Shall I have a word with Ian and Caroline?" asked Lucinda. "To see what they want to do?"

"Yes, do that," said Charles. "I'll get a valuation and let them know to see if they are interested."

Mrs Harris announced dinner was ready, and the three of them convened to the dining room, where Charlotte Elizabeth joined them wearing her best dress.

Now the decision had been made to relocate, Charles travelled to London several times over the next few weeks to explore opportunities at one of the hospitals. Eventually a letter arrived from University College Hospital offering him a position to lecture and carry out research. He was to begin after Easter, which was a month away. He accepted it without hesitation and then began the preparations to move.

He wasted no time getting Acacia House valued and asked Dr Burns if he were interested in the property. Ian told him he would talk to Caroline and would let him know.

The next day there was a polite tap on the sitting room door and Dr Burns entered. He knew the family would be together at that time, just before dinner.

"I hope I'm not disturbing you, but can I have a wee word?" he said.

"Yes, of course, come in," replied Charles, getting up to get him a drink. "What can I get you? A whisky?"

"I never refuse a dram, thank you." He took the glass offered and had a sip. "I've spoken to Caroline," he began, "and we would very much like to purchase Acacia House."

"That's splendid!" exclaimed Charles, looking thrilled. He looked over at his wife and mother-in-law.

"I'm so glad," added Lucinda. "I'm sure you and your family will be very happy here, as we have been."

Sapphire nodded in agreement.

"It's just what we wanted," Ian replied. "I've always felt very at home here. We're getting married at Easter, I don't know if that fits in with your plans."

Lucinda laughed. "We haven't started looking for a house yet. I don't know how long it will be before we find one."

"You folks take your time, Caroline and I can wait."

There was so much to do, and Sapphire began to feel stressed. She dreaded telling Mrs Harris the news but gathered up her courage and went down to the kitchen the following day.

After imparting the news about the move to London, she added, "We shall be so sorry to let you go, but I presume you would not want to move to London with us?"

She could see that Mrs Harris was shocked. The woman stopped her work at the kitchen table and kept wiping her hands on her pinafore. She looked distressed.

"Oh, Miss Sapphire, I'm sorry you're going, I've loved looking after you all, but no, I wouldn't want to move all the way up to London."

"Dr Burns is going to buy the house," Sapphire continued. "He and Mrs Bailey are going to get married and live here with his daughter and her two girls."

Mrs Harris's eyes lit up. "I *am* pleased. They make such a lovely couple."

"I could ask them if they would like you to stay on," suggested Sapphire.

"Yes, yes, I would, definitely," Mrs Harris responded brightly.

Sapphire let go of her reserve and hugged her. "You've been such a treasure," she said. "I don't know how I would have managed without you."

Mrs Harris looked embarrassed and bowed her head. "Thank you, dear."

Charles was having discussions with Brian about the need to move the surgery to his house.

"Do you think there will be room?" he asked his partner. "And what does your wife think about it?"

"We've talked it over," said Brian. "It will be a squeeze, but I think we can manage for a while. We would have to extend onto the back of the house at some point to enlarge our living accommodation."

"There's been a surgery at Acacia House for a long time. It will mean quite a change. We need to make an announcement at some point soon and let the patients know."

Brian nodded in agreement. "We shall all be sorry to see you go, Charles. You and your family have done a lot for the village."

Charles dreaded the time he would have to tell his patients. Many had become friends, and he had known about their families as well as their problems—not always medical ones. He knew they would continue to receive good care with Brian, and that reassured him.

One of his other problems was his daughter. When told about the move, she pouted and said she did not want to move away and go to a new school. She was adamant she wanted to stay at the Academy, as Miss Langdale had told her she was very talented. Sapphire and Charles did their best to persuade her she would be able to continue with her singing lessons, albeit with a new teacher. At this point she stated she did not want another teacher and flounced out of the room. Her parents were perplexed, and even Lucinda was unable to talk her round.

As time went on, Charles could see that it was all getting too much for his wife. One evening she burst into tears.

"Oh, Charles, I can't cope with all this. There are so many loose ends, things we must sort out, and I don't know what to do about them. We haven't even found a house yet!"

Charles put his arm round his wife's shoulders. "I'm sorry to put you through all this," he began. "Let's go through all your worries and see what can be done."

He fetched Lucinda, and they sat down together.

"Now, tell me what your concerns are."

"First and foremost is Charlotte Elizabeth. I hate making her leave her school. She loves it there and is enjoying her singing lessons."

"Perhaps she and I could remain here until July," suggested Lucinda. "I could ask Dorothy again. Charlotte Elizabeth loved staying there, and it would only be for a few weeks."

"Dorothy and Billy have been very generous to us," observed Charles. "It would certainly help us to get the new house ready. What do you think, Sapphire?"

She looked relieved. "That sounds a very good idea. Thank you, Mummy." She got up and kissed Lucinda on the cheek.

"Now, what else?" enquired Charles.

"My gallery."

"What do you feel you want to do with it?"

"I don't want to let it go, but I shall have to find someone to run it."

Charles had no solution to give, but told Sapphire he would ask round the village to see if anyone wanted to manage it.

Lucinda then voiced her concerns about Ben.

"I know my pa will miss us greatly," agreed Charles. "He may not be able to travel to London for much longer. We must reassure him that we'll make regular visits to see him and my sisters."

"Have you and Brian sorted out the arrangements for the surgery?" asked Sapphire.

"More or less," said Charles. "He has some changes to make at their house. His wife isn't too happy about losing their front room."

Charles reassured his wife and mother that everything was organised for the surgery, and Brian was going to get a locum to help for the time being. This would free him so he could get on with the house move.

Charles and Sapphire travelled to London several times and stayed with Lionel and Amanda while they searched for a suitable property. Charles realised that London house prices were high, and they would have to settle for a smaller house than they were used to. He decided to ask his mother-in-law if she would consider selling her London flat, and this she agreed to do. That, together with the money from the sale of Acacia House, would enable them to find a suitable property.

Eventually they found a Victorian two-storey house in Highgate, a pleasant area of northwest London that had kept the appearance of a village. Charles would be able to travel to the hospital from there quite easily on the newly improved underground railway. Lucinda joined them in London to look it over. It was slightly smaller than Acacia House, but the rooms were spacious enough, and there was a garden at the rear. After she had been shown round, Charles asked her what she thought.

"It's a lovely house," she replied. "You and Sapphire have chosen well, and I'm sure we shall be very happy here."

CHAPTER THIRTY-ONE

FAREWELLS

SAPPHIRE HAD ASKED CAROLINE AND Ian to Sunday lunch. Ian was still living with them but spent most of his time at his fiancées house. He entered the living room at Acacia House in full Highland dress, much to Charlotte Elizabeth's delight. She took his hand as soon as he and Caroline arrived, smiling up at him. He put his arm round her.

"I shall miss you, my wee young girl," he said affectionately. "Who will you beat at draughts now?"

"You did win sometimes." She laughed.

"You must come and stay with us," Caroline said to her. "I'm sure Dr Burns's daughters would love to see you again." Charlotte Elizabeth's face lit up. She had been told she and her grandmother would be staying on until the end of the school year.

"When are they moving down here?" asked Lucinda.

"Next week," answered Caroline. "They're just bringing their personal belongings. Eleanor decided that it would be too expensive to move their furniture here, so they have sold most of it."

"You'll have to buy some pieces to fill all the rooms here," observed Sapphire.

"So much to do," agreed Ian.

"And you have the wedding to organise as well," added Lucinda. "Please let me know if I can help."

"You have quite enough to manage," said her friend. "We have the church booked, and we are arranging to have the reception at a local hotel." She looked at Charlotte Elizabeth. "Are you excited at the move?" she asked.

"Yes! Mummy says I can go to a special school in London and have singing and dancing lessons."

"That sounds very exciting."

"She's mad about performing," explained Sapphire. "Charles once told me I had a good singing voice and should have gone on the stage."

"You did sing beautifully," he said. "I think I was trying to flatter you at the time."

"Ian tells me you want to keep the gallery."

"Yes, but I need someone to run it for me."

Caroline nodded. "I may be able to help there. I wrote to Eleanor, and she is interested. She wants to be able to support herself and not live off her father, so she would like to take it on, if you're agreeable."

Sapphire sighed with relief. "That would be *marvellous*. I hope it won't be too much for her."

"I think she would love doing it."

"She's a very independent lassie," added Ian.

"We now need to start saying our goodbyes to everyone," said Lucinda. "We'll be going to see my brother William and his family first and then Charles's family. It's going to be very emotional," she added as they all went into the dining room.

Lucinda had written to her brother, telling him of their move and asking to come and see him. A date was arranged, and they set off to Somerset one morning the following week. On their arrival Lucinda embraced her brother and his wife warmly. He had been good to her when she had been expecting Lionel and had taken her into his home. She enquired after Madelaine, her niece.

"She's in France," replied William. "She spends a lot of time there doing translating work. She's met some man. I'm not sure how serious it is."

Sapphire and Madelaine corresponded occasionally, but Sapphire had not been told about a boyfriend. She knew Charles had once shown an interest in her cousin, but she had held back, having only just broken off an engagement with a clergyman friend of her father's. William had been none too pleased and had blamed Charles for the breakup. Afterwards Charles had rekindled his affair with Sapphire. All this seemed forgotten as William wished his sister and her family well and said he hoped they would be very happy in their new home.

The visit to Ben was on Easter Sunday when Charles and Sapphire went to Forge Cottage to say their farewells, taking Lucinda and Charlotte Elizabeth with them. Florrie had organised an Easter egg hunt for the children, and the two boys ran round the house and garden excitedly looking for the hidden eggs, led by Charlotte Elizabeth. Little Sarah was admired; she was sitting up and engaging with everyone now. Charles examined her and told her parents she was looking very well. Florrie said they were still going for regular checkups at the Plymouth hospital, and they had been pleased with the child's progress.

The three children came rushing into the parlour with handfuls of eggs, which they tipped onto the table. Florrie had decorated the hardboiled ones they had collected, and she now handed them each their chocolate one. Jonny's eyes shone when he was given his, and he gobbled it up in no time.

Ben watched him. "Are you going to share some of your egg with Grandpa?"

"All gone," said Jonny, his mouth full of chocolate.

Ben pretended to look upset. "Are you sorry you didn't give me any?" he asked his grandson with a doleful face.

Jonny shook his head and ran from the room, leaving everyone laughing.

"He's a little monkey," said his mother. She turned to Stephen. "I hope you're looking forward to having him when he starts at your school."

"He'll be fine," Ben said in the boy's defence. "He just needs some firmness from time to time."

"He plays you up, and you let him get away with it," commented Florrie.

Ben gave his daughter a conciliatory look and shrugged his shoulders.

"Your family's growing up fast," said Lucinda. "Have you finished planting all the fruit trees, Ben?"

"Just about. There's little room left in the orchard—I now have seven grandchildren."

Florrie handed round slices of her Simnel cake, which she always made at Eastertide, and then went to find out what Jonny was up to. Christopher and Charlotte Elizabeth settled down at the table, colouring in pictures that she had provided.

"I wonder what these children will do when they grow up," mused Lucinda. as she placed a small piece of cake daintily into her mouth.

Christopher heard her and promptly said, "I'm going to join the navy!"

Not to be outdone, Charlotte Elizabeth stated that she would become a famous actress.

Florrie returned holding Jonny's hand.

"What are you going to be when you grow up?" asked Ben, addressing him.

Jonny thought for a moment. "Footballer," he replied.

"Oh, no," his grandpa exclaimed. "That means I shall have to play with you. I'm getting too old for that now."

Jonny pouted, and Ben looked at Stephen. "Your daddy will play with you," he said, making Stephen pull a face.

The final visit planned was to go to Plymouth. to visit Rosa and Danny, and this took place shortly after Easter. Sapphire and Charles took Charlotte Elizabeth with them, but Lucinda decided to stay at home, as Rosa might not be that pleased to see her after the upset of her and Ben's holiday together.

They parked outside the terraced house, causing some interest from the neighbours, who were not used to seeing such a posh motor in their street. Rosa welcomed them in, and Charlotte Elizabeth went straight to Digger, who was wagging his tail furiously. Hilda calmed him down, and they all crowded into the small sitting room, where the twins were sitting in their highchairs. A row of nappies was airing on the fireguard and the room felt warm and cosy.

"They look bonny enough," said Charles as he looked at each one as he came in. "How's the feeding going?"

"Stop being a doctor," said his wife, nudging him.

"Very well," replied Rosa. "They're growing fast and have voracious appetites."

Rosa asked her brother about his new job. She said she was very impressed with what he was doing, especially as she had young children herself now.

Danny told them his work at the garage had not been affected too much by the stock market crash in America. He said he was more than grateful to have a job, as many men at the dockyard had been laid off. "Our church is manning a soup kitchen," added Hilda. "We also run a clothes exchange, which is very much used."

"I hope things will be better when my boys grow up," added Danny, wistfully.

When they left, they passed by rows of terraced houses with children playing outside in the street. Men in cloth caps were hanging about outside seedy-looking public houses.

Sapphire turned to her husband as he drove along. "Thank you for looking after us," she said.

It was now time to begin packing up the contents of Acacia House in earnest. The crates were piled up, and removal vans ferried the larger items to the new house in London. Lucinda's apartment was to be left untouched, and it was decided that Charlotte Elizabeth would sleep there when she came home at weekends, before rejoining her family at the end of July. Charles cleared his personal items from the surgery, telling his colleague it would be very strange not doing general practice work any longer. He said he would "miss the patients, even the difficult ones."

Finally, with most of the contents removed, Charles and Sapphire wandered round the empty rooms hand in hand. Sapphire surveyed the wallpaper she and her mother had chosen together. They would have to begin again in the new house, which needed decorating. As they walked back down the bare stairs the sound of their steps echoed. Sapphire collected her coat and handbag and followed Charles out to the motor. She paused on the step and turned round one last time.

"Goodbye, Acacia House," she said quietly.

Towards the end of July, Florrie passed Ben a letter from Lucinda as he settled into his chair after breakfast. He recognised the writing immediately and waited until Florrie was preoccupied with Sarah before he opened it.

Dear Ben,

The time is coming when we shall part our ways, although I hope we can visit you in the future. I know you will want to see Charlotte Elizabeth, who is growing up fast.

We are both getting old, and who knows what the future will bring. It is well that you are happily settled with your daughter and her family and not so far from Rosa either.

Our lives have been entwined in a strange way. Who would have ever thought that your son would fall in love with my daughter? And yet it was all meant to be, and I am glad of it. Your loyalty has meant so much to me as we shared our wonderful son together. I am so grateful to dear Sophie for being so generous and forgiving us. We did something very wrong, but I think we have tried to make amends, and now we are a united family.

I shall come and see you before Charlotte Elizabeth and I leave at the end of the month. She is loving her time at school and adores Miss Langdale! She will be so sorry to be leaving you, as will I.

Your loving friend,

Lucinda

Ben folded the letter carefully and tucked it into his waistcoat pocket. He sat for some time, lost in his memories, until Florrie asked him if he wanted to walk to the shop with her. He stood up and found his stick.

"Come on, Jonny," he called out, and they made their way to the village.

Two weeks later, Ben was standing before the mirror in his bedroom brushing his hair. Unlike many men of his age, he had not gone bald, but his sandy-coloured hair was now becoming grey. He straightened his necktie and stood back to view himself. Feeling presentable, he made his way down the narrow wooden staircase to wait for his visitors. Lucinda and Charlotte Elizabeth were coming that afternoon to say their farewells.

Florrie was in the kitchen putting the cake she had made onto a plate. She handed it to her father to take into the parlour.

"Have you made some of those special cakes Charlotte Elizabeth likes?" he asked.

"Yes, they're already on the table," she reassured him.

As Florrie took off her apron to hang behind the door, a motor drew up outside.

"They're here," she called to her father. Charlotte Elizabeth was first in.

"Hello, Gandy," the girl said, putting her arms round his neck. Lucinda came in, followed by Billy.

She embraced Florrie, then Ben, who led his guests to the parlour.

"What a wonderful spread," enthused Lucinda. "You have gone to a lot of trouble, Florrie."

Florrie joined them with Sarah and Jonny. Lucinda took a package from her bag as she sat down.

"This is for you," she said, looking at Jonny.

The boy took it, saying "fank you" without being prompted, which made Billy laugh at him.

Lucinda had brought a game of snakes and ladders, and Charlotte Elizabeth sat at the table to show him what to do.

"Ladders and worms," he shouted in excitement.

"That should keep him quiet," said Ben hopefully.

"Has Charlotte Elizabeth finished school now?" asked Florrie.

"Yes, they've broken up early, as it's a private school. She was very sorry to leave," answered Lucinda.

"It was a good choice, then," said Ben.

They all made a fuss of Sarah, who appeared very alert.

"Dorothy can't wait to begin these piano lessons," commented Billy.

"I'm convinced she's going to be musical," added Florrie. "She loves it when I sing to her."

"Just think," mused Lucinda. "Wouldn't it be wonderful if she accompanied Charlotte Elizabeth one day?"

After tea, Ben and Lucinda wandered round the garden, arm in arm. The sun was shining through the trees, leaving patches of sunlight and shadow beneath them on the grass.

"I hope you'll settle happily in your new home," Ben said.

"I'll be able to see Lionel and Amanda and little Edith quite often. We can get there quite easily by train."

"London will seem very busy after life in Devon."

"I hope you can come and see us."

"I doubt that, Lucinda. I'm really feeling my age now. I don't think I could manage the journey." Ben squeezed her arm. "I shall miss my visits to you."

Lucinda stopped and turned round to face him. "Kiss me, Ben," she said suddenly.

Without hesitating, he took her in his arms and kissed her gently, then released her. For a few moments, they looked into each other's eyes, bound by the same memories.

"It's time to go," she said, slowly moving away from him. Ben followed her but hung back. His emotions were overwhelming him, and he had to steady himself as he entered the cottage.

When it was time for them to go, Ben and Florrie stood by the gate to see their visitors off. Florrie was holding Sarah, and Jonny was waving.

"Goodbye, girl!" he shouted.

"Shush. Her name's Charlotte Elizabeth," his mother remonstrated.

"She's my friend," he answered.

Billy started the motor and drove them away. Jonny ran back inside, while Florrie and Ben lingered.

"Are you all right, Pa?" asked his daughter, looking at him.

"Yes, my love, thank you," he replied, hugging her.

They went inside, where Jonny was sitting in Ben's chair, looking mischievous.

"Out of there," Ben commanded, tapping him lightly on his legs with his stick. Jonny jumped out quickly and waited for his grandpa to sit down. He then climbed on his lap, and Ben enfolded him in his arms as they settled down together.

He bent over and whispered in his grandson's ear. "Whatever you do in this life, young man, don't fall in love with two women."

EPILOGUE

MANY YEARS LATER

A CAR CAME DOWN THE LANE and parked outside Forge Cottage. A young woman and her partner emerged and stood looking at the property. Peter zapped the car, locking it, and as they approached the cottage, his mobile phone rang. It was the estate agent, telling him she was running late but would arrive in about ten minutes. Lynne opened the gate, and they went in.

"Look, Pete, there's an orchard!"

They walked down the garden together.

"The trees look quite old," said Lynne, looking round.

"They may have a few years in them," observed Peter.

They wandered leisurely hand in hand until they saw the young woman estate agent putting the key in the door. She was wearing a smart jacket, and her hair was tied neatly back in a ponytail. They went back to meet her, and she led them inside. The first room was the kitchen, and it smelt musty.

"I know what you're going to say," said Peter, looking at Lynne. "Needs a refit!"

"These old properties can look quite transformed," the woman assured them.

Peter and Lynne looked at the paper peeling off the walls, the brown-stained oven, the patchy linoleum, and yellow-painted cupboards. The sink was dirty, and it contained an unwashed cup.

Peter pointed to a wide alcove with a mantelshelf above. "There must have been a range there," he said.

The three of them walked into the next room.

"This is the sitting room. It's a decent size," said their guide. "The cottage seems to have been extended at some point." She waved her hand from side to side. "This room was enlarged, and an extra bedroom was added upstairs."

The couple climbed up the narrow wooden staircase on their own. There they found the main bedroom and two smaller ones, with one leading off the other.

"This would make a lovely en suite," said Lynne enthusiastically when they reached the third bedroom. She continued looking round, peering out of the windows, and opening closet doors.

Back in the main bedroom, she called out, "Pete! Come and see this." She held up a small rusty horseshoe tied with a frayed, slightly yellow ribbon. "I found it in this cupboard." She indicated where it had been at the back of the shelf. They both examined it.

"Isn't it lovely?" said Lynne. "These would have been hung up for good luck. I wonder if this one is from a wedding bouquet. It had a white ribbon. Do you think the bride married the blacksmith and they lived here?"

"It's an appropriate thing to find in a place called Forge Cottage."

They went back downstairs. The smart young woman had gone outside and was on her phone. Peter put his arm round his fiancée.

"Well, do you like it?"

"Yes, I do, very much. The cottage has a lovely feel to it. I think the family who lived here must have been very happy."

"It needs quite a lot of refurbishment," said Peter. "We must think of our finances."

"We shall have plenty of time for that," replied Lynne. "There are some outbuildings—you could have one for your writing."

"If you're happy, shall we put in an offer?" he asked.

She nodded enthusiastically. Peter went outside to announce their decision while Lynne stood in the shabby kitchen, examining the little horseshoe in her hand.

"I wonder who the bride was," she said quietly to herself.

The End

ABOUT THE AUTHOR

Penelope Abbott is a retired teacher who lives in the Chilterns with her husband, John. She has two grown up children, a son James, and daughter Ros. Her hobbies are writing, painting, gardening, and playing her violin.

To find out more about the background of *Sophie's Story* and this sequel, *Sophie's Children*, please contact :

pennyabbott.author@btinternet.com

or

visit the website penelopeabbott.com.